**Praise for the Novels
of Holly Lisle**

I See You

"Likable characters . . . plenty of action. . . . This is obviously a one-sitting read." —*Midwest Book Review*

Last Girl Dancing

"Add Lisle's name to the list of exceptional romantic suspense authors. Gritty drama, eerie paranormal twists, and heart-pounding suspense make *Last Girl Dancing* well worth the price." —*Romantic Times* (Top Pick)

"Exciting . . . fabulous . . . a fine suspense thriller that keeps the audience in a state of high tension."
—*Midwest Book Review*

"Edge-of-your-seat reading."—Suspense Romance Writers

continued . . .

Midnight Rain

"Chilling."

—Lisa Jackson, *New York Times* bestselling
author of *Deep Freeze*

"*Midnight Rain* is an engrossing read. It's every woman's
dream—and every woman's nightmare."

—Linda Howard, *New York Times* bestselling
author of *Killing Time*

"Haunting suspense fills the pages of *Midnight
Rain*. . . . a spine-tingling and riveting reading experience. The characters are deeply detailed, and the reader
is drawn into the plot, the emotions, and the intensity of
the story from the first page. The pace is fast, the story
enthralling, and the conclusion explosive! For a tale that
will keep you reading late into the night, I highly recom-
mend *Midnight Rain*, and award it [a] perfect 10. A novel
of intense emotion, chilling suspense, and ghostly haunt-
ings, *Midnight Rain* is a guaranteed winner."

—Romance Reviews Today

"Wonderfully moody and atmospheric . . . [Lisle's] writing is strong and her characters are compelling. This is an
emotional and suspenseful read." —All About Romance

"*Midnight Rain* is dynamic romantic suspense."
—*Midwest Book Review*

"This thriller has just about everything you could ask for. . . . suspense, intrigue, a broad brushstroke of the paranormal, and topped off with a great romance that makes it sizzle. To put it bluntly, this was one heck of an absolutely riveting suspense/paranormal romance—totally awesome! Such an adrenaline rush, I could have jumped out of my skin. Bottom line: This is a superb, fascinating ride of a suspense-filled romantic thriller. Do yourselves a big favor and find this book for a great read by an author who I predict has a fabulous future in front of her." —Suspense Romance Writers

"Lisle explodes onto the suspense scene with a book so chilling and a voice so original that she's sure to become a major player. Creepy and thrilling, this book is truly unforgettable." —*Romantic Times*

"Though this is her first foray into romantic suspense, Lisle proves herself a master. . . . Her story does everything right. Lisle has also created one of the creepiest bad guys to come along in a good while—Michael could give Hannibal Lecter lessons. *Midnight Rain* is the first in what I hope will be many more thrillers from this very talented author." —BookLoons

NIGHT
ECHOES

Holly Lisle

A SIGNET ECLIPSE BOOK

SIGNET ECLIPSE
Published by New American Library, a division of
Penguin Group (USA) Inc., 375 Hudson Street,
New York, New York 10014, USA
Penguin Group (Canada), 90 Eglinton Avenue East, Suite 700, Toronto,
Ontario M4P 2Y3, Canada (a division of Pearson Penguin Canada Inc.)
Penguin Books Ltd., 80 Strand, London WC2R 0RL, England
Penguin Ireland, 25 St. Stephen's Green, Dublin 2,
Ireland (a division of Penguin Books Ltd.)
Penguin Group (Australia), 250 Camberwell Road, Camberwell, Victoria 3124,
Australia (a division of Pearson Australia Group Pty. Ltd.)
Penguin Books India Pvt. Ltd., 11 Community Centre, Panchsheel Park,
New Delhi - 110 017, India
Penguin Group (NZ), 67 Apollo Drive, Mairangi Bay,
Auckland 1311, New Zealand (a division of Pearson New Zealand Ltd.)
Penguin Books (South Africa) (Pty.) Ltd., 24 Sturdee Avenue,
Rosebank, Johannesburg 2196, South Africa

Penguin Books Ltd., Registered Offices:
80 Strand, London WC2R 0RL, England

First published by Signet Eclipse, an imprint of New American Library,
a division of Penguin Group (USA) Inc.

First Printing, April 2007
10 9 8 7 6 5 4 3 2 1

For Matt, with love and thanks

ACKNOWLEDGMENTS

Grateful thanks to:

My guys, who are magnificent, and who made me laugh
when the writing got frustrating.
And
My wonderful agent, Robin Rue, for getting us to "Go,"
and for support and encouragement throughout the
entire gestation of this story.
And
To the many folks who cheered me on
through my weblog (http://hollylisle.com/writingdiary2).
And
To Claire Zion, for hanging in with me
over the writes and rewrites.
All success is shared.
These are the people who share mine.

Prologue

Three in the morning, and once again Emma Beck stood in her bare feet, in her sleep shirt, with her eyes almost closed, painting. The gessoed board sat unsecured on her easel, bouncing as her palette knives gobbed paint onto the board in a dark, impasto style she barely would have recognized as coming from her hands. The painting that grew out of her frenzied work was of a subject she would never have chosen to paint—one man dressed in the style of the mid-nineteenth century feeding wood into a bonfire on which burned the bodies of a young woman and a small child. The painting, technically proficient, was ugly, angry, frightening, disturbing.

More disturbing, though, was the fact that Emma Beck had risen shortly after falling asleep every night since she had moved into the house two weeks earlier, and each of those nights she had created at least one angry, strange painting. Each night when she finished, after no less than three hours but no more than five, she cleaned up her supplies and hid the canvases away in a secret room in the rambling old house—a room her waking self did not know existed. She then returned to bed, unaware of anything she had done since going to bed the first time.

Chapter 1

Emma pulled to the side of the road as she came over the rise. Down below, white against brown, old and friendly and weary and rambling and waiting, it sat. The House. Her new home.

She got out of the moving van and walked to the overlook. A chill breeze bit through her thin sweater, her feet crunched in the gravel, her hands slid along the cold metal of the guardrail. She stared, unbothered by the cold, unworried by occasional passing traffic. She was coming home—in ways she could not rationally explain, and to a place where she had never lived—and she discovered she was having to get there in steps, because doing it all at once felt overwhelming.

The house below was a classic southern farmhouse, pre–Civil War though just barely, two stories high with a tin roof, hand-scrolled gingerbread, a wraparound front porch and a big separate back porch, and small-paned hand-blown glass windows. There had once been a swing on the front porch. She intended to see that there would be again. There was still a fine row of live oaks along both sides of the front drive. An old carriage house and a livestock barn sat to the north, on the back of the cleared property, covered in briar tangles that in the summer would be a mass of wild rambling roses. On the south side of the land, a stream cut its banks in meandering curves through one of two large pastures.

She smiled, almost afraid to get back into the moving van, almost afraid that if she turned away from the scene below, it would disappear behind her.

But she got in anyway because she couldn't stand on the overlook forever, and she finally steadied her hand enough to turn the key in the ignition. She drove down the little rise, around the curve where the trees still grew up to the road and arched over it, and then turned right. Going home, she told herself. Going home.

She hadn't known anything about Benina, South Carolina until her mother died of a heart attack when Emma was twenty, and her mother was fifty-three. That was when her father, then nearly sixty, told her that she probably didn't have to worry about a bad ticker because she'd been adopted.

Five years later, when Emma was twenty-five, her father died, too, leaving her a great deal of money from the sale of his prosperous Wisconsin dairy farm, and an old folder she'd never seen before, containing a detective's report. In it she'd learned, as her adoptive parents had, that Emma's birth mother had been from Benina. It also disclosed her birth mother's name—Maris Kessler—and the fact that she had died at Emma's birth.

Though Emma had always loved her parents, she'd never felt like she belonged in Wisconsin. From the time she was old enough to legally do so, she had traveled, painting and subconsciously searching for the place where she did belong. She was a professional artist, not well known, but she had managed to eke out a living doing science fiction and fantasy cover paintings for a few publishers, and doing commissioned portraits of people's children and pets when things got really tight.

Only now things wouldn't be tight anymore. She'd set up most of the money from her inheritance so that she would receive a small monthly stipend—enough to cover her basic needs, not enough to touch the principal or prevent her nest egg from growing. Frills she would pay for with her artwork, which she would be able to pursue without the constant fear that she would be unable to pay bills, buy food, keep her car on the road or a roof over her head.

The remainder she had spent buying The House, and setting aside a healthy remodeling fund to pay for the renovations.

Finding the old home had been like walking around a corner and crashing headlong into her muse.

She'd been painting since she was five. She'd been painting variations of The House just as long.

Twenty years, and in those twenty years, she had slipped echoes of the graceful front gables, the deep wraparound porch, the broad wash of azalea and rhododendron bushes and the twin rows of live oaks into almost every painting she'd done. She hid the images, and those fans she had acquired over time found pleasure in finding them. Hers was an odd obsession, but harmless. It amused her, it amused the people who bought her work. Where else might they find fierce aliens or elves and fairies and in the same picture, shadows and hints of a mysterious house?

When she was a child, she hadn't realized the style of The House was purely Southern. She never considered the fact that it looked nothing like the house where she lived, or any of the houses she saw every day. The gables, the porch, the tin roof, the broad swaths of flowering shrubs, were all imprinted in her mind as "The House," as if that form were the template from which all other houses had evolved.

As she got older and began studying art and architecture, she discovered the origins of the style she'd painted so many times, and came to wonder at her affection for it. It hadn't come from personal contact.

Her parents had never taken her out of Wisconsin. She had never seen a structure like The House in her life, except, perhaps, on television or in a photograph. But how could even a glimpsed image of a house have so captured her attention as a young child. It was a simple country farmhouse, most likely built by the hands of the people who then lived in it. Not the sort of house that would enrapture most people.

She found The House—now *her* house—driving into Benina the first time. It sat on the left side of the road, neglected, shabby, abandoned. She saw the oaks lining the driveway first, and slowed because they seemed so familiar. Then she caught sight of the old home itself, crouched behind its swag of overgrown azaleas, its porch in sad disrepair.

Her heart had thudded and seemed for a moment to stop completely. She'd pulled off the side of the road and stared at it. And then she'd driven down the weed-choked drive, and sat parked with the house on her right, with the old carriage house and stable straight in front of her but set back a ways, and she'd started to cry.

She couldn't explain the tears, any more than she could explain the wild elation that overcame her after the tears had passed. Any more than she could explain the moment when she'd taken complete leave of her senses, had gotten out of the car and walked up to the door and knocked. No one lived there—she could see by peeking through the sidelight windows that the place was empty. One of the door's sidelights had broken, so, she did something she never would have considered before; she reached through and worked the old-fashioned lock, and let herself in.

The house had been neglected, but the inside was not as bad as she'd feared it would be from its outside appearance. All of the upstairs windows were intact, most of the downstairs ones were, and the deep porch had kept water damage from the few that were broken. In fact, she found no indication of water damage inside. No vandalism. No signs that the house had been disturbed since the previous owners left, taking most of their belongings with them.

She'd walked through the house, alternately laughing and crying. She'd touched the doorframes, looked out the windows, pressed her face close to the walls and inhaled the old-wood scent of the place, as sweet to her as the scent of old books in a library.

All of the rooms were in the right places. She could not explain how she defined right places, except that this house fit her. She stood in the center of the front room, and felt the late afternoon sunlight pouring through the west windows, and the house—The House—had whispered "home."

Her heart listened.

Emma hadn't even considered moving to Benina.

The trip was simply to see the place where she had been born.

But The House changed everything.

She'd thought, *This must have been where my mother lived. This must be why I've been seeing this place all my life.*

She'd gone into town, walked into the office of the first real estate agent she located, and said, "I want to buy the abandoned house out on Bricker Road."

There'd been a bit of a furor, and a few legal hassles with deed checking and land surveying and searching for anyone who might have had a claim when the house fell empty. That was when she found out that her mother had never lived there—that the house had been in the possession of members of the Barnett family since it was built, and that it had been sitting empty since the last Barnett died. No one came forward to claim it, no one wanted it, and in the end, it had become hers.

The House had called to her, and she'd answered. She still couldn't explain why. But she'd answered. And here she was.

Emma pulled into the driveway.

Her driveway. She'd never owned a driveway before. She stopped again, right by the mailbox, and just sat there staring at the three live oaks on the left and the three on the right, trees that were so old they almost had to have been planted by the original owners some time in the early eighteen hundreds. And now those magnificent trees were her trees, and she'd never owned trees before, either. Or a porch, or doors, or windows.

It was stupid, she knew it was stupid, she had promised herself she wouldn't do it. But she did. She started to cry again.

Between the last time she'd seen the place and this time, the man she'd hired at her real estate agent's recommendation had already started to fix the place up. He'd removed and reglazed the broken windows, he'd scraped off the peeling paint and covered the exterior with a coat of fresh white and—at her request—had painted the shutters dark green. He and his crew had fixed the porch and the outside stairs, put new locks on the doors, trimmed the overgrown shrubs, cleaned and swept up the indoor living areas, and mown the grass around the house.

Beyond the neat square of the area where they'd worked, the place still looked wild. She owned ten acres, half of it in woods and meadows, one-fourth in overgrown pastures, and the rest in yard.

From the overlook, the grasses of the pastures had looked like the gold-tipped waves of a sun-drenched alien sea. Up close . . . well, they would have been a lot prettier if the real estate agent hadn't mentioned the varieties of poisonous snakes in the area.

Thanks to her contractor and his crew, she would have running water and electricity, and the floors would be safe to walk on, and she would have heat in the winter, and the dust bunnies wouldn't choke her in her sleep. It was livable, so long as she was willing to be flexible about her definition of livability.

She had an enormous amount of work ahead of her, though, because she intended to restore the place to its original condition. She wasn't concerned about the size of the task she'd taken on; one thing she'd learned from her childhood on a Wisconsin dairy farm was how to work. She'd make the place gorgeous again, piece by piece, in between doing her paintings and traveling to shows and the conventions where she sold some of her work.

She started unloading the few things in the rental moving van, and a thought struck her. She hadn't even mentioned—to her real estate lady, Lorelei Bushhalter, or the contractor she'd spoken to over the phone—that she'd been born in Benina.

She laughed a little. It seemed an odd thing to forget.

Mike Ruhl saw the rental moving truck in the drive as he drove past the old Barnett place on the way home for lunch.

He was surprised. The moving van was small, one of those little rentals that wouldn't accommodate much in the way of clothes or furniture. A battered pickup truck was hitched to a carrier behind it. Mike had assumed the new owner would have a huge moving van there, and a nice car of some sort, or maybe a flashy SUV—people who renovated old houses always seemed to Mike to have a lot of money when they started in.

He considered stopping by, just to see if Ms. Beck was satisfied with his work. The real estate agent had told him she was young and pretty, and that she thought Mike would like her, but Lorelei was pushy that way. She was always recommending this girl or that girl to Mike, because, as she put it, "I can't stand to see you with your heart broken."

His broken heart was entirely in her imagination, a fact he'd reminded her of more than once. Worse, though, Lorelei was working her way through her fifth marriage, and rumor had it she was already holding try-outs for husband number six. So Mike wasn't inclined to look too hard at candidates she proposed for him.

Besides, the house had always given him a sick feeling—from the time he was a kid, he'd hated even riding by it on his bike. He'd had the creeps the whole time he and his crew were shoring it up and making it livable. Mike figured if the new owner had any comments about his work, she had his card. Lorelei told him she had made sure of that.

Emma's cell phone rang while she was dragging her boxes of paints out of the van. It made a nice excuse to put the current, very heavy, box down and breathe for a moment.

She didn't recognize the number on the screen, but it was local.

"Emma," she said.

On the other end of the connection, she heard a throat clearing, and a stiff, precise voice, pitched deep. "Ms. Beck, this is David Halifax. I'm getting things caught up in the office today, and it has come to my attention that the paperwork for your house, including your deed and plat, are still here. Are you planning on picking them up, as you said you would, or should we mail them to you?"

The weight of the disapproval in those words—*as you said you would*—dripped like acid across the connection. Emma's heart sank. David Halifax had been the late-fortyish, upscale local lawyer who'd handled her closing on the house, and while he had been polite, the way he'd looked at her while they were going through the endless forms had left her so uncomfortable she'd hoped she would never have to see him again. She couldn't say what it was about him that had made her skin crawl, exactly. He never did or said anything that was less than utterly professional.

But when she was done, she had to force herself to shake his hand, and to walk out of the office, rather than running.

She almost had to thank him for calling, though. He'd handed her the perfect excuse to not see him again. "I'm just moving in today," she told him. "And I have a deadline that's going to make it impossible for me to get by the office anytime soon." This was only marginally true—she did have a tight deadline, but she could also have diverted herself from a grocery run to pick up the papers. "Mail them to me, would you?"

Even the pause that followed sounded disapproving. "Of course," he said after a moment. "To your old address, or your new one?"

"The new one. I'm here for keeps."

"I see. I'll have them in the mail to you on Monday."

She hung up and shook her head. There hadn't been too many people in her life that she'd met and instantly disliked. He was, however, a memorable example of one she had.

Emma jammed her cell phone back into her pocket and hoisted the box again.

And, thanks to his call, she never had to deal with him again. Exhausted as she was, that was still good news. She grinned.

Chapter 2

"Susan? It's Emma."

Emma leaned against the open door, staring out the dining room window at the part of the road she could see between the lace arch of tree branches. Early-morning sunlight poured into the room through the side windows to the east. Everything was beautiful, beautiful. And so quiet.

"Have you decided you've lost your mind yet?"

Emma laughed. "You have to come visit. The guy I hired did a great job on the repair work. You would not believe the views I have here; you'd kill to paint some of them."

"You're just saying that to lure me down there."

Susan had been Emma's friend since they swore undying passion to the goal of becoming famous artists, back when they were both eight. Halfway through art school, though, Susan had gotten married. Several years later, she and her husband Tad were expecting their first child in just a few weeks. Emma had dated, and had once even been engaged, but had never ended up keeping anyone. Men to her had been like places. She'd never found one that felt like home.

"I'll send you pictures as soon as I hang up," Emma told her. "I know you can't come down now, but you and Tad need to plan a week down here once the baby is old enough to travel. I'll put you up—I have tons of room, and by then I should have a couple of beds and everything."

Susan laughed. "Send the pictures. And . . . we know what it's going to be now."

"I thought you weren't going to find out."

"The last ultrasound was unmistakable. He's a boy. We have a name picked out."

Emma closed her eyes and said a quick prayer that it wouldn't be Tad, Jr. Susan's husband was a great guy, but Emma thought he couldn't have been more misnamed if his parents had called him Jane. "What did you choose?"

"Bryan Sherman Hacksell."

"Your dads' names, huh?"

"They're both so happy they're about to explode. And we got away with telling my father he got chosen second because the baby was a boy, so Tad got first pick. We told him that I'd get first pick next time."

Emma laughed. "It's a good name. And you're going to be a great mom."

"You've got to try this," Susan told her. "You need a husband and a kid or two."

The smile fled from Emma's face though she tried hard to keep her voice light. "You know me. Dying for a house full of kids, but too picky to settle on the father."

"It's not you. You just haven't met the right guy yet."

Emma did not want to pursue that conversation any further. She said, "My cell phone is about to die on me, Sue, and most of my stuff is still in the moving van. I'd better go get it unloaded. I want to turn it in today so I don't get charged extra."

"Go. Unpack. Call me again when you get a chance," Susan told her. "Keep your phone charged. I want to be able to reach you when I go into labor. I can't believe you're going to be there instead of here."

"I know. Me, too. But maybe I can still be there. You aren't due for weeks, and I'll be back that way as soon as I can."

She hung up and stared out the window. Susan had been steadfast in her belief that the right guy for Emma was going to show up any day since the two of them had been nineteen. Susan's perfect man had landed in her life when she turned twenty.

Emma wasn't losing hope. Not completely, anyway.

It was well past noon, and she wasn't even half finished unpacking the van. She slid her back down the living room wall and leaned against it, hands clutching her knees. Sweat ran into her eyes and down her neck, she was breathing hard, and already, every muscle she had hurt. She hadn't realized how far she'd gotten from farm chores in the last few years. Time was, she wouldn't have felt a twinge from the heavy labor. But she'd been lulled into a false sense of sturdiness by friends who'd helped her pack the truck; she hadn't imagined how different the job of unpacking it alone was going to be.

She'd thought she was being smart when she made sure no bundle, box, or piece of furniture was more than she could handle on her own. She'd failed to take into account the effects that stairs and unwieldy furniture shapes, and weariness, and even loneliness, would have on her.

She'd gotten her paintings out of the van the night before, and then her art supplies, and moved them quickly to the room she'd chosen to be her studio. Fix up on that room was the one real splurge of cash she'd put into the house before moving into it. She'd invested in full insulation, new thermal windows, and a quality climate control system, because she didn't mind living with drafts and the vagaries of humidity while she fixed the place up, but her work couldn't.

Once her art was safely stored, though, she had to face everything else. She'd dragged in her futon mattress, flopped on that, and promised herself that unpacking in the morning would be easier than after a long drive because she'd be fresh in the morning.

Only she wasn't.

Emma hadn't bothered bringing large furniture, like the couch or her bed, with her. The furniture she'd had in her apartment didn't match her new home, and she wanted to haunt flea markets and antique stores, buy old things, and refinish them to match the vision she had of what The House would be when it was finished.

She had chairs, however, and all the disassembled pieces of a dining room table; boxes of reference books and favorite novels; trash bags of clothes; her futon frame and mattress—which would be her bed until she found just the right one for the house; and other items she couldn't bear to leave behind. She had enough to fill the front room from wall to wall, and in the end, she gave up on putting things where they would eventually belong, and satisfied herself with the idea of just getting everything out of the van. That way, she would be able to move things around at her convenience, and she'd still be able to turn the van in before six.

Emma walked into the dining room and stared out the east window. She had a wonderful view of a neighbor's fields in the distance; they hadn't yet been plowed under, so they were ragged with the skeletal crops of the previous season. She could make out cotton and corn from her vantage point. Closer was her east pasture with its ragged fencing. And right up beside the house, she realized she could just make out the outlines of a rose garden. She studied it, frowning. She hadn't noticed any garden before she bought the house.

Granted, there wasn't much left of it. Weed-strangled roses, bare-branched in the dead of winter, one falling-down stone bench, and in what must have been the center, a small, broken fountain. But she could imagine what the garden must have been like when it was still being cared for. Shaded and cool during the hottest part of the day, illuminated and dewy and radiant first thing in the morning. She could almost smell the sweet, rich perfumes of antique roses, echoes from another time.

She could feel the presence of the woman who planted those old, battered roses. And loved them. Who knelt, trowel in hand, carefully placing each young plant in the rich, dark earth.

Abruptly, Emma found herself shivering, with the hair standing up on the back of her neck, and her arms covered with goose bumps.

Behind her, from somewhere in the back of the house, she realized she could hear water dripping.

She sighed and pushed herself away from the win-

dow. She could track down the open tap, then get back
to unloading the moving van. Hunting down the drip
would give her a breather from slogging heavy things
into the house.

The sound seemed to be coming from off to her left.
That would make it the kitchen. Easy enough.

She walked through the empty dining room, wincing
at the peeling wallpaper, and stepped into the kitchen.

The sink sat on the far end of the enormous room,
next to the space where the refrigerator would go when
the delivery truck got around to delivering it. The spigot
was bone dry.

Emma could still hear water dripping, but the sound
was behind her again.

She turned, annoyed, and half closed her eyes, and
started to work her way through the house, following
the alternately fainter and louder drips. The sound was
steady enough that it suggested a lot of water leaking. If
it was coming from someplace other than a sink or tub,
she could end up with serious water damage in a hurry.

She followed the dripping upstairs, trying not to
creak on the steps, tuning her ears for the faint sound.

A soft, steady plink, plink, plink came from the first
door to the right of the landing. Emma opened that door,
and for a moment she almost couldn't breathe. The
sense of something *wrong* rushed out at her and overwhelmed her. Without questioning, without thinking,
she pulled the door shut again, and stood there with her
heart pounding and her hands shaking.

She'd been in the room before, once on the day that
she'd discovered the house, and again on the day that
she'd come down to pay for it and take possession of the
deed. She'd never felt anything like that either time.

The room had been empty. She hadn't seen anything out of place. What had been, at one time, a child's bedroom, was at that moment a simple square of space, one window on the east side, one closet, no furniture. No item left behind. A single bare bulb in the porcelain socket in the ceiling.

Emma tried to slow her pulse, to make her hand reach out for that door and open it again. The dripping noise was gone. The room had no taps in it, and because of its location, would have no pipes running through it, so the dripping noise couldn't have been coming from there. Further, nothing had been *in* that room, nothing had been *wrong* with the room. She had no reason to recoil from it.

And yet she was as bone-deep terrified as she had ever been in her life, so scared her knees were weak and she couldn't catch her breath. She had to sit down on the top stair, and force her muscles to relax, and count her breaths—four in, hold for twelve, exhale for six, hold for four, inhale again—to get any control over her heart rate or her rushing respirations.

Ten breaths and her heart no longer felt like it was going to claw its way out of her rib cage.

Ten breaths, and she realized that she could hear dripping again. Downstairs.

She glanced over her shoulder to the door behind her. She didn't like having that door at her back. Her gut feeling was that, if she didn't watch it, it would burst open.

Emma clenched her fists tight enough that her nails dug into the palms of her hands. Nothing wrong, nothing to be afraid of in this house, The House, her home that had felt like home from the moment she saw it.

She wouldn't be stupid. The problem was leaking, and she didn't have time to deal with leaking. She had a van to unpack.

So she walked down the stairs, grabbed her cell phone out of her purse, and called the number of the man who had done the renovation work.

Mike Ruhl had just dragged out his tackle box and his fishing rod, looking forward to a well-earned afternoon of fishing, when the phone started ringing. The number wasn't local, but he recognized the name. Emma Beck.

So she was out at the house, and calling from her cell phone.

"Should have stopped yesterday," he said to thin air, and answered the phone. "This is Mike Ruhl."

"Hi, Mike. This is Emma Beck." On the other end of the phone, he heard the same voice he'd talked to pretty regularly while he and she were getting things set up for her before she moved down. She sounded funny, though. Kind of tight. Stressed.

"You all right out there?" he asked.

She laughed, and it was not a happy laugh. "I hate moving. And I'm really hating unloading that van. But that isn't why I called. Water is dripping somewhere in the house. I can hear it, but I can't find where it's coming from."

He wasn't entirely surprised. He and his crew had gone over the pipes before they signed off on the project, and everything had been tight then. But the place was old, and so were most of the pipes. It was entirely possible that something had gone wrong between the old pipes and the new fittings in the couple of weeks since he'd finished the work.

The temptation to pass her off to a local plumber hit him hard. He was hungry, and he'd just wrapped up a long job for miserable people who had been impossible to satisfy, and he desperately wanted to take the day off.

He'd done the job, though, and when he finished, he took her money, and she'd paid promptly and on faith, without even coming down to check everything out first. He had an obligation to make sure he'd done the work right.

"Mr. Ruhl? Are you there?"

He said, "I'll be right out." The largemouth bass would just have to wait.

Emma had managed to drag the pieces for her futon into the house, and was sitting on the floor with a wrench, a screwdriver, and pliers, trying to get everything to go back together the way it had been in her apartment, when Mike Ruhl knocked on the door.

She could see the side of truck through the sidelights around her front door, and MIKE RUHL CONSTRUCTION, YOU DESERVE THE BEST painted on the side.

"Come on in," she yelled. "The door's open."

It opened, and he stepped in.

Emma stared at the man in front of her—a man of average height, with sandy hair, and a good body under a loose T-shirt and tight jeans—and she felt a little woozy.

She got to her feet, trying not to stare at him. But she was staring at him anyway, frozen, wordless, lost in the most ridiculous, insane, idiotic wave of desire that she had ever felt. She had never in her life been so overcome with passion that she'd actually undressed a man in her mind. Not once. And yet here she was, staring at him and visualizing him as naked as the day he was born, but a whole lot better developed.

Her reaction to him was so over the top that she would have laughed out loud . . . if only she could have breathed.

And then he asked her, "Have we . . . met before?"

She realized that he was staring at her as intently as she was staring at him.

"No," she said.

Except, in a funny way, they had. Sort of.

She had painted him in her work. She knew the planes and angles of his cheeks and jaw, the line of his nose, the lift of his brow, almost as well as she knew the curves and lines of her own face. His was a face she thought she'd dreamed up. It was the face of her ideal warrior, her ideal hero. It wasn't a handsome face. It was . . . fierce. Clean, rugged lines—no hint of the femininity that she loathed in the male-model faces on book covers painted by so many other artists. His was the face she'd painted on lean, hard-muscled fantasy heroes in barbarian furs, and his, too, the face she had created for space-faring pirate captains. She'd changed the hair color, the eye color, the clothes. But when the face of her live model was too pouty-lipped pretty, the face Mike wore was the face she'd substituted.

Only . . . she thought she'd made him up.

Looking at him in the flesh, she discovered she was having to tell herself, *Inhale. Exhale. Inhale. Exhale.*

His hair was military-cut short, and sandy blond, his eyes were a calm, steady gray.

She wanted him. Not in the polite, hi-nice-to-meet-you way that would let her get through this awkward encounter with her dignity intact. She wanted him naked, on her futon mattress on the floor. She hoped her face didn't reflect her thoughts.

And still they stood there, staring at each other, while the silence grew longer and more awkward.

Abruptly, Mike shook his head and blushed, and said, "Um . . . where did you hear the leak?" But he didn't seem interested in his question, or her answer. He hadn't been able to take his eyes off her since he stepped through the door. He hadn't even moved.

She forced herself to turn away from him, to point toward the kitchen. "That's the first place I heard it," she said. "It seemed to be coming from a couple of different locations, but that was the first one."

He cleared his throat. "I'll go take a look."

Neither of them moved.

She nodded. She didn't say anything else. She couldn't. She waited, and after another awkward pause, Mike Ruhl turned and looked away from her, and headed toward the kitchen.

Whatever spell had bound their feet to the floor broke as he walked away, and Emma sagged.

God, she wasn't a drinker, but right then a shot of straight whiskey seemed like it would have been a good idea.

She went back to putting her futon together instead, though she kept looking at the pieces and seeing the whole, and then imagining him on it. Them on it. Hot. Sweaty.

She shook her head, and listened to him thumping around and tapping things, and opening and closing doors. Going upstairs, coming back down.

She finished the futon frame, dragged the mattress onto it, and shoved it against the back wall. She'd had

her little break. She couldn't justify putting the futon together before she'd emptied the moving van, because
she could always just sleep on the mattress on the floor
again. But she was so sore and tired, she'd pretended
getting the futon put together was the most important
thing she had to accomplish that day.

The van still had a lot of stuff in it, though. She
dragged herself out the front door and returned to haul-
ing it in, one box at a time.

She came off the back of the truck and across the
ramp with a box of books that had gained about fifty
pounds between Wisconsin and South Carolina. Sweat
dripped down her nose and she was panting. She
bumped the door open with her hip, staggered inside,
and there he was, just inches from her. She almost
dropped the box on his feet.

"I can't find anything wrong in your kitchen, or anywhere else that you have pipes, and I can't hear any
dripping anywhere, or find any signs that you have a
water leak." He looked apologetic when he said it, as if
finding a water leak would have been the good alterna-
tive.

She carefully slid the book box on top of other boxes,
making a largish pyramid of them in the center of the
floor.

She turned and he was still right there. Too close. Too
close for reason, too close for logic, too close for control. She willed him to back up, but he didn't. And she
didn't.

She could envision herself moving forward, wrapping her arms around him and kissing him with everything in her. Starting to cry, so grateful to be with him
that she could not even find words. Some wild, reckless

part of her wanted that, and told her that was what she should do.

"I'm sorry to have called you out," she said, struggling to get those words out of a mouth that seemed to fight her over every one of them. "I'm sorry I wasted your time. How much do I owe you?"

"You don't owe me anything," he told her, and backed up at last. "These old houses make funny sounds and do funny things, and you don't want to run the chance of ignoring something that could leave you with a mess."

"No. I don't," she agreed.

He looked past her, to the pile of book boxes behind her.

"Let me help you get the rest of your stuff into the house before I go. You don't have much more until you're finished." They stared into each other's eyes.

"You don't have to," she said.

He grinned, and it was the first time she saw a smile on his face. It melted her knees right out from under her. "I don't," he said. "But I figure I will anyway."

She followed him out the front door, watching the way his shoulders moved under his T-shirt. "Thanks," she told him. Maybe she could just follow him back and forth for a while, watching his muscles move. He was a whole course in Anatomy for Artists.

She picked up her own box, though, and hauled it in after him.

An hour later, they were through. He'd moved about seventy-five percent of the stuff still in the van, and they'd brushed against each other a dozen times in the process, and Emma felt like her nerves had been strung out in all directions and tightened like guitar strings.

Finished, they stood at the door. "Guess I'll get the thing back in time to not owe another day now," she told him, smiling. "Thanks. I don't think I could have done it by myself. Today, I mean."

"S'alright."

He was standing close enough that she could feel the heat of his skin brushing against her. She thought, *I could give him a thank-you kiss,* and knew as she thought it that it was a bad, bad idea. She said, "Let me repay you for the help."

He shook his head. "You don't owe me. Consider it me being a good southern gentleman."

"I'll make you dinner sometime," she blurted, and heard the words come out of her mouth and was horrified that she couldn't stop them.

No chance to take them back, though. He considered her offer, and nodded. "All right. I'll hold you to that." And then he turned and left.

She didn't want him to leave, and at the same time, she couldn't get the door shut behind him fast enough.

She closed the door, and when she'd locked and double locked it, she leaned her forehead against the door.

And started to cry.

The tears were totally out of character. She didn't understand. They were as stupid as the tears she'd shed while sitting in the driveway. She wasn't a crier, or she never had been before.

She'd been exhausted before, she'd felt overwhelmed before, she'd been scared before—and sometimes all three at the same time. Moving into her house and meeting Mike Ruhl in person should not have affected her the way they did.

It took an inordinate amount of effort, but she made herself stop.

She made herself go outside. Hooked her car to the back of the moving van again. Drove it in, turned it in, and drove home.

And started weeping in her damned driveway again.

"This is nuts," she told herself.

She made sure she locked up. Then she lay down on her futon in the living room, and closed her eyes, and willed her trembling body to stillness.

It had to be exhaustion. The drive from Wisconsin had been long and dismal. Leaving hard winter behind had been pleasant enough, but she could still feel the road on her. Her mind was tired from the constant demands for alertness, her eyes were heavy, her body ached. She'd slept her first night in the house but she hadn't rested. She'd dealt with noises that seemed to be imaginary. Her emotions were out of whack. If she thought she was hearing things, with sounds of dripping water that weren't coming from anywhere; if she suspected herself of seeing things, with the familiarity in Mike Ruhl's face that would no doubt be considerably less striking when she was rested; if she'd turned into a weepy idiot for no apparent reason, her solution was still simple.

A nap would fix everything.

Mike sat at his kitchen table, an uneaten microwaved dinner in front of him, staring at his hands. They were shaking, his heart was racing, and he felt like he'd backed into live wires and been kicked across the room by the shock.

He'd been inches—inches—from getting himself in real trouble. The instant he saw Emma Beck, he wanted to grab her and kiss her and drag her onto that mattress she had lying in the middle of her floor, and tell her he was never letting her go again. It had taken every ounce of will in his body to keep his distance.

As far as he knew, he'd always been a normal guy. He'd been married once, it hadn't worked out, and his wife had moved on after a year to a man who would provide for her in the style to which she wanted to become accustomed, leaving Mike alone but relieved. He'd dated since, he'd had a little fun, but he'd comfortably avoided anything that might be mistaken for commitment. He'd done marriage, it was nothing but a way for a woman to demand all his money while using sex as a weapon, and the rare half-assed home-cooked meal when she wanted something just wasn't worth it.

He had no answer for why he'd responded to Emma Beck like that. He couldn't explain why, with his brain telling him to get out, get out, *get out* after he couldn't find the leak she thought she heard, he then helped her carry stuff into the house. Or why, with his brain saying *No, thank you, that's not necessary* to her offer of dinner sometime, his fat mouth had said, "I'll hold you to that."

He knew he couldn't go back to her house again. He would have to send one of his guys out. Or refer her to another contractor.

Except that even as he thought about sending someone else out there, he knew he wasn't going to do it.

What if all men responded to her that way? The caveman part of his brain, the part that was saying *Ugh. My woman*, was also visualizing Bill Chesney, Mike's main business competitor, pushing her back against a wall and kissing her until she squealed.

At which point, Mike visualized smacking Bill over the head with his caveman club.

This sort of lunatic possessiveness over a woman he did not know unnerved him.

He needed a dose of reason. A good, rock-solid, inescapable kick in the side of the head.

So he left untouched food and unopened beer on the table and drove over to his sister's house.

Cara opened the door when he rang the bell and stared at him. "You look like hell," she said. "And not even a shower first? Ick."

"I'd say it had been a weird day, but it only got strange around lunchtime. Drew around?"

Cara shook her head. "Hospital called him in on an emergency. Sounded pretty bad—I'm guessing he won't be home for hours."

"Good."

Cara raised her eyebrows.

"Not good about him not being here. You know I love the guy. But good, because if I'm going to prove I'm crazy, I only want to do it in front of you. Something happened to me that doesn't make any sense, and your job is to talk me back to sanity. And you don't get to tell Mom or Dad, and you don't get to tell Drew. Okay?"

Cara stared at him. "I have dinner getting cold on the table, and I'm hungry. If I'm going to listen to this, I'm going to eat. And you are, too."

"That works for me."

They sat and ate, and Cara listened to Mike while he

carefully explained his connection to Emma Beck, and his reaction to their first meeting. And he downed some fine, fine pork chops and gravy and greens and pinto beans; Cara had learned to cook from their mother, and nothing had gotten lost in the translation. When he was done, both talking and eating, he sat back.

And Cara stared at him and shook her head, and started to chuckle. "I would never have guessed you to be the sort of guy who could fall in love at first sight, Mike. I've watched you with women, and your approach has always been to let them get just so close, and no closer. You were like that with Bria—I know she had her bad points, and I agree with you that you weren't in your right mind when you married her. But she never had a chance with you."

"Bria was a disaster."

"Given. But I'm not talking about Bria. Bria was a shallow, grasping, greedy bitch, and everyone knows that. Including her poor hubby number two, who, every time they come into the office, looks like he's been whipped hard, spurred till he bled, and ridden into the ground. You and Bria never had a chance because she's hell on two legs. But she never had a chance because you wouldn't let her get close, either." Cara tipped her head and studied him. "I want to meet the woman you can't get out of your head."

"No," Mike said. "Cara, you don't understand. We're not talking love here. We're talking *crazy.* We're talking about me looking at a complete stranger and seeing naked and sweaty and having this stupid feeling that . . . that . . . never mind . . . but . . . dammit, there I was, bumping into her on purpose while we were carrying boxes into her house just so I could touch her." He leaned forward and stared into her eyes. "I don't know who the hell I was when I was in that house with her, but it wasn't me."

"I'm *definitely* going to meet her," Cara said. "Because that was the way I felt about Drew when I first saw him. I had to have him. And eventually I did."

"Hell. So what you're saying is, crazy runs in the family."

"Bite me." Cara laughed. "You are a pain in the ass, little bro, and a know-it-all. I have to do laundry, though, and iron my stuff for work tomorrow, and wash dishes, and all the rest of that mess, and unless you're going to help me, you need to get out from underfoot."

Emma woke shivering and lost, with her breath curling in pale white clouds across her face. She ached everywhere. She didn't know where she was or how she had come to be there.

All she knew for certain was that something was watching her.

Moonlight carved pale white squares on the floor, but outside curtainless windows, the sky she could see was black.

Above her, a floor creaked. Outside, an owl hooted, something screamed. *My new house*, she thought, and then, *I'm in my new house, I'm on the futon. I was just going to take a nap.*

She didn't dare move.

She could feel whatever it was staring at her, but she couldn't see anything. The towering stacks of boxes, the furniture jammed and piled in no order, the bags of clothes—all made perfect cover for anyone.

She'd locked the door.

She'd turned on the heat, too, hadn't she? Surely she'd turned on the heat?

But no. She'd been in and out the door, she'd been working hard, she'd been sweating, and it had been the middle of the day, and warm—

Behind her, something rustled.

Emma's heart took off at a gallop, and she tried to make herself smaller. Still. Her breath plumed, radiant in the moonlight.

Outside, a car drove past her house, tires humming on concrete. She could see the headlights illuminate the rows of live oaks, branched low and twisting, reaching.

The light did not make it to the front room.

None of that light made it to the front room.

A heavy thud, right behind her. She turned, sat up.

Saw movement from the corner of her eye.

She started to scream, started to recoil—

And something big, and furry jumped over her and landed on the back of the futon. Pale eyes that glowed green stared down into hers, big paws kneaded the cushion, and, as the animal settled into a watchful sitting pose, the white-tipped tail wrapped primly around the feet.

"You're a *cat*?" she said.

She could barely see his outline. He was a big cat. Heavy. Easily twenty, twenty-five pounds. He was long, rangy, broad. His fur looked thick and glossy—smoke-tabby patterned with perfect tuxedo marks. He wore no collar. She watched him watching her, wondering if he was a neighbor's cat that was up to date on his shots, or some feral animal that would bite her and give her rabies.

He studied her with an air of calm confidence, as if he were certain of his welcome. Emma decided she didn't seem in imminent danger of being bitten. She stood and said, "You scared the skin right off me. Get down. I need to turn the lights on in here, and get the heat going, and then we're going to open the door and send you home."

He arced from futon to the floor, liquid as water tossed from a cup, and landed lightly between boxes and bags, disturbing nothing.

"How did you get in here?" she asked him as she started turning on lights, checking doors and windows, making sure the house was secure. Everything was locked up tight. "Did you come in while I was bringing things into the house? While Mike Ruhl and I were making fools of ourselves?" The cat padded along beside her, companionable and silent.

In the light, he was just as big as he'd looked in the dark. The glossy black stripes in the swirling pattern overlaid elegant gray and bits of fox red, and the spotless tux of white at the muzzle, white bib, four white feet gave proof to his careful grooming. Pale, pale yellow eyes watched her. He was a beautiful animal.

And seemingly content to walk with her as she made her rounds, downstairs, then upstairs. She picked up a broom as she started up the stairs. It wasn't much of a weapon. She was going to have to do better.

She went room to room, starting with the empty bedroom at the top right of the landing, the one that had so terrified her earlier in the day. This time when she opened the door, it was just a room. The rest of the upstairs rooms were equally benign. Everything in the house was as it should be.

Emma went downstairs, finding odd comfort in the presence of the cat as the two of them finished their rounds. "I'm all for a little hot chocolate," she said as she headed into the kitchen. "Before I kick you out the door, do I have anything at all that you'd like?"

She looked down at her side and discovered he was gone.

She didn't have a cat box, but she had plenty of boxes, some of them opened but not emptied, with items in them that would not be improved by being used as a cat litter substitute. She went back through the house, feeling like an idiot as she called, "Here, kitty, kitty."

"Here, tiger, tiger," would have felt more appropriate. Less demeaning. That cat had never been "kitty."

She spent a good two hours looking for him, from three thirty in the morning to five thirty in the morning, but he had managed to disappear completely.

She decided the missing cat was good incentive for her to get the boxes unpacked and cleared as quickly as possible. Doing so would prevent her finding nasty surprises in with her knickknacks, and eliminate a lot of the places a cat could hide. The tuxedoed tiger would show up again before too long, she decided, needing to be let out. She would let him out, and be careful not to let him back in. Even if she did like him, he seemed too well mannered not to belong to someone. She didn't want to be the woman who broke some little girl's heart by stealing her cat.

Emma's uninvited guest made her think, though, that a kitten might be nice. Company in a big old house in a place where she knew no one. *Almost* no one, she thought, trying to erase the image of Mike Ruhl that had popped into her mind. A kitten would get her through the empty places before she made friends.

Tired, achy, but filled with purpose, she started emptying boxes and finding places for things.

Chapter 3

THE THIRD DAY—Monday

He had to stop.

Mike refused to let himself slow down as he drove past her house for the third time that morning. The moving van was gone, her truck was parked on the west side of the house, beside the porch, and he had no doubt whatsoever that she was inside.

He was making excuses to run out for things his crew didn't really need, and he was taking the long way back every single time, and sooner or later she was going to register that the same damned truck had driven in front of her house in the same direction all morning. She was going to call Driscoll Cavanaugh at the police station and have him come out to see who was stalking her.

Mike did not need to develop a reputation as a stalker. He and Dris were finally getting past Mike's less-than-angelic adolescence, and Dris had started creeping around to the opinion that Mike might, now that he was twenty-eight, have grown into a respectable adult and a solid citizen.

He wasn't likely to look as kindly at stalking as he

had at toilet-papering the courthouse, or Mike and his buddies moving Driscoll's beloved VW Beetle up onto the pedestal that was going to hold some artist's modern art disaster in front of the new library.

He hadn't been all that kind about those incidents, come to think of it. Especially the VW.

"Perspective," Mike muttered. He would get back to the site, he would get into the work, and he would cut and measure and hammer until he was exhausted. He would sweat the woman out of his system, and then he would drive home, eat, have a cold beer, and watch the news until he fell asleep.

One o'clock in the afternoon, and an entire morning of floor scrubbing lay behind her.

Emma hurt in places she hadn't remembered she had. She winced her way out to the truck and eased herself in, trying her damnedest not to whimper out loud.

Once inside and seat-belted in, she looked at her list again. Aside from three varieties of over-the-counter pain reliever on her shopping list, she'd written down every variety of food she could think of that did not require refrigeration. Plus a large cooler, which in the middle of winter would probably be hard to find. Bags of ice. She was tired of running out to the town's lone burger joint for breakfast, lunch, and dinner. The fifteen-mile round trip was getting on her nerves. So was the cardboard food.

She'd also listed shelving boards and brackets from the local hardware store. A good wallpaper stripper. Necessary hardware. She knew she needed to be doing the cover art for the book, but she didn't feel like painting. She wanted to work on her kitchen.

She drove into Benina, admiring the charm of the place. The major superchains hadn't found it yet, so Main Street was still alive. Not thriving, exactly. But between the little thrift shops and the corner banks and the diner of questionable quality and the used bookstore and two department stores that still did a decent business, it looked a lot like most towns must have looked twenty or thirty years earlier.

Hardware store on the right. To the left, the real estate office she'd walked into the day she found her house.

Big green square in front of her at the end of Main Street, with the courthouse behind it old and regal and picturesque.

Emma had never gone all the way down to the courthouse. So, because she didn't have anyplace she had to be at any particular time, and because driving hurt less than getting out of the truck and walking, she decided to look around. Just for a few minutes.

The square was beautiful, verdant with close-mown winter wheat, jeweled with pansies and some bright, decorative cabbage-looking plants, with a war memorial in the center of the square and benches and sidewalks around the perimeter and laced across the green in curving patterns. The beautiful old courthouse, brick with a patinaed brass cupola on the top and ornate arches and pillars, could have been a set from a movie. To the left, back where it couldn't be seen from up the street, sat a square yellow-brick police station. It was small and stern and sure of its purpose. To the right, totally at odds with the rest of Main Street and the slice-of-the-past square, sat a modern library in front of which squatted an appalling embarrassment of modern art that looked mostly like a melted orange toad jammed onto a marble cube. The LEGO-block construction of the library had to have been approved by hippies, Emma thought. Deeply stoned hippies. Its slab panels in primary yellow, blue, and red, angled through white concrete, making it look more like a messy room a child had failed to clean up than any respectable architecture.

She found herself driving around the back and into the parking lot, just to see if it was as ugly from that angle as from the front.

It was.

She parked.

Got out.

She hadn't planned to visit the library, but now that she was looking at it, she had to go inside.

She went in, thinking that the inside had to be an improvement from the outside, but she was wrong. Inside, the colors were orange, green, and purple, and they covered everything from the librarian's desk to reading tables to shelves. The walls were stark white, the carpet a not-quite-geometric pattern of stark, sharp-edged purple, orange, green, red, yellow, and blue that had not worn well.

Emma stood in the center of the main room, turning slowly, looking up and down and around, and winced.

"No one on the town council that approved this building was reelected," a woman said behind her. "Ever. Unfortunately, we could neither run them out of town on rails, nor burn down the building."

Emma laughed. "It doesn't fit the rest of the town." She turned to look at the woman, who looked to be in her mid-fifties. She wore a proper sweater set, a gray wool skirt with pleats, flats, hose, and a single strand of what looked like, to Emma, real pearls.

"I'm Emma Beck," she said, smiling. "I just moved here, and was scoping out the possibility of getting a library card. If this library still has books, that is."

"Gwen Carlston, and nice to meet you, Emma." The librarian sighed. "It makes you wonder, doesn't it? We had a fine old Carnegie Library on this very spot, up until the early eighties. Burned to the ground one night following a lightning strike, all except for the brick outside, and the town council went looking for something a lot less stuffy—that was their word. They wanted an edifice that would inspire a new generation to read. This . . . this monstrosity . . . is what some fool sold them instead. And here it is, and we can't pray lightning back to this spot to save our lives."

Emma laughed. "So. What do I need to get a library card?"

"A driver's license and a utility bill with your name and address on it."

Emma sighed. "I don't have either of those yet. Well, I have a driver's license, of course, but it's from Wisconsin. And I haven't gotten my first utility bills yet. I just moved last Thursday."

"Where'd you move?"

Emma smiled. "You know the old Barnett farm out on Bricker Road?"

"*You're* the one who bought the old Barnett house?"

The look of shock on the woman's face did not fill Emma with warm feelings. "Why do you say it that way?"

"As long as I've lived here, everyone has been afraid of that house. Up until about ten years, maybe fifteen years ago, a descendant of the original Barnett who built it lived there. She was old and reclusive and crazy, and she talked about hearing voices and having things moved around when she woke up in the mornings. I wouldn't live there on a bet."

"The real estate lady didn't mention anything about it being haunted."

And Gwen just raised an eyebrow. "Did you ask? The town has been trying to figure out what to do with that place since the last Barnett died. She didn't have any offspring, and she had written into her will that the place had to be sold by the town to a new owner. There hasn't been a soul willing to offer a penny for the place in ten years. And then you come along and just up and buy it? No one would want to mention anything about it being haunted."

Chatty, Emma thought. The library looked empty except for the two of them—if it was like that most of the time, she could understand Gwen being happy to have someone to talk to. Still . . . she was definitely chatty.

Emma thought about the room at the top of the stairs. Then she quashed that thought. Exhaustion had caused her to react strangely—that was all. She said, "It doesn't seem haunted. In need of a lot of work, definitely, but not haunted."

She leaned against the horrible purple reading table beside her and said, "Have you lived here all your life?"

"My family has been in Benina for as many generations as there's been a Benina," Gwen said.

"Did you ever know a girl named Maris Kessler? I was told she was from around here."

Gwen seemed to cool a little. She gave Emma a hard look, and took a half step back, and crossed her arms over her shoulders. "Who might have mentioned her?"

"It's a long story," Emma said, wondering what she'd said that had raised the librarian's guard. "I was at an art show in Wisconsin, and got to talking to someone about one of my paintings. She noticed the house in it, and said she'd seen one that looked a lot like it, back where she used to live."

Emma listened to herself lying, stunned by her duplicity. She could easily have said, "She died in childbirth, and I'm her daughter. I was adopted by folks in Wisconsin." What would have been wrong with the truth? But she couldn't get the truth past her lips. Something in her was . . . afraid.

The librarian nodded. And waited.

Emma continued, "Anyway, we got to talking about where she used to live, and small towns, and how much she missed Benina, and I have no idea how it happened, but we got onto the subject of lost friends. It was a sad conversation. And she mentioned Maris Kessler, who she said had been a good friend of hers, but who had died young. She said it was a sad story."

The librarian was still cool. Still wary. "What was her name?"

"Amanda, I think. Or Alana. Something that began with an A, anyway." Emma shrugged. "She didn't buy any of my work, so for me it was just one of those conversations you have with people that float out of your memory."

Gwen was staring into the middle distance, an expression of deep concentration on her face. "Maris's friends . . . The ones who moved away. . . ." she murmured. "Amy?" she asked suddenly. "Did you talk to Amy Kirkbride?"

Emma said, "I honestly can't be sure. It could have been Amy, but she never told me her last name, and I did talk to quite a few people that night."

"It was probably Amy," the librarian said, and suddenly she was warmer again. "They were very good friends, right up to the tragedy. But I knew Maris. She was a lot younger than I was, but she sang in our church choir. She had the most beautiful voice."

Emma sang a little, but no one would have remembered her for her voice. She smiled, discovering this bit of her mother still around for her to find. She said, "Maris's friend and I never got to finish our conversation. A customer came up to me wanting to talk price, and I had to go. But I've always wondered about the rest of the story."

The librarian leaned in a little. "Well, Maris died when she was sixteen. She got pregnant, and according to just about everyone, she never told anyone who the father was. Amy knew, though, I'm pretty sure. But Amy and her whole family moved away right after Maris died." She frowned a little, considering that. "Anyway, we knew she was pregnant, and then she disappeared from school." Gwen paused. "And then she died, and the rumors surrounding her death were awful. The least awful one was that she had complications because she was so young, and the baby was stillborn and Maris died in childbirth. The second was that she went crazy a month or so before she delivered, and tried to kill her doctor, and then tried to kill one of the nurses when they put her in the hospital, and when the baby was born she tried to kill it and then somehow did manage to kill herself." Gwen frowned and shook her head. "And the last was that she was murdered by the parents of the baby's father."

"Oh, my God," Emma whispered. She felt light-headed.

Gwen stared off in the distance, lost in her own thoughts for a moment. And then she looked back at Emma, and added, "I'm almost certain the 'died in childbirth' story was the official one, but the rumors about the craziness and the murder and suicide have never gone away. It was awful," Gwen said, not noticing the effect that the story was having on her listener. "But the funny thing is, I never believed the bad stories about her."

Emma paused in the midst of her panic. "No?"

"As young as she was, Maris was . . . practical. As practical as any teenager back then, anyway. She was the sort of girl who helped her mother, who listened to her mother. She was never flamboyant, never all that visible. But if you watched her—if you listened to her— you knew she was a nice girl. A good kid. She wanted to please people. I always suspected the boy who took advantage of her was the real problem."

Emma had a hard time getting through her list of chores. The librarian's story of Maris and the doubts and questions surrounding her mother's death had left her shaken. The detective hadn't hinted at any questions surrounding her mother's death, no whisper of either madness or murder.

Clearly, Emma hadn't died at birth. So at least that part of all three stories was false.

But an attempt to kill a doctor or a nurse during pregnancy? Emma wondered if that might have been hormone imbalances. Or schizophrenia.

She suppressed a shiver.

That was supposed to be hereditary, wasn't it?

She managed to gather up everything she needed

back at the house, but her mind was trapped in an ugly loop.

Schizophrenics heard voices, didn't they? Or sounds that didn't have any connection with the real world? Like dripping water. Maybe they fixated on things, too. Maybe they saw The House that had been an obsession to them for most of their lives in some ordinary, run-down house. Maybe they saw The Face in the face of some ordinary guy who walked into their living rooms and didn't look much like the image they had embedded in their minds.

Maybe Emma's mother had been crazy—violently crazy. And maybe Emma was headed in that direction, too.

The cat was sitting on the back of her futon couch when she walked into the house.

"Where have you been?" she asked him.

And then she wondered whether he was really there or not. She knew he hadn't gotten in with her—or when she went out, either. She had scoured the house for him the night before.

He was watching her, pale eyes solemn. He had a dead mouse in his mouth.

When she put her bags down, he poured himself off the back of the futon and trotted over to her. He dropped the mouse at her feet, then disappeared into the back of the house.

She stared down at the little corpse on her floor. That certainly looked real enough, and it was something that she was going to have to clean up. She made a face, and carried her bags into the kitchen, and returned to the foyer with a broom and dustpan. The mouse was still there, and still dead. She was grateful entirely out of proportion to the situation.

Her cell phone rang as she was dumping the mouse into her trash. She fished the phone out of her pocket and pressed the answer button without looking. "Hi, Susan, I'm dealing with a dead mouse. Hang on."

"I wasn't a Susan the last time I checked," the male voice on the other end of the phone said, and Emma shoved the mouse-inhabited trash can under the sink, closed the cabinet door, and checked the name on her phone, which she should have done in the first place. As she did so, she heard the voice say, "But it's good to hear you can deal with dead mice."

It was a local number. "Mike?" she said.

"That would be me."

"I'm sorry I didn't check first. I've been half expecting to hear from my friend from back home all morning. She usually calls in the morning, and she's expecting, and could be due any time."

"That's fine. I just called because I had an idea about that drip sound you were hearing. I thought I'd offer to come out and track it down this afternoon, check my theory."

"What's your theory?"

"That you're getting condensation from your roof that's running into the house somewhere. It might have a couple different drip lines, which would explain why you hear it at different places. And if there's enough of it, you could still be getting water damage."

At that moment, having a man tell her the dripping noises she'd been hearing the day before might still have a genuine physical cause made her as happy as having to dispose of the body of the dead mouse.

Funny how perspective could make even bad news good.

And she had to admit, the idea of having someone else nearby was a little bit comforting. Emma had always been comfortable with her own company, but the story the librarian told her had left her uneasy.

"Come on out. I'll be here all afternoon. The appliance guys are supposed to be delivering and installing my refrigerator, my stove, and my dishwasher today."

"I'll be by, then," he said. He sounded good.

He sounded obsessively, painfully, heart-poundingly good.

Emma shoved her phone back in her pocket and closed her eyes.

Maybe the detective had been wrong. Maybe she wasn't the daughter of Maris Kessler. Maybe Maris Kessler's daughter had died at birth, and the detective, tired of looking for the truth, had come to rest in a random small town and on a convenient lie.

Maybe schizophrenia wasn't something she would ever have to worry about.

And then again, maybe the way she was feeling about Mike Ruhl was less about magic than it was about madness.

"Cara, you have to meet me at the door with a baseball bat," Mike said into his cell phone.

"You need to club somebody?"

"I need you to club me."

Cara laughed. "Uh-oh. What did you do? Get into another bet with Scooter?"

"I invited myself over to that woman's house, ostensibly to check for condensation that was causing drips under her roof."

"Sounds like a reasonable thing to check."

"It would be if I hadn't already checked it, Cara. I've driven by her house three times already today. I caught myself making excuses another three or four times to go off the job to fetch things back, and managed to stop myself all those times. But then I called her, and told her I had an idea what was causing that drip she heard—and it was just an excuse to go out there and see her. I don't want to do this."

"Sure you do," Cara said. "If you didn't want to do it, you wouldn't have done it."

"I don't want to *want to* do it, then."

"That's because deep inside, kiddo, you are a coward."

"I don't know why I called you," he said. "I can call my own self names." He could see Emma Beck's house ahead, and her truck in the drive, and an appliance delivery truck parked right in front, with burly men offloading enormous cardboard boxes.

"Because you wanted to hear me tell you what I'm going to tell you. Go ahead and get to know her. No harm in it. Maybe she'll be someone wonderful, and maybe you'll discover that she's the woman you've been waiting your whole life to meet. Maybe she's just a nice woman who caught something in your gut, but it won't be anything to change your world. Maybe she'll be no one special, maybe you'll walk away. And if you do, at least you'll know. If you don't, she'll end up being this enigma that you never had the belly to unravel, and you'll spend the rest of your life wondering what you missed. You don't have anything to lose, Mike."

"You're right," he said. "I know you're right."

And he pulled into the drive, his heart racing and his

skin prickling and his nerves on edge and his mouth dry. Dust dry.

He wasn't sure what he was going to say once he was in there, but he knew he couldn't just keep driving by her house.

Fish or cut bait, his dad would say. Mike decided he wanted to fish.

The delivery men sounded like a herd of buffalo doing the tango in her kitchen, and Emma retreated to her studio, shutting the door behind her. They were unboxing and untaping and hooking things up, and she would be glad to have the appliances (and to be rid of the dingy, chipped, mid-sixties horrors whose places they would be taking), but she was amazed at just how much noise two men could make.

With her door closed, it wasn't so bad.

She had a fantasy cover-art painting to finish for Elvish Books. Fairies dancing around a girl in blue jeans stretched out on a lawn reading a book, apparently unaware of the strangeness going on right beside her.

Emma didn't get to pick the subjects of a lot of her paintings; advertising departments and book salesmen and publishers and editors got together and came up with ideas, and then sent her a one-page treatment of what they wanted. Sometimes, they'd send her the manuscript for the book, too, or at least a part of it. Not often, though. This time she was working straight from the treatment and the book's title (which was *Anna Beyond*), and she found herself wondering what in the world might be going inside the eventual covers.

She checked the partially finished painting on the easel. It wasn't secured by the clamp at the top—something she couldn't figure out. She was certain she'd left it clamped. She hated working with her support loose, because the fine-grained gessoed boards she preferred to paint on were bouncy if they weren't clamped into place.

She squeezed acrylic paints onto her palette, added a little slowing agent so the paint wouldn't dry too quickly, and reached for a brush.

It was wet.

The bristles were wet and had been left unshaped, the ferrule was wet . . . even the handle was wet.

She put it back down and looked around her room. Nothing was out of place—not that she could see, anyway. But she hadn't painted the day before. She'd just set things up so that she could spend time painting the next day.

She hadn't even put water in her paint cup. She'd brought that in with her.

How did the brush get wet?

She looked up at the ceiling, wondering if perhaps the drip she'd heard had, in the most unlikely fashion, come through from the floor above and sought out that paint-brush, of all her paintbrushes, to drip onto. The ceiling, though, was pristine.

She shook her head. It was going to have to remain the Mystery of the Soggy Paintbrush, because she was on deadline, and she'd already spent a lot of her day *not* working toward her deadline, and she could feel herself slipping behind. She didn't have the time or the energy to backtrack her motions of the day before to figure out exactly how she'd soaked one of her brushes. It shouldn't have been wet, it was, she'd live with it.

Someone knocked on her door, and she jumped.

"Come in."

She turned, expecting one of the delivery guys to tell her the buffalo ballet in the kitchen was done. Instead, Mike poked his head in. He said, "I'm going to head up to the attic. Just wanted you to know I'd be thumping around up there."

She couldn't help grinning at him. "Thumping seems to be the theme of the day."

He was looking past her. "That's . . . really good," he said. "Beautiful."

She turned to look at the painting. "It needs more cobalt blue," she said.

"You do that for a living? Or as a hobby?"

"For a living, but it's a fairly small living. I do book covers, mostly. Portraits of pets and kids. Some families, too, but mostly kids. A few fine-art paintings that I sell through gallery showings. I'm small potatoes, and the fact that I do commercial art makes it harder for me to sell fine art. The snob factor, you know."

He shook his head. "I don't know a damned thing about art. I like to look at it. I prefer paintings where you can tell what the artist was painting, and I don't think that jackass who peed in a cup and dumped a crucifix in it was any sort of artist. Or the one who wrapped a bridge in cellophane, or whatever it was he did." He shrugged. "What you're doing—that looks like art to me."

She liked him a lot right then, beyond him just making her heart race like a hamster on a wheel.

"Thanks," she told him. "That's pretty much the way I look at art, too. It isn't too popular a position among art buyers."

"Since when was popular ever right?" He didn't give her time to answer. "Going to check that attic. If I find anything, I'll let you know."

She nodded.

And started back painting, working cobalt blue shadows into the undergrowth that surrounded the girl, and into the shadows the fairies cast. It made the painting more intense. Then she worked on the fairies' wings for a while, losing herself in the pursuit of photorealistic iridescence. She was working from several photos of Japanese beetles—much maligned insects, but quite lovely.

The delivery men came for her to sign off the worksheet, and after she'd checked to make sure everything worked, she tipped each of them and they left.

The house got quieter immediately. And in the relative quiet, she could hear the sounds of Mike's work boots upstairs. Steadily walking along one wall. Slowly, patiently.

And then walking down the stairs, slowly and ponderously, as if he were carrying something heavy. She wondered what he'd found up there that would be interesting enough to drag down the stairs. He brought it over to the door—she could hear him dragging it.

She waited for him to knock, but he didn't. She said, "Mike? What did you find?" But he didn't answer.

She finally walked over and opened the door of her studio, expecting to see him setting up something large and awkward.

No one was there. Nothing was there. And then she heard him thumping across the floor up in the attic.

Her skin started to crawl.

She carefully closed the door to her studio. Then locked it. Then stood in the middle of the room with her arms wrapped around herself, trying to keep her hands from shaking.

Someone had been outside her door. Someone. She wasn't willing to explore the avenue of "something" just yet. She'd heard heavy footsteps, the sound of someone dragging something. She'd heard it.

But maybe she hadn't. Maybe she hadn't heard footsteps, and maybe she hadn't heard dripping, and maybe she was sliding into the dangerous realm of schizophrenia. Going crazy.

Like her mother.

She didn't know what she wanted, but she knew she didn't want to be alone. She rinsed her brush, dried it on a paper towel, and shaped the bristles with her fingertips. Returned it to her brush rack. Covered her palette with the airtight plastic lid that clamped over the base to keep the paint fresh longer.

And then she went up the stairs, past the room that made her shiver, around the corner, and to the narrow door that would admit her to the attic.

She opened the door and yelled up, "Find anything?"

"Nothing that would explain a drip," he told her.

"Great," she muttered. If he'd been able to find proof of a leak right then, she would have had a party.

Instead, she trudged up the steep, narrow attic stairs. She hadn't been in the attic before.

It was dusty. Hot. Cobwebby. Full of stuff that Emma guessed hadn't been worth selling in an estate sale. In other words, the typical attic.

"Everything's good up here," he told her. "And the ceiling is high enough that you could turn this into a nice room of some sort, if you wanted to. You'd have to pull out some of the trusses and redo the support system a little for it to be really comfortable. And add insulation, which frankly I think you should consider doing anyway. And get rid of that half wall in the middle of the room."

She looked at him, standing in front of the chest-high divider built where the attic turned at a right angle to accommodate the L-shape of the kitchen wing. Sun from a slatted vent illuminated him from behind, and the dust he'd kicked up gave him a halo. He looked delectable. Desirable in ways she had a hard time accepting. She'd always liked to think that she was in control of herself, that she couldn't be knocked off her feet by emotion. But looking at him, she was flat on her ass.

"When you came down the stairs earlier," she asked, "what were you carrying? It sounded really heavy."

He frowned. "I haven't been down the stairs since I came up here."

"I thought I heard someone," she told him.

"One of the delivery guys run up the stairs for something?"

"This was after they left." She shook her head. "I guess I'll get back to work. I need to go shopping later today. Now that I have a fridge, I need some fresh fruit and some fish. Maybe a couple of steaks. Tomatoes."

"With which to make us dinner?" he asked. But he winked when he said it.

Something impish inside her, maybe boosted a little by the realization that she didn't want to be alone in the house the next time she heard footsteps on the stairs, took hold of her. "Precisely," she said. "Tonight. It will give me a chance to break in all my new appliances."

He raised an eyebrow, considering. Then said, "Done. What time?"

"Seven?"

"I'll be here in my Sunday best."

She turned and walked downstairs before he could change his mind. She didn't understand why she was so sure she could trust him. She wanted to understand where she kept getting the thought that she knew him.

He was a stranger. She should never have invited him to dinner.

She refused, though, to turn around and beg off, in spite of the shreds of sanity and self-preservation that tugged at her. She wanted to be with him, she wanted to talk, she wanted to get to know him better. He'd been trustworthy in dealing with her house. He'd done a good job, he hadn't overcharged her, and he wasn't looking for ways to gouge her—had he been, he would have had the perfect opportunity to convince her she needed a whole new roof. She would have been happy to believe him, too.

"So what time are you going to be there tonight?" Cara asked. She'd called at a damned inconvenient time.

Mike, with his cell phone in his pocket and an earbud in one ear, was digging through his closet, looking for something that wasn't a T-shirt and jeans but wasn't a suit, either. He'd reconsidered the whole "Sunday best" thing, and was only half listening to his sister as he tried to come up with the appropriate clothing to wear for a first date with dinner at her place. "Uh-huh," he said, pulling out a navy blue pullover that would work pretty well. He bought clothes in three colors: navy blue, gray, and black. Plus white for shirts, of course. He also had things his mother and sister gave him for Christmas— sweaters in bright green with stripes, plaid shirts, shirts with freakin' cowboy yokes or pearl buttons, sweaters in iffy shades like moss green and salmon. Those he put on in front of them, then jammed into the back of his closet, where they would never see the light of day again.

Men wore navy blue, gray, and black. With the occasional white shirt.

He had charcoal gray slacks that would look okay with the sweater. A white shirt to go underneath it. Gray socks. Black shoes.

It had taken him years to figure out his system, but as he pulled his clothes out of the closet and dragged them toward the dryer for a quick tumble to get the wrinkles out, he was confident that he'd pass inspection.

"That wasn't a yes or no question," Cara said. She sounded annoyed, Mike realized. "You aren't listening to me."

"I'm doing something," he said. "What did you ask me?"

"What time you were going to get there tonight."

He stopped in the middle of the kitchen, arms still full of clothes. "Did . . . we have something planned tonight?"

"It's Monday."

"Monday," he repeated. And then memory kicked in. "Dammit. *Monday.* I'm not going to be able to make it. I . . . something came up. I'll have to tell Mom and Dad. Tell Drew I'm sorry I missed him."

"You were just going to not show up?"

Mondays, Mike's family got together for dinner at his parents' house. They sat around the table, eating his mother's cooking and talking late into the night. They discussed books, science, the arts, music, politics, religion, current events, UFOs and alien invasions, their work, and anything else imaginable. He loved Mondays. He made it a point not to schedule dates on Mondays. And yet, he hadn't given it a second thought today.

"I forgot what day it was, actually . . . but this is important. Something that I have to take care of."

"Mmmm." Cara didn't sound like she believed him for a minute. "You're going to tell me what's so important," she said.

He tossed his clothes into the dryer, turned it on, and headed back to the shower. "Not right now, I'm not. I have to call Mom and let her know I can't be there, and then I have to go. I'm on a tight schedule here. But . . . I'll talk to you later. Tell you anything that's worth telling."

"Count on it," she said.

Emma studied the steaks, seasoned and waiting in the fridge. The casual salad, bright and colorful and already in two bowls. She could smell the potatoes baking. She had garlic bread on the counter. She'd already split the loaf, basted it with olive oil, and pressed a couple of cloves of garlic to spread onto it. Salted it. All she'd need would be to put it in the oven to brown, when he got there.

She looked at the clock. Six fifty-five.

She turned to look toward the door. The cat was sitting in the doorway between the kitchen and the hallway, watching her. She hadn't heard him. "How in the world did you get in here?"

He hadn't come in with her. She would have bet any amount of money that she had been unaccompanied every time she went through her doors in either direction. She'd had two bags of groceries in her arms, but she was certain she would have noticed him. He was a big cat.

Yet there he sat.

"I bought some food for you," she said. "If you're going to keep visiting, I guess I ought to feed you. I'll have to think about a litter pan, too, though you don't seem to have any trouble getting in or out of the house, so maybe that would just be a waste of time. I have to tell you if you didn't have such good manners, I'd chase you out with a broom."

He watched her, unperturbed by suggestions of violence.

Behind her, she heard the sound of dripping again. It was *clearly* coming from the sink area.

She frowned, walked over to the sink, and studied the single faucet, which was dry. She ran her fingers around the base of the handle, but it was dry, too. She opened the cabinet doors beneath, got down on hands and knees, and felt the pipes and the wood floor of the cabinetry. She could find no moisture anywhere, but she could clearly hear it.

"He's going to think I invited him over to hunt down my plumbing leaks again," she told the cat, turning. But the animal was gone.

She heard a truck pull into the drive, and headed for the front of the house. Through the sidelights, she could see Mike pulling up the drive. He parked beside her truck, at the side of the house, and stepped out, and she watched him walk toward the porch steps.

He looked good. Better than good. Her reaction to him was totally unreasonable, unprecedented, a little bit crazy. She didn't know him well enough to want him the way she did, and the intensity of her response frightened her. He made her breathless. He was dressed conservatively; sweater over shirt, slacks, casual shoes. He looked so different from the man in the T-shirt and jeans she'd seen first. He was less raw. Less nearly naked.

She watched him come around the side of the house, not seeing her, simply walking, and she could see him naked again, and realized that he wasn't different. She saw his clothes, but neither the T-shirt and jeans nor the slightly dressy outfit seemed like him at all.

She felt her hands tightening into fists, felt her nails biting into her palms, and her heart started racing and her mouth went dry. She might have been thirteen, going on her first chaperoned date. She could not remember having been so nervous even then.

He knocked on the door, and her heart thudded faster. She opened it, and smiled at him, and felt her lips tremble. In his eyes, she saw the same shock of recognition that she felt.

"Wow," he said.

She managed a faint, "You, too," and then she caught the movement of the cat right at her feet, and she looked down to find that he had dropped another dead mouse for her.

With his gift recognized, he trotted to the shadows beneath the staircase that curved upward on the right side of the entryway.

"Ugh, don't step on that," she told Mike.

He looked down at his feet, and saw the dead mouse. "Ugh. Where did that come from?"

"Cat brought me a present."

"I love when they do that. Want me to dispose of it for you?"

She grinned. "I don't mind, usually. But I do have

dinner just about finished, and well, food and dead mice. . . ."

"I'm on it," he told her, and trotted into her kitchen to return a moment later with a paper towel. "I saw your trash can pulled to the road outside. Want it to go straight in there?"

"Perfect. I'll get the steaks and the garlic bread in right now, and we can eat the salads when you get back."

He came back in and she heard him washing his hands in the downstairs bathroom, whistling. It was a really old song, something she had heard somewhere, and knew well. But she couldn't remember the name of it right then.

They settled down to eat, and he said to her, "I wish I could understand why it seems like I know you."

"I wish you could, too," she told him, "because then you could tell me."

"Were you ever here before. Ever?"

Emma considered telling him that she'd been born in Benina, but as much as she felt like she knew him, as much as she wanted to touch him, as much as it seemed the two of them had been eating dinner at right angles from each other at her kitchen table forever, she couldn't bring herself to admit that truth. And it didn't change anything, anyway. He hadn't known her as a baby. Her adoptive parents had received her when she was only days old, according to her birth certificate.

"I haven't," she said. "And if you've never been to Wisconsin, you never met me, either, I'm pretty sure. If you were at Myrtle Beach the week we vacationed there when I was twelve, maybe. But I don't think the chances of that are very good."

"Never been to Myrtle Beach," he told her. "My parents used to take us to the mountains. You live around here long, you get all the hot you can stand. A summer vacation means going someplace cool."

"It's just funny, is all," she said. He nodded, and they ate the rest of their salads in silence, while the smells of baking potatoes, broiling steak, and browning garlic bread filled the room.

When the timer went off, Emma was almost grateful to get up and turn the steaks. Mike joined her. "Everything going all right with the house?"

"So far," she told him. "Mostly. Except you can hear that leak now, louder than it was."

He frowned. "Really?"

She flipped the second steak, pushed the broiler pan back in, and closed the oven door. "Yeah. I can't figure out why."

She beckoned him over to the sink. She could clearly hear the dripping, which sounded like it was coming from inside the cabinets. "You hear that?"

He stood with his eyes half closed, his head cocked a little to one side. "Dripping?" He frowned.

"Right under the sink. You don't hear it?"

He shook his head and, dropping to one knee, followed the same procedure under the counter that she had. "Dry under there."

"I know. That's part of what's driving me cra—that's making this so frustrating. I hear the dripping, but it's always, always dry when I check." She crouched beside him, looking into the recesses of the cabinetry, puzzling along with him. "But you don't hear the drip."

"I don't hear water." He stood. "I hear . . . something."

The timer went off again, and Emma hurried to the

stove to retrieve the garlic bread and check the steaks, which were not quite done.

She said, "Something? What kind of something?"

"It gets louder, then softer. Then stops. More of a . . . a . . ." He frowned. "A wind-through-a-crack sort of sound, though not entirely. Not exactly." He came over to stand beside her. "And not under the sink so much as just under the house. These old places are built upon brick pillars," he told her. "Wind blows right through the lattice and board and whistles around down in the crawl space."

"No. What I hear is clearly water. Dripping water."

He said, "You have a tape recorder?"

"No." She laughed. "Not for years. Does anyone even use them anymore?"

"I have one. I'll drop it by tomorrow. See if you can capture the sound you're hearing, and I'll use that to fig- ure out what you've got going on here."

"All right," Emma said.

She put thoughts of the drip that Mike couldn't hear behind her. They sat down to a dinner that had come out as well as she could have hoped.

"This is excellent," he told her. "I'm afraid I'm not much of a cook."

She said, "I got plenty of practice. My mother was a huge believer in competence in the kitchen. She started teaching me when I was little, and if I didn't take to it like a fish to the river, I did eventually get the hang of it. I can make a fair number of dishes without recipes. And I know how to can and pickle and smoke and dry foods, too." She grinned a little. "We lived on a farm, so I'm handy. Not so much with tools. Tool-wise, I'm only good at framing pictures."

"I'm impressed," he told her. "Seems like the majority of women don't have any idea how to cook anymore."

Emma shrugged. "Society tells girls they'll demean themselves by cooking food or cleaning house or raising their own children. Schools and TV and other influences make it clear to girls that if they don't want careers, they're failures. My mom was a farm girl, though. She never tolerated that crap, and she made sure I didn't buy into it, either. She said family could be a career, and raising good children was an art. So I learned to cook, and I grew up wanting a family." Emma's voice faltered when she said that. If what she'd heard about her birth mother was true, family might be an option she didn't have anymore.

"And yet somehow you didn't stay on the farm."

Emma smiled a little. "I didn't. Both of my folks made sure I knew they'd support me in anything I wanted to do. They just didn't want anyone telling me that I couldn't be a mom, if that was what I wanted." Her smile died. "I figured painting was a job that would let me stay home with my kids, if I ever had them."

He helped her clean up after dinner, and then the two of them put on jackets and went walking out in her yard. *Her* yard. It still sounded so strange and foreign to her.

They wandered down the drive to the road, beneath the arches of the massive live oaks. "The trees were what made you love the place, weren't they?" he said.

"No. I mean, I loved the trees. Don't get me wrong. But I knew that I belonged in the house the moment I saw it. I drove by and was so taken by the place, I almost drove into the ditch."

"It's not that good-looking a house," he said. He

sounded doubtful. "Not that it won't be once you get it fixed up. I have no doubt that you'll turn it into a show-place."

Emma watched the cat jump off the railing that went around the front porch. He trotted across the drive and into the tall grass on the other side of it. "He got out again," she mused.

"He? Who?"

"The cat," Emma said. Mike had been looking back down the drive toward the house, right at the cat.

"Really?" He looked around.

"The cat that just jumped off the porch and ran into the tall grass," Emma said.

Mike looked where she was pointing, then glanced over at her, then looked back to the porch again. "Guess I didn't see him," he said after a moment. But he wore an expression of faintest doubt, and that doubt made her stomach tighten.

He hadn't seen the cat, even though he had been looking at it.

Was there a cat? Was the cat like the dripping water? Just something in her mind?

Except the cat was bringing her dead mice. The mice were not just appearing out of thin air. They were not spontaneously generating out of dust. The cat was killing them and dropping them at her feet. And Mike had seen one—and disposed of it. She was not imagining the cat.

Mike simply hadn't seen it.

She sighed. "I want to show you the rose garden," she told him. "I first saw it when I looked out the window, after I moved in, and I've been captivated by the possibilities."

She led him around to the south side of the house, and back to the patch of ground where the fountain and the bench seat and the sad old rose bushes and ramblers waited.

And watched him recoil.

"I guess I mentioned to you that your house gave me the creeps," he said.

"You said something along those lines."

"Nothing in the house makes me feel like a goose standing on my grave, but this rose garden . . . I don't know. There's something wrong with it."

She tried to see the garden objectively, not through eyes that could imagine it as it had once been, and as it might be again.

It was grim. Bleak, thorny, dreary, lost in long shadows, haunted by neglect and the aura of despair. But it still compelled her.

She walked forward, feeling in her gut the story behind its creation—feeling that it had once been loved. It seemed such a sad place to her. Tragic, but at the same time, it promised renewal. She could imagine it in springtime, as it would become after she had worked in it, cutting back the old roses, tempting them to new blooms. She would plant old-fashioned flowers in it. None of the fancy hybrids, nothing that did not grow from seed and set seeds that would grow the same flowers as their parents. She would bring it back to life.

"Emma?"

Mike was a ways behind her, and she realized that she was kneeling beside the fountain, touching the ground at the base of it, and that tears were welling in her eyes. She blinked them back and stood, embarrassed at her behavior and that she had permitted herself to behave so strangely in front of him.

She walked back to Mike's side and said, "I don't know why, but I love this garden. I love this house. I feel like an idiot for looking at it like it was my child, but that's almost how it feels."

"You're unique, Emma," he told her. "I don't think it was coincidence that after all the years this place sat empty and for sale, you came out of nowhere to buy it. I suspect that there might be one true house for every woman, just like one true love."

And then he winked, and she realized that he was teasing her.

She laughed. "You're making fun of me."

"Only a little. Mostly, I'm making fun with you. With you living here, I don't hate this place the way I used to." He turned away from the rose garden, though, and led her back into the house. "I want to see you turn this place into the great home you evidently see when you look at it," he told her. "I have to confess that I don't see the possibilities through my own eyes. But getting glimpses of it through yours, it seems like it will be wonderful."

Her hand slipped into his. She wasn't sure how it happened, whether he reached for her, or she reached for him. But their hands fit into each other's perfectly. They walked around the front of the house, along the drive, back to the carriage house.

Emma said, "I have a question for you." She turned to face the back of the house, and pointed toward the second story. "The window on the left is my bedroom. The window on the right is the spare back bedroom. But what's the window in the middle? I can't find it inside the house."

Mike laughed. "I wondered about that, too. I got up there when I was painting, and I discovered the window is a dummy. I mean, it's a real window, but the only thing behind it is boards and plaster. It's just there so there will be three in back to match the three in front. If you figured spaces, you'd find the closet in your bedroom and the closet in the other bedroom meet in the middle."

She shook her head. "I wonder why they didn't just open the window to the closet, then. It's a dark closet."

He said, "In these old, owner-built houses, I've seen stranger things. Maybe the owner's wife dressed in the closet or something. From the outside, that window adds a lot of balance, though. You'd have a big, blank expanse of siding if it wasn't there."

"You're right," she said, trying to picture the house without the window. "It would look completely wrong."

They ambled back between the carriage house and the tobacco barn, back into the trees behind the main property.

"Old pecan orchard," he told her, pointing to the stark outlines of old trees in neat rows, all of them shaped like those martini glasses James Bond drank from. Between the rows, brambles and young pines and scrub oak and a thicket of weeds scrambled for growing space.

"It must have been beautiful once," she said.

"Could be again. The pecan trees are too old to do much for you; they'll leaf out all right, I'd guess, but you can't expect much in the way of pecans from them. You could get someone out here to clean out the scrub, though. Put some grass down, and maybe put in azaleas and rhododendrons, and you'd have a regular park back here."

"That sounds beautiful."

"It would be fitting," he said, turning to face her. Their hands were still entwined. Beneath the pale light of the moon, he stood in silhouette, his breath pluming out in short, uneven bursts. "There's a certain craziness about this," he told her. "About me, and the way I feel about you. I'm trying to make it make sense to me, and it just won't."

She tried to say, "I know," but the words stuck in her throat.

"The thing is," he said. And then he said, "Aw, hell."

And kissed her.

His lips were firm on hers, and she melted inside, and kissed him back, at first tentatively, and then with everything in her. They fit. He fit her; she fit him. It was the only thought she could hold in her head as her hands slipped loose from his, as she slid them under his jacket, as his arms went under her sweater and around her waist and they pulled together tighter, closer, more desperate with each passing instant, with each new touch. She felt tears run down her cheeks and did not know if they were hers or his. When she brushed her hand against his face, she felt wetness at the corners of his eyes. But she was crying, too, and could not explain why. Could not understand why.

She was lost.

He picked her up and held her tight against him, and she wrapped her legs around his waist as if she had done it a thousand times. His hand worked its way beneath the back of her blouse, while hers seemed of its own accord to unbutton his shirt, so that she could get closer. They were not close enough. They were not all the way inside each other's skins, and nothing short of that was going to satisfy her.

It wasn't a question for her anymore of what was going on between the two of them. She didn't care. An explanation wouldn't have made her want him any less, or any more. All she knew was that they fit, and that she was incomplete without him.

He started back toward the house, carrying her, seemingly without effort. He walked, they kissed, they touched.

They moved inside and he locked the door behind him one-handed, and she turned out the light, and the two of them moved into her living room, to her futon pressed against the wall.

She had only ever been to bed with one man, and that after months of dating, when they were engaged, and she was sure they were going to get married, and have children together and grow old together.

She had never taken sex lightly.

She was not taking it lightly with Mike, either. She was lost—in forces she did not understand, in voices and images that kept showing her the two of them together, him and her, naked and moving in each other, in sunny meadows and shadowed bedroom and kitchen and carriage. She knew his touch as well as she knew herself. She knew the shape of him, the feel of him, the way to please him, the way to respond to him to get the most pleasure for herself.

They had done this before, not just once, not just a hundred times. More. Much more.

She knew him, and as they shed their clothes, as they moved together, whispering endearments she had never said before in her life, but that came to her tongue as if she said them every day, she knew that he was her future.

They were naked, their bodies ready, and in the back room where her art supplies were, a piano began to play.

She froze, and shivered in the sudden chill of the room.

He pulled away from her, and she wrapped her arms around herself, covered with goose bumps and feeling the hair standing up on her arms and the back of her neck.

"Do you hear that?" she asked, and then wished she hadn't said anything, because his expression suggested that he hadn't heard anything at all, and further, that she was spooking him.

"Hear . . . something?"

"Nothing," she told him, as the piano played on, from her studio where there was no piano. "I just . . . thought I heard a thump at the back of the house."

He was shaking. He fumbled with his pants as she pulled her own clothing back on. "Back of the house, you said?"

"A thump. It was . . . probably the cat."

"I'm going to go check," he told her. He put his shirt on and buttoned it as he walked away.

She was glad. Glad he was getting dressed, glad he was walking out of her sight. She didn't know what had happened to her, what had almost happened with the two of them. For a while, she'd seemed like someone else. The piano sounds were gone, and for the moment at least, so was the insane craving that touching him had caused. She could breathe again, she could get herself back in order. She could look at what had almost happened sanely.

More or less sanely, she amended when she realized that she ached to have him touch her again.

Dressed, still shivering, she listened to him walking down the long central hall, checking doors, going into her studio, returning to the kitchen, then coming back.

"I didn't see anything out of place," he told her. He looked wary. And rattled. "Everything looked fine."

She nodded. "It must have been that cat again."

"I think . . . I should be going," he told her. "I have an early job tomorrow."

It was a thin lie, but she appreciated him taking the trouble to make it. She knew he was leaving, and she didn't think for a minute that he'd call again. From his perspective, she must have seemed insane, leaping on him the way she had, acting like a crazy woman.

From her own perspective, she was pretty sure she was insane. The melody from the piano that didn't exist still echoed in her memory.

"I'll drop the tape recorder by tomorrow," he said. "So that you can try to get a clear recording of the dripping you're hearing."

"Sure," she told him. "Thanks. I'll get it back to you as soon as I can."

The good-byes were awkward. Emma and Mike were careful not to touch.

Mike couldn't stop shaking as he drove away from the house. The sick feeling he'd always had about the Barnett house was still there. But now he could add actual fear to it.

He'd done a quick check of the downstairs because that's where the noise he'd heard had been coming from. He couldn't tell her what he'd heard, though. Not when she'd just heard a thump at the back of the house.

He knew she didn't have a piano, but he'd looked,

just in case. Just so he could get verification that he was losing his mind. He didn't find a piano. He found her portable stereo, set up in her studio. Plugged in, but not on. Nothing else that might have suddenly gone on, playing a recording of a slightly out-of-tune piano and a sad lament from another era.

It was wrong, the whole thing. His bizarre obsession with her, the way he'd lost control when he kissed her, the way the two of them had almost ended up in bed together. He'd pushed her, he'd taken advantage of her.

Well, he hadn't. She'd jumped right in with him, giving as good as she got. But he'd done a hell of a lot more than he'd planned to on a first date with a woman who he thought might mean something special to him.

And the worst part of it was, he didn't feel like himself when he did it.

He pulled into his own driveway and sat there, staring at the little house, trying to put the events he'd just experienced into some sort of coherent order.

Dinner. Dinner had been fine. Her insistence that she heard dripping in her kitchen had been weirdly and wonkily endearing. Their walk after the meal—good meal, too—had started out pleasant enough. Things had started going wrong when they walked around to the garden she wanted to restore. Watching her walking forward, an enraptured expression on her face, he'd been lost in the certainty that he'd seen her in that place before, the same expression on her face.

And both yearning and horror had dug their talons into him and pulled.

Away from the garden, walking back into the old pecan orchard, he'd felt better. Then, though, he'd touched her, and he almost felt like he was two men in one body, and both of them wanted her, but one of them was determined to have her right then, right there.

He'd lost control. He didn't want to admit that, but while the two of them were kissing and touching and pulling clothes off themselves and each other, he had been a spectator in his own skin.

"Bullshit," he muttered, and got out of his truck and slammed the door, hard. "Bullshit. You were a horny bastard and if that damned piano hadn't started playing, you'd have done something you'd have a hard time apologizing for."

He trudged to the front door, hands jammed into his pockets, head down, angry with himself for making excuses for his behavior, for pushing her as hard as he had, and conversely, for pulling away in the moment that he thought he heard music. Because he discovered that he didn't care how badly the evening had turned out. He could still feel her naked skin against his, the full heaviness of her breasts, the soft, rounded curve of her belly, the way her thighs had tightened around him when they'd been outside.

He wanted her more at that moment than he had the first time he saw her.

He stormed into the house, checked his phone for messages, and when there were none, stripped down to T-shirt and underwear and went to bed.

Her knife moved over the board, smearing paint, slashing it in hard lines and sharp curves. Red, bloody red, and then black to mark out two staring eyes. Titanium white faintly tinted with umber and cobalt became a bluish skin, stark and pale. The face that emerged was that of a child, dark-haired, sweetly beautiful, tragically dead.

Emma's hands moved of their own accord, angry hands. Her muscles bunched and tensed, her shoulders tight, her spine rigid. But her head seemed almost disconnected, relaxed, with eyes almost closed, face expressionless in sleep.

In the corner of the room, the cat sat motionless, watching her.

When she put the palette and knife down and started putting things away, he waited. He followed her when she put the painting in the secret room beneath the staircase. And then he faded away.

Chapter 4

Emma woke to the ringing of her cell phone. The sun was pouring into the room at the high angle of late morning. She'd overslept.

She rose, looked at her hands, and saw smears of red and black on her fingertips.

She frowned as she answered the phone. "Here," she said, and heard Susan's voice on the other end.

"You okay?"

Emma lay there considering that. "I think I may be coming down with something," she said. "I'm exhausted, and my whole body aches."

Susan sounded concerned. "You don't have anybody there, Em. Who's going to bring you soup and make sure you're all right?"

"Don't worry," Emma said, sitting up. "I'm not alone. I had a date last night."

Susan said, "Wow. Met someone that quickly?"

"It's a dull story," Emma told her. "I went out with the contractor who got my house ready for me."

"Good date?"

"Well . . . we had a good time initially. I think I screwed things up at the end, though. I doubt he'll call me again."

"I'm sorry. First dates are so treacherous."

"How's the baby?"

"I'm so big I can't move. The kid has heels wedged under my right ribs, and I can't breathe, and I have to pee all the time."

Emma watched the cat stalking across the field and toward the house. He had a dead mouse in his mouth. She sighed. "And you're trying to talk me into doing this. It sounds like such fun. Seriously, all I need is a guy I can keep and I'll be ready to join you. But you and I both know I haven't found him yet. So I should try to talk you into sharing my fun with me."

"What? Dating again? No, thanks."

"No. Just dealing with restoring a really old house. This place is full of sounds that take you by surprise, and a neighborhood cat has found a way in. He visits whenever he wants, bringing me dead mice as housewarming gifts. I need to find out how he's getting in, because I'm afraid if he can get in, snakes can too. And I keep hearing this leak, but I can't find it."

"I'll stick with my problems." Susan laughed. "I couldn't bend over to pick up kitty gifts right now, anyway."

They talked a while longer, and when Emma hung up the phone, she felt better. Still sore, but happier.

She tried not to think of Mike, and of the ruin of a start that had seemed so magical. She didn't think she was the sort of woman who was cut out for grand passion, anyway. She'd always been careful, wary, just a little distant. It was as if, even before she started dating, she carried the weight of having been badly hurt.

She showered and dressed and headed into her studio to work on the cover art.

The painting was sitting on the floor, leaning against one of her stands. Mike had gone in there the night before, looking for the thump she'd claimed to have heard. He hadn't found the cause, of course, because she'd been lying. But why had he moved her painting?

At least he'd been careful. It had no smudges on the edges, no scratched areas in the still-soft paint.

She put it on the easel and clamped it down.

Reached for her palette. The airtight cover on it was loose, and the paint she'd prepped the day before, and which she had been using, was gone. It didn't take long to figure out *where* it had gone. It was in her trash can.

How it had gotten there was another matter. She could have believed Mike would move the painting, though she couldn't imagine why. But he hadn't had enough time to move the painting, unlatch the airtight cover on her palette, lift it off, pull off the sheet of palette paper, throw it away, and put the lid on, not even in the half-assed state that she'd found it.

And he hadn't had time to tinker around with her paints, either.

She stared at them. Alizarin crimson, titanium white, cobalt blue, raw umber, and lamp black were spread across her worktable. The caps were on, but each had been squeezed from the middle, something she never, ever did. Ever. One of her brushes was out of place. And one of the palette knives she used for texturing gesso over prepared boards when she was going for a differ-

ent effect was in the center of the scattered paints, and
bore a smear of the crimson.

She frowned.

He sure as hell hadn't had time to do all that.

She'd had red smears on her hands when she woke
up.

But she hadn't done anything with the paints. Or the
painting knife. . . .

She jumped as the cat leapt onto the table beside her.
"You're in here?" she asked. She saw the dead mouse he
dropped, and sighed. "Thank you. You're very noble,
trying to provide for me. But, really, I don't need any
more food. Why don't you take that one and eat it outside?"

He turned and strolled out of the studio, and she used
a paper towel to pick up the mouse and dispose of it in
the kitchen trash.

And then she returned to the puzzle of the paints and
the palette knife and her dumped palette of paint. It
didn't make any sense. She couldn't see that anything
was missing. There were no new paintings in her studio,
either.

She tried to come up with a sensible explanation for
what was going on, but she couldn't.

She heard a knock out at the front door, and put down
her work. She hoped it was a representative from the
phone company. They were supposed to be sending
someone to wire the house for phones in most of the
rooms.

But it wasn't the phone guy. It was Mike.

He had a tape recorder in one hand.

"Get anything you can, noise-wise," he said, handing
it to her.

She took it, but she was nervous about doing so. She could tell herself that he hadn't had time to mess with everything that had been tampered with in her studio, but the fact was, he was the only person besides her who had been in the house much since she moved in. He'd put in the locks, so he might have had spare keys made for himself. The only big problem she had with her theory was that for the life of her, she couldn't imagine what he might have accomplished by messing with her paints, moving her painting, or dumping her palette.

What could he have accomplished?

She said, "You have a minute?"

His look was wary. "I do. Maybe we should talk out on the porch, though?"

She raised an eyebrow.

"I . . . acted out of hand last night," he told her. "I hadn't intended for our date to go like that. I'm sorry. And I thought you might prefer to talk with me out on the porch, where people could see us."

She couldn't help the faint smile that twitched at the corners of her mouth. "*What* people?"

"Oh." He flushed. "I mean the general idea of people, I suppose," he said. "Being outside where people could see. If they were around."

She nodded. "I understand that. But you can't take the blame—"

A car she didn't recognize pulled into her driveway. It was a nice little silver compact, American made, and the woman who got out of it had a bright grin on her face that made Emma like her instantly.

"Mike," the woman yelled. "I didn't think for a minute you were going to be here." She reached back into the car and pulled out what Emma recognized as a cake carrier. The woman started up the drive, and Emma heard Mike mutter under his breath, "What the hell?"

He told Emma, "That is my sister, Cara. With a cake. I have no idea what she's doing here."

"That's fine. Think chaperone," Emma whispered. And then she brushed past him to go out and meet Cara. "I'm Emma Beck," she said.

"Cara Jackson. Mike's big sister."

"You two look about the same age."

Cara laughed. "I love you for that. I'm actually six years older than he is, and if he hears you, Mike will act all uppity, though." They walked together toward Mike, and Cara continued. "I've been hearing from Mike how nice you were, and all the exciting things you're planning for this house, and I just had to come out and meet you, and say hello, and see the place for myself."

"It's good to meet you."

"You look surprised. He forget to tell you he had an older sister?"

Emma nodded. "We've only had one dinner together, and I think we ended up talking more about the house than about families."

Cara said, "I'm surprised he didn't tell you about his wild childhood. Never mind that most of our childhood adventures started out as my great ideas."

"Your great ideas just about got us killed," Mike said. He turned to Emma. "Her favorite trick was to point to me when something went wrong, and convince our parents that she'd had nothing to do with any of it."

Cara laughed. "Half the time. Half the time he was pointing the finger at me first. And whereas the folks took the stand that since I was older, everything was my fault just on general principles, he got away with everything."

Emma smiled, but said nothing.

"You don't have a bunch of stories about your brothers or sisters?" Cara asked.

"Only child," Emma told her. She led the two of them into the house.

Cara's cell phone rang, and she answered it. "Hey, sweetheart. No, I'm out at the old Barnett place, the one Mike's been working on . . . No. He's here, too, and we're talking to the woman who owns the place . . . Emma. She's the one who had dinner with Mike last night . . . Right. Sure. I'll see you then."

She hung up the phone. "My husband. He was on his way back from playing golf with his cousin, but since Mike and I are here, he's going to drop by."

"I thought doctors did golf on Wednesdays," Emma said.

"They do," Cara agreed. "One Tuesday a month, though, Drew and his cousin, who's a lawyer, go out for a game. They've been doing it since David was in his teens." She winced a little. "He's been curious about the person who bought this place. He and David spent years trying to get the city council to tear it down."

"Lawyer . . . David Halifax?" Emma asked.

"You know him?"

"We met when I closed on the house," Emma said. The words came out grimmer than she would have liked.

Cara's smile was meant to be reassuring. "Don't worry. Drew didn't have anything personal against the house. I don't *think*. He just treated more than a few kids who got hurt out here, trying to break into the place or playing around in the buildings in the back, and David suggested that the property as it was could generate lawsuits for the town. His stance was that it was an attractive nuisance."

"So having someone living here—" Emma started to say.

Cara cut her off with a laugh. "As long as he doesn't have to drag himself out of bed after midnight to treat another teenager with a broken arm or leg he got from those barns back there, I think he'll be a happy man."

"I don't think his cousin was," Emma said. "He gave me the strangest looks the whole time I was signing papers."

Mike said, "David is a jerk. I think Drew tolerates him because he's a good lawyer, and cheap because he's Drew's father's sister's kid. Apparently he used to follow Drew around like a puppy when he was a teenager."

Emma led Mike and Cara into her kitchen, and got out plates and glasses. She figured the thing to do was serve the cake promptly, and share it with her guests. She was never going to be able to eat the whole thing herself; it was huge.

She changed the subject from the unpopular David to Cara's husband—he sounded like a much more pleasant topic. "Your husband is a doctor. General practice, or a specialty?"

Cara smiled. "General practice. I run his office, but, it being the first Tuesday of the month, we close up. Benina doesn't have a lot of specialists in town."

Emma nodded. "Is he taking new patients? I haven't had a chance to search for a doctor, or a dentist, or any of the other necessities yet."

"He's . . . ah . . . getting on in years," Cara said.

Emma heard a knock at the door.

"He's a lot older than her," Mike added.

"Excuse me for a moment," Emma said, and heard the two of them talking quietly with each other as she went to answer the door. Mike sounded annoyed, Cara sounded amused.

She'd missed out on the whole sibling thing. She had friends with seven or eight siblings, and she loved the feel of big families. Listening to Mike and his sister trying to disagree quietly made her feel wistful all over again.

She could see two men at the door through the side-light as she approached. The first was David Halifax. Her stomach flipped.

The second was considerably older. He looked like he was in his early sixties, Emma guessed, with silver hair, a lean build, and a golfer's unfortunate taste in clothing. He was wearing a vivid pink shirt, plaid pants in lime green, lemon yellow and flamingo pink, and tasseled black shoes. Cara hadn't been exaggerating when she'd said he was getting on. He had his back to the door.

Emma opened the door warily. "Hello, David. And you must be—" she started to say.

Dr. Jackson turned around.

The expression on his face mirrored the shock and amazement on hers. "Tom? Tom Jackson?" she squeaked.

"E.J. Beck?"

They stood staring at each other. "Oh, my God," she finally said, and told him, "Come in. Come on in. I can't believe this."

"Neither can I," he told her. She led him through the house to the kitchen. Cara rose to offer introductions, but Emma said, "I can't believe this, but I already know Tom. Er . . . Drew. He and I go back a few years. He bought a couple of my paintings back when I was getting started."

This statement drew bafflement from both Mike and Cara.

"The E.J. Beck paintings, darling," Drew told his wife. "This is the artist who painted them."

"Tom. I mean Drew. Or should I call you Dr. Jackson? I had no idea you lived around here," Emma said. "For some reason, I thought you were from Kentucky. Or . . . Tennessee."

He shook his head. "My full name is Thomas Andrew Jackson, because my parents had political aspirations for me when they named me." He grinned and shook his head. "I was supposed to grow up to be president. I go by Tom generally. Drew is what friends and family call me. Please call me Drew. And no, I think I mentioned the South, but I don't believe I gave a state. I'm from here—all my life." He paused and shook his head. "E.J. Beck. How in the *world* did you end up living in this ruin of a house?"

David Halifax said, "She refused to take good advice." His mouth smiled when he said it, but his eyes didn't.

Both Drew and Mike gave him sharp looks, and Cara sighed.

Emma laughed the comment off. "It's such a long, strange story. But, Drew—this is *the* house. From the paintings. I think the better one of yours had the left half of the front porch and the left two gables."

He said, "How can that be?"

Emma waved off his look of disbelief. "Oh, I don't think it's actually the house I made up, that I've been painting since I was five. That's ridiculous. But I saw this place, and it looked just like it."

Mike interrupted. "So you two knew each other, because Drew bought your paintings, but you didn't know he was from here, and he didn't know you were moving here, and you just accidentally ended up with me doing your renovation because of the real estate lady, and Cara happens to be my sister and Drew's wife."

Emma nodded. Drew nodded. Mike and Cara looked at each other, and Cara said, "This could not possibly be weirder if the two of you were like those identical twins who accidentally meet while having coffee one day, and discover that they've both just moved to the same city that week."

"It *could* be weirder," Drew said. "Doctor and artist end up living in the same town. Nothing like the identical twins thing."

Cara said, "You're such a spoilsport, Drew. It was so much more mysterious the way I put it."

Emma was dishing out the cake. "Some for you, too, David? Drew?"

David gave her a stiff, "No, thank you."

"If Cara made the cake, I'd be crazy to turn it down."

Emma cut him a slice. "Everyone calls me Emma," she said. "E.J. is my, ah, art name. The gallery owner who first displayed my work told me I'd never get anywhere with a name like Emma. I believed him." She shrugged.

Everyone but David sat there eating cake, which Emma had to agree was the best cake she'd ever tasted. Finally Drew asked her, "How in the world did you end up down in this neck of the woods, a big city girl like yourself?"

"I was wondering the same thing," David said.

Emma smiled. "Madison is hardly New York City, and the whole city-girl image, like the name E.J., is something the gallery owner stuck me with. My folks had a dairy farm. They were older; my mother died five years ago, and my father died earlier this year. I wanted to go someplace different, and . . . well . . . my father accidentally pointed me in the direction of Benina. I came down to see the place, and ended up falling in love."

Neither Mike nor Cara seemed inclined to pursue that, but Drew said, "Pointed you in this direction? Why in the world? I can't imagine Benina ending up on anyone's map of places to see."

Emma didn't want to get into that, especially after learning that her birth mother's history had been a grim one. She didn't want to admit that she was from Benina. She felt David watching her, and she didn't feel . . .

. . . safe.

So she lied. "Apparently he'd been here once. I'm not sure why he was interested in the place—it was just one notation I found after he died. But it caught my curiosity because as far as I knew, he'd never been interested in anyplace but the farm. I came. I looked around." She ran her hands over the old, wide boards of the doorframe and said. "I found this house and I fell in love."

David snorted. But his response was what she would have expected.

Drew was watching her, though, and in his eyes, she saw disbelief. Not anything he was going to make a big deal about. But his left eyebrow flicked up once, down once when she looked at him, and then he turned to Cara and said, "You did something different with this cake. You have to do it again, you know."

And Cara laughed. "No, no, I can't. The different thing I did was put coconut in it."

Drew put down his fork and stared at the cake. "But I hate coconut."

"I know. That's why I never use it when I bake for us."

"But this is *good.*"

"I know. That's why I used it baking for Emma."

He took another bite, this time looking like a man having his first taste of deep-fried rattlesnake and discovering it suited him.

Emma would have laughed, but that quick flick of the eyebrow had disconcerted her. Drew didn't believe her.

Why didn't he believe her?

Six in the evening, already dark—everyone had left, and Emma was alone in the house again. She had more lights on than she needed. She didn't want to question that; she wanted to think keeping lights on in every downstairs room was perfectly normal. But she could hear water dripping, and shortly after everyone left, she heard what had sounded like footsteps up in the attic.

She had the tape recorder running, out in the kitchen where the dripping sound was loudest.

She was in her studio painting.

The cat had gotten in somehow, and was sitting on the windowsill, watching her.

But painting wasn't in her right then.

On a whim, she decided she wanted to go out. She got in her truck and drove into town, to the library. It was still open. Would be until seven p.m., which seemed kind of late to her. The parking lot was almost empty. She walked across it, and into the ugly building, and found Gwen Carlston shelving books.

Gwen spotted her and smiled. "You're back. Give me

a minute. I found a few things I thought you might be interested in."

Emma was surprised. She wouldn't have thought the librarian would have given any thought at all to her interests.

It took Gwen about ten minutes to finish putting things away. When she was done, though, she said, "After you left, I looked into the girl you asked me about."

"You did?" Emma was startled. "Why?"

Gwen's smile didn't quite work. "I hadn't thought about her in years, and your bringing her up made me remember how odd everything was back then—how many rumors there were, and how many questions that just went away unanswered. My whole job is finding things out and answering questions, and I have a lot of resources now that I didn't have back when I was young." She shrugged. "I found a few things on the microfiche from around that time, and talked to a friend of mine who knew the girl a lot better than I did. If you're genuinely interested in what happened back then, you want to go into Jennibelle's Flowers and Baskets tomorrow and talk to Aileen Wilkes. She's the owner."

"Jennibelle isn't?"

"Jennibelle was the owner twenty years ago. Aileen didn't want to change the name when she bought the place, and now there's no point."

"And Aileen knew Maris?"

"Quite well. And she said she'd be happy to talk to you." Gwen sighed. "Don't get sucked into her conspiracy theories, though. She's been quiet about her suspicions ever since Maris died, but she has this dramatic turn about her. She's certain Maris and Maris's mother were both murdered." Gwen shook her head. "It's a small town. People get worked up about things, and there isn't enough going on to ever get them pointed in another direction." She smiled. "In any case, I printed copies of the news articles that related to Maris's story. I figured you might want to see them."

Emma was genuinely floored. "Thank you so much. I can't believe you went to so much trouble."

Gwen gestured toward the empty library. "I have a lot of time to spend. When I'm not trying to figure out how to encourage people to read more, I usually end up making new bulletin board displays. Actually looking for information that someone else might find interesting was refreshing. At the same time, it scratched an old itch for me."

"Well, thank you so much," Emma told her. "I'm grateful. I wouldn't even have thought of checking microfiche."

"I would have pointed you in that direction." Gwen rummaged under the countertop, and pulled out a manila folder that held a few sheets of paper. "These are all the items I found. There might be more, but I'm not sure where."

Emma got directions to Jennibelle's, and drove home, both excited and a little scared by the prospect of reading the old articles.

She was afraid to find out more about her mother, terrified that her next news would be as bad as the last.

With the things going on at her house, she was already thinking she might be edging toward crazy. She wanted a sign to reassure her that she was okay. That she hadn't inherited something from a young girl she had never known that would one day turn her into a violent, dangerous woman who might destroy someone else's life, or her own.

In the end, the articles didn't tell her much. They were typical of small-town reporting of delicate matters. One mentioned that Maris had died in the hospital, though it didn't mention anything about suicide, pregnancy or childbirth, psychosis, or violence. The next told about Maris's mother's suicide—that one was a bit more informative, mentioning that following her daughter's death, neighbors reported the mother had been deeply depressed. There was a third article noting that in spite of the fact that the mother had left no note, her overdose of pills, taken with a large amount of alcohol, had been ruled intentional suicide rather than accidental death since as far as anyone knew, the mother wasn't a drinker.

And that was it.

Emma read them, feeling disappointed. From talking with Gwen, she'd been sure there would be more to the story than the scant references contained in the paper. She knew small towns, though. The real story was always in what *didn't* make the news.

The phone guy had come by while Mike and the Jacksons and David Halifax were still there, so she had her new phone line, her old phone, and a new phone book. She decided to put them to use. She called Jennibelle's, but all she got was the answering machine, telling her that she had called after hours, and that the shop would open promptly at eight in the morning.

Mike had eaten food from a bag for dinner, and he'd made an effort to absorb himself in the Discovery Channel's all-night Modern Marvels marathon, but his heart just wasn't in it. He sat in his recliner and stared at the television, but he wasn't actually seeing it.

He was seeing Emma. Watching her talking about why she'd come to Benina, watching Drew respond to that with that little tic of disbelief that he came up with sometimes.

Mike had to agree with Drew. Some part of Emma's story of how she'd come to find Benina didn't ring true.

He couldn't say that it was the part about how she met Drew. Both of them had seemed totally shocked to find the other in Benina. Mike didn't think Drew was much of an actor. He didn't know about Emma. But they'd both been open about how they'd met, and where, and though Mike had watched for any signs that Drew might have decided to break his sister's heart by replacing her with a woman somewhat younger, in the end he had to let that go.

Emma had not come to Benina to be near Drew. At least he was fairly sure she hadn't.

Drew seemed like a good husband for Cara. The two of them had what seemed to him both a good friendship and a deep and abiding affection for each other. And if Mike couldn't help questioning Drew's occasional medical conferences, which he attended alone, there had certainly never been any tangible evidence that his brother-in-law was up to anything. To Mike, being voluntarily apart from the woman you loved didn't make sense. But he'd conceded that his imagined ideal for the perfect relationship might not fit everyone—and that Cara and Drew made each other happy.

Drew had, of course, been married before Cara. He'd had a beautiful wife and two gorgeous children. His

wife, Hannah, had died in a car accident a long time
ago. Following her death, he'd put the kids in exclusive
private boarding schools, and after they graduated and
left home, he had been alone. He'd done his work, and
he'd been viewed by the townsfolk as something of a
solitary saint, dedicating himself to his patients. His
kids had been less generous—they'd blamed him, and,
Drew guessed, his dedication to his work, for their
mother's death. They grew up and left him. And then
Cara had come into his life, and had pursued him with
the sort of dedication that only Cara could manage.
Drew had fallen to her determined charms. She had won
him over, he had eventually asked her to marry him, and
the two of them had been, for the last five years, as
happy a couple as Mike had ever seen.

Still . . .

Mike didn't like himself for being suspicious, and he
had hated having to look at Emma and wonder about her
intentions. The thought that she might be in town to try
to win Cara's old, settled-in husband away from her had
been an ugly one.

He got up and went into the kitchen to make himself
some popcorn. He wasn't even seeing the television.
Drew invested in artwork, and a fair amount of it was by
people Mike had heard of. He loved art. And Mike had
no trouble believing that he'd seen something in
Emma's paintings that had made him think she'd be
worth collecting. He'd shown Mike the paintings with
tremendous pride when he brought them home, talking
warmly about the beauty of line and the depth of color,
the quality of subject matter, and the interesting quirks
of E.J. Beck work that he thought would make it worth
a fortune one day. After his own lifetime, of course,

he'd said with a laugh. But the best thing men of vision could do for young artists, Drew always said, was to support their work before men with no vision discovered it and made it valuable.

The popcorn popped in the microwave, and Mike paced in the kitchen.

Coincidences happened. Of course they did. They happened all the time, with people thinking about each other, and then running into each other in the most unlikely places the same day. Serendipity, it was called.

Problem was, it was easy to claim coincidence as a cover for . . . other things.

Emma had a secret. Her secret might not be Drew. Drew might, in fact, be a genuine coincidence. But he suspected that Benina was not. Drew had hit the nail on the head. Why, in all the world, would a promising young artist choose to buy a house and settle down in Benina? And why *that* house? That rattrap, falling-down, money-pit, creepy-ass house that had made his skin crawl every time he walked through the doors—until Emma moved into it. The creepiness had gone away since she arrived there, he had to admit. But everything else he had disliked about the place was still true.

Emma, he decided, had a secret. Before he let himself get carried away with her—well, before he did so again—he was going to find out what that secret was.

Chapter 5

Morning came before Emma was ready for it. For the first time in her life, she was having to set her alarm in order to get herself out of bed, and when she did, it was all she could do to drag herself into the shower, and force herself through breakfast with her eyes open.

Farm girls learned to wake early. Emma had made the five o'clock wake-up a part of her life by the time she was six, and old enough to start helping with chores around the house. Her parents were up at five, she was up at five. It had come naturally to her. She had bounced out of bed ready to take on the world.

Now, she stared blearily at the clock in her studio. Seven thirty a.m., and it was all she could do to stand in front of her painting and figure out what she needed to do next.

And her supplies were out of place again. Her palette was opened, a fresh, empty sheet of palette paper faced her, the paints she had left on it the day before were in the trash, and another sheet of palette paper was in the trash, too. She pulled the second sheet out and looked at it. Lamp black, and lots of it. Prussian blue. Cadmium red. Cadmium yellow. And zinc white.

Ugly, ugly combination of colors. She hated black— her feeling was that the absoluteness of it killed a painting, so her darks were either rich blues or earthy umbers, depending on the overall palette and the effect she was trying to achieve. She didn't trust zinc white in most cases and for most uses. And she didn't like the way prussian blue mixed with the cadmiums.

Whoever it was who was smearing her paints around on her palette paper was working from an entirely different approach than made sense to Emma.

She looked around her studio. Nothing else seemed to be disturbed. Her brushes were all dry and in place. One of her palette knives was out, but it was clean. She could find no sign of a hideous painting done by a color-blind artist. Maybe she'd somehow forgotten that she'd put them out. Maybe she'd put them away incorrectly herself. Maybe she'd been so tired she'd put the wrong paints on the palette, and didn't remember doing it, and then realized her mistake and dumped the whole mess.

Whatever the truth was, she was, frankly, too damned tired to pursue the matter further—at least for the moment.

Nothing else in her house was disturbed, nothing was missing. She could find no signs of a break-in.

She decided she was going to call the police in anyway, though. And maybe have an alarm system put in.

The paints weren't putting themselves on her palette paper.

She stared at the painting a moment longer, and then said, "I need a day off. I need a whole day off, and I need to take a nap."

Weary, sore, and bewildered by everything going on around her, she went back to curl up on her futon.

She woke a little past noon, well rested and considerably less sore, but horrified at the waste of her day.

She couldn't even contemplate going back in her studio to paint, though. She decided she would go into town, meet Aileen Wilkes, and then stop by the police station, explain her problem in terms that didn't make her sound insane, and see if she could get a policeman or a sheriff or whomever to come out and look at her house.

The drive into town was charming. She loved the curves in the road, the folds in the land that hid and then revealed each new vista as if it were a gift just for her. She loved the compactness of the tiny town, with its brief outskirts of little houses, its charming business district, and its air of determination to hang on to its main street in an era when massive department stores had killed off most main streets in the country. She turned off on Willow Branch, the cross street before the library, and found herself on a two-lane side street lined on both sides by enormous oaks that formed a cathedral arch over the road, with a handful of large houses that had been turned into businesses. A funeral home. A law office. And a flower shop turned crime scene.

Emma parallel parked in front of the funeral home and got out to see what had happened. Yellow crime scene tape marked off the parking lot and the sides of Jennibelle's Flowers and Baskets. Three police cars—one from out of town—and an ambulance blocked a good part of the street. A cop in uniform stood directing

traffic around the obstacles. One other cop stood in the
parking lot—talking to a man in a dark suit and white
shirt and tie. Emma guessed the man in the suit to be a
police detective.

A crowd had gathered around the perimeter of the
scene, and Emma saw Gwen standing in the midst of it.
She got out of her car and walked up the sidewalk to
join her.

"What happened?" she asked.

Gwen turned and saw Emma, and looked startled.
"You haven't heard?"

"I was just coming to talk with Aileen. This is the first
I've seen of this."

"Aileen is dead," Gwen said. "I don't know any of
the details, but her assistant left to take a load of deliv-
eries. When she got back, she couldn't get into the shop.
The doors were locked, and she didn't have a key. She's
only a part-timer."

Emma nodded.

"Aileen's car was there, and when the assistant went
around the building and knocked on windows, trying to
get Aileen's attention and to see what was going on, she
saw something in one of the windows that made her call
the police."

"What did she see?"

"I have no idea. Driscoll Cavanaugh isn't saying, and
Pearlie was hysterical. They took her off to the hospital
because she started fainting and complaining of chest
pain."

"Older lady?"

"Twenty-two."

"Ah."

Gwen gave Emma a sidelong look. "Precisely. She's

certainly going to be a suspect. She was the last person
to see Aileen alive."

"With the police here, I'm guessing Aileen didn't just
have a heart attack."

Gwen gave an exasperated sigh. "I wish I knew. No
one is saying anything. The EMTs haven't brought her
out yet, but, as you said, with half the Benina police
force here and a detective from over in Anderson, I'm
guessing they found something that makes them sure
what happened wasn't an accident." Then she arched
an eyebrow. "Or that makes them hope it wasn't an accident. The boys don't get a lot of excitement, you
know. She could have tripped and hit her head on
something sharp, and they would have dragged out
everything but the SWAT team. If we had one, of
course."

Emma managed a smile, but it was a wan one. "My
timing is awful. If I hadn't gone back to sleep, I could
have been here earlier. I might have been able to stop
whatever happened. I might have been able to make a
difference."

"And you might have gotten yourself killed," Gwen
said, "if it was a murder. You could have been there at
just the wrong time."

Emma considered that, and she shivered. Gwen was
right. Had she been out the door on time this morning,
she might have been in the flower shop when a mur-
derer arrived. She watched the EMTs appearing at the
front door, a stretcher between them, a black body bag
strapped to the stretcher.

She could have been in that very bag.

Of course, so could a lot of other people who had
walked into and out of the shop that morning. People

who had only thought about stopping in the shop would tell their friends how they had narrowly escaped their own demise. People who shopped there regularly, but who hadn't been anywhere near the place that day, or who had not even considered going in, would mention that they could have been victims.

In all, Emma thought, probably half the town would end up narrowly escaping death. That realization made her own situation amazingly less special.

"I keep thinking," Gwen told her, "that it could have been me in there. I stopped in to talk to Aileen from time to time, ordered flowers from her for my home, sent flowers to friends. I'd thought about stopping in to tell her I'd talked to you again. I could have been in there this morning."

Emma nodded. "You were lucky," she said. Behind her, she heard a woman whispering to another woman, "I was going to get a basket of mums to send to Elizabeth Cottril. Can you imagine? It could have been me they are putting into that ambulance."

Half the town. Considering the size of the town, Emma thought she might have to revise her estimate upward.

Still, Emma felt a pang of connection with the dead woman. Aileen Wilkes had known her mother, and had been willing to talk to her about what she'd known. If Emma had only gotten out the door early, instead of allowing herself the ridiculous luxury of a morning nap, she would have known whatever it was that Aileen knew.

She shook her head and let out her breath slowly.

"Are you all right?" Gwen asked.

"Fine. It's just scary," she said. But she wasn't fine.

She'd lost a connection to her mother that she could not replace.

"I'm more curious now than I was before," Gwen said. "About Maris, I mean. I'm going to ask around and see what anyone else might remember. Maris wasn't one of the popular girls back then, but people liked her. Maybe someone else still remembers her." She glanced at Emma. "Do you want me to let you know if I find anything?" Her voice was casual, but her eyes were curious.

Emma knew someone who was only casually interested would say, "No, that's okay." But she couldn't say that. This was her mother. Her own past. A mystery that she needed to unravel.

So she said, "Thank you." She dug through her purse and pulled out a pen and a pad of sticky notes. And then pulled out her wallet and retrieved the piece of paper that held her new phone number, which she had not yet completely memorized. She copied the number onto the pad, and added her name, and handed the paper to Gwen. "Call me. Any time." She took the paper back, and scribbled her other number on it. "My cell phone. Not sure how much longer this will be valid. I have to see if I can transfer my account to here. But for now, it works, and if you need to reach me, the cell phone is a good backup."

Gwen rested a hand on Emma's arm. "Who was she to you?"

"Who?" Emma asked, watching the ambulance turn on its lights and silently drive away.

"Maris."

Emma glanced at Gwen and bit her bottom lip. "I'm still trying to find that out," she said at last.

*   *   *

Driscoll Cavanaugh, the chief of police, referred Emma to Farley Waites, the sheriff, because she lived outside town limits, and because, as he put it, "We're up to our necks in murder around here."

Farley Waites—clearly envious of the excitement in town—listened to Emma's story of palette paper in her wastebasket with raised eyebrows and barely concealed boredom, and then sent out a deputy to go over her house with her.

The deputy, Jimmy Pate, showed Emma how her door locks had not been tampered with and couldn't be loided—demonstrating by working one of his own credit cards into the doorframe and showing her how the frame itself blocked any attempts to wiggle the thumb lock open—how the window locks would keep out any thief who wasn't willing to break the glass, and how, so long as she wasn't an idiot who slept with her doors unlocked—and he'd given her a hard look as he brought up that possibility—no one was going to get into her house unless she wanted them in. He did give her the name of a local security company. He was polite about it.

But when he left, he left her with the very clear impression that he didn't think much of her problem. That an extra sheet of paper in her wastebasket and her paints disorganized was not really anything the sheriff's department was going to be willing to expend a lot of energy trying to solve.

He let her know the county did have real emergencies, real crimes, and real problems.

She ended up apologizing for taking his time.

It was stupid, she decided. No one would break into a house to mess with her paints. She'd done what she needed to do, though. She'd talked to the police, she'd talked to the sheriff, she'd had a deputy out to the house, and she'd made a fool of herself on the record.

Other people in the world had bigger problems, some of them closer to home.

Murder. She shuddered. Why in the world had someone murdered that poor florist? Was it a robbery gone bad? Revenge? A love triangle? Some dark small-town secret?

Emma didn't feel like painting, but she had a deadline, and she was hell-bent on meeting her deadlines. Regular misses would ruin her business. She had a reputation for reliability to uphold.

So she went in and put paint on her board, working through the blades of grass and the carefully detailed dandelions in the foreground. She was about done with the thing. Another day, maybe two, and she'd have it drying and be e-mailing photographs to the publisher.

And she'd be done on time.

She could hear water dripping. She could hear creaking up in the attic. And the cat was sitting over in the corner again, watching her paint. When she looked down, she saw he'd brought her another dead mouse.

"I don't need them," she told him. "Really. You can keep them and eat them. You'll enjoy them. I have lots of food of my own."

He gave her that silent meow that cats did sometimes, and blinked at her.

"Right. You've made me your project. You're going to teach me to eat wild mice and hunt them to support myself, right?" She grinned at him. "I appreciate the effort. It's nice having someone around who wants to take care of me."

She needed to remember to fill his food bowl. That taking care of business went both ways.

Mike heard about the murder from his sister.

"Drew was doing rounds when the ambulance dropped her off at the hospital morgue," she told him. "He got the whole story. You know you can't tell anyone about this, you hear me?"

"I never tell."

"I know, but we don't know yet whether your girl out there can keep quiet, so you can't talk to her about this either."

"She's not my girl, and I'm not going to talk about what Drew found out."

"Aileen was murdered, and it was bad. Someone bashed in the back of her head with one of the vases she carries in the shop. It was horrible. The cash register was cleaned out, too." Cara sighed. "Drew was just sick. Aileen had been a patient of his forever. She was a *nice* lady, too. He can't figure out why anyone would have hurt her. She wouldn't have fought for the money in her cash register. He's sure of it."

"I knew her a little," Mike said. "I got flowers from her for a few of the women I dated. She *was* a nice lady. She did have a tongue on her, though."

"She heard the best dirt," Cara agreed. "I guess she was in a business that made it possible. She knew when men were buying flowers for women who weren't their wives, and I'll bet she had . . ." Cara faltered.

"Yeah," Mike said, "we're hitting the same conclusion at the same time. I'll bet she knew a lot of secrets. Maybe somebody realized that she wasn't very good at keeping them. Or found out she'd told one that had hurt him." He was frowning. "One of those guys who was buying flowers for a woman not his wife, for example."

Cara was quiet on the other end of the line. "The money might have been taken to make it look like a robbery."

"Might have been," Mike agreed. "And then again, it might have been a robbery. Let's not go turning it into a mystery, Cara. It is probably exactly what it looked like—some asshole who needed drug money or something, who realized she was in there by herself and killed her before he took it from the cash register."

When Mike hung up, he pinched the bridge of his nose and then pressed his thumbs into his temples to try to ward off the headache that he felt coming on. He'd started having them the last few days, and he had just about never had headaches before.

He thought about Aileen, who'd been someone he knew well enough to nod to in the grocery store. She'd had him out once to fix a leak in her roof, but mostly she used Taylor and Sons, who had been established a lot longer. He figured he got the nod on the roof leak because she wanted to keep him as a customer—he was, in fact, a pretty big flower buyer.

She wasn't someone he would have ever thought would be murdered. Cara was right in noting that she was a sweet, friendly woman. She'd been easy to talk to, and sympathetic, and more than once, buying flowers, he'd found himself telling her more about the woman they were for than he intended to.

Had someone else done the same thing?

He was sure the police would be looking into that angle. They didn't have a lot of this sort of thing going on. He couldn't remember the last time there had been a murder in town. But Dris and his boys were a dedicated bunch, and the Anderson detective, rumor had it, looked pretty sharp. They would figure this out.

He rubbed at his head again, and decided to see what he had in the medicine cabinet. Headaches. All of a sudden, too.

Chapter 6

She didn't even hear the alarm go off. The sun in her eyes woke her, and when she sat up, her body was so sore she yelped.

Emma stared at the alarm clock beside the futon. Ten thirty a.m.

She couldn't believe it. She'd slept so long the alarm had shut itself off. She had never done that in her life. Not once.

She crawled out of the covers and glared at the futon. It wasn't a particularly comfortable bed, but it had never actually inflicted pain before. She said, "You know what? I can replace you."

After dragging herself through a shower that loosened up her stiff muscles only a little, and taking a couple of pain relievers to shake them the rest of the way out, she went into town to buy a bed. Enough was enough, and maybe at the ripe old age of twenty-five, her body had decided it wasn't going to tolerate cheap mattresses anymore, or hippie sleeping arrangements.

She was going to go for nothing fancy, but driving

down Main Street on the way to the bedding place on the other side of town, she passed an antique store. Something about it caught her attention, and she went in.

The place was a jumble, of course. Everything jammed into limited space, headboards and footboards stacked along one wall, big armoires crammed edge to edge along another, horrible horsehair-stuffed Victorian sofas almost climbing on top of each other.

Knickknacks abounded. Someone, somewhere, had fallen deeply in love with the iconic chicken, and then had died, leaving the proprietor with a porcelain poultry yard to dispose of. There were a few lawn jockeys. A lot of tin signs for products no one made anymore.

One headboard caught her eye. It was flame maple, very clean and elegant, with delicate posts. It was expensive. But when she looked at it, she could see it in the master bedroom. She could put a little frame over the top of the posts from the ceiling, and drape gauzy cloth over it, and the whole thing would look elegant and beautiful. And still old.

She talked to the owner, who agreed to have the headboard and footboard delivered.

She then went to the bedding place and bought herself a real mattress, the best she could find. And some fancy sheets, and a down comforter.

She wasn't doing what she'd planned to do. She'd wanted to redo the bedroom before she moved into it. She'd wanted to paint and refinish the floor and the woodwork, and she wasn't sure what else. But, dammit, she needed to get a decent night's sleep, and she needed to wake up feeling like she hadn't been playing football with the UW Badgers. As the football.

Some things took precedence. She could always make the room prettier later.

By the time she got home, she felt better. Her muscles had stopped aching, her mind had relaxed, and she was able to focus on her painting. She had stopped setting up her palette for more than one day, and she made a point of not looking in the trash, so she didn't have anything to distract her. She finished and signed the work and moved it to her drying rack. She'd photograph it the next day, and send print-quality images to the publisher. They could use those for dummies while the original dried and she boxed it and shipped it.

She was just realizing that it was almost two in the afternoon and she'd missed lunch when she heard a truck in her driveway. Neither the bed nor the mattress was supposed to be delivered until the next day, but she sort of hoped at least the mattress would arrive.

However, her heart took a little jump when she saw that it was Mike.

She met him on the porch. "Hey," she said, "I did that tape recording for you."

He nodded. He was rubbing his forehead, and he looked kind of distant.

"Are you okay?"

"Headache," he told her. "I almost never have headaches, but the last week or so, I've had one just about every day."

"You talk to your doctor?"

"No," he said. He gave her the same look she'd seen on the faces of men who had just had it suggested to them that they ask for directions.

She laughed. "Never mind. You need an aspirin or anything?"

"Maybe." He smiled at her, then, and his whole face changed. Her heart skipped a few beats, and she thought about being in his arms, kissing him, touching him . . . pulling his clothes off.

"Tape recorder," she said, trying to rein in her wild lust. "Come on in, and you can hear what I got. I set it up where the sound was loudest, and just let it run. I hope you'll be able to make some use of it."

"Have you listened to it yet?"

"No," Emma said. "I've been finishing a commission. Deadlines, you know."

"I do. They're the bane of my existence," he told her, and followed her into the house.

"I sort of like them," she said. "They mean I'm employed."

He laughed at that. "True."

While he was moving the tape recorder over to the kitchen table and sitting down, she got him a couple of aspirin and a glass of water. Then she sat down next to him. She glanced over at the cat's food dish, and realized he hadn't eaten anything.

Well, he was getting fresh mice. Dried food probably wasn't much of a temptation. Maybe she should get him some of the canned stuff.

Mike turned on the tape recorder, and for a moment neither of them heard anything but Emma sighing and then moving off.

As the sound of her footsteps receded, though, Emma heard something that sounded like a whisper. She couldn't make out what it was saying, but it didn't sound anything like a drip. She stared at Mike, who looked back at her, his expression blank and tense.

The whispers got louder. And then she could hear what they were saying.

This is wrong. We shouldn't be together.

I know. But I can't leave you. A pause. *I love you.*

What if he comes home?

He's dead. If he were not, he would have come back to you long before now.

More whispering, but Emma could not make out the words any longer.

Mike stopped the recorder. "What did you hear?" he asked her.

She wrapped her arms around herself. Suddenly, she was cold. "I don't want to say. What did you hear?"

He bit his lip. "Has anything strange been happening here?"

She said, "Aside from me hearing dripping where there was no water, and being so terrified of walking into the room at the top of the stairs that I've avoided it like plague, and having my palettes end up in the trash mornings, along with palettes of paint in color combinations I wouldn't use except at gunpoint? And hearing footsteps in my attic, and something heavy being dragged down the stairs?"

He said, "I don't think you should live here, Emma."

"You heard . . . ?"

"Voices," he told her. "I heard voices."

"I love this house," she said. "I feel home when I'm here, in a way I've never felt before in my life."

"But you heard . . . ?"

"I heard voices," she admitted. "Two people talking about how they shouldn't be with each other."

"That's a bad thing," he said. "That's not the sort of

thing you want to find in a house you plan to live in. You don't want footsteps on stairs, or voices, or mysterious dripping water. . . ."

She glanced over Mike's shoulder and saw the cat, out in the hallway, staring at her. She glanced down to see if another mouse was at her feet, and was grateful to find that one wasn't.

"What?" Mike said, realizing that she was looking past him, and turning to see what she was looking at.

"Just the cat," she said.

"Where?" He kept looking where she was looking. Staring straight at the cat.

"You're looking at him."

"I'm looking at an empty hall."

She saw a cat. A big, elegant cat that brought her mice. A nice cat, that kept her company while she worked, and trotted by her side while she inspected the house, and that kept his distance—he was a little wild, she supposed. That thudded down the stairs like he was two kids jumping in gunny sacks.

A very real, very tangible cat.

And Mike didn't see him.

"Come here, kitty, kitty," she said, and dropped her hand, and wriggled her fingers, hoping to tempt him over to her. Instead, with one long gaze at her, he turned and trotted away.

"You *saw* the cat," she said. "This is the same cat that has decided I need a complete dead-mouse collection. Big cat, swirly stripes, white tuxedo markings. Friendly. Short-haired. You've seen him before. He's been here just about every time you have."

"I've heard you talk about the cat, and I've seen that

you're feeding a cat, and I've seen the mice he leaves for you . . . but I've never actually seen the cat. I figured he was shy."

Emma closed her eyes.

This wasn't right. Something about all of this wasn't right, and suddenly she felt stupid. Suckered, though she wasn't sure yet by whom.

She *knew* the cat was real. He'd never let her pet him, but he brought her mice. He didn't eat the cat food, but . . . well, it was dry food, and he'd already clearly been eating well.

She didn't know what to think. But suddenly she realized that every untoward thing that had happened in the house had happened either while Mike was around, or in direct connection with Mike.

The tape recorder, for instance. Maybe Mike and his sister had prerecorded the tape. The footsteps. He'd been the other person in the house when Emma had heard footsteps down the stairs, and the sound of someone moving something heavy. The first time, anyway.

Dripping? No, that she heard on her own. But he was the one who was saying he couldn't hear it, and pointing to reasons why there was no dripping.

The scare she'd had in the room upstairs? He hadn't been there for that, but that she could write off to simple idiocy. Nothing—absolutely nothing—was wrong with that room. Even if she didn't intend to go into it any more than she had to.

She looked at Mike with a sudden, deep distrust. She wasn't sure why she felt so attracted to him, but he had been quick to take advantage of her attraction. He'd gotten her naked in record time. If they hadn't gone through with the business, that had been because Emma heard . . . a piano. Well, he'd been there for that, too, hadn't he? And he'd been the one to go hurrying off in search of whatever it was he'd set up in the first place, while she was cooking dinner. He'd been out of her sight more than once. He'd had plenty of opportunity.

And what would he get out of it?

The only thing she could think of was something he'd said earlier. That she shouldn't be living in her house. Drew Jackson had said something similar.

Cara hadn't. But Cara and Mike could have taken turns playing good cop, bad cop.

If she liked the three of them as much as anyone she had ever met, if she felt drawn to them, all *that* suggested was that they were damned talented con artists.

"I think you'd better leave," she said, turning to Mike.

He looked shocked. "What got into you?"

"Sanity," she said with careful evenness. "Sanity, and adding things up, and realizing the only time anything strange happens around here, you're here to put your spin on it. You don't see the very ordinary cat who dumps mice at my feet. You don't hear the piano playing in a house that has no piano. You don't hear the sound of booted feet dragging something heavy down the stairs. You don't hear the dripping." She glared at him. "And you hear the voices on the tape, but those whispery voices could just as easily be you and your sister, and the tape recorder a nonfunctional one. Or the tape prerecorded and fixed so that it can't be taped over."

His eyebrows had been sliding steadily upward during her tirade. Right at the end, he managed to look pissed off while smiling.

"And why would we conspire against you, my sister and I?"

"*And* Drew. To get me out of this house," she said. "Because while you were in here working on the place, you found something valuable, or maybe found out that something valuable might be here."

"I would have said I found the only valuable thing that had ever been in this house on the day you moved in," he told her. His voice was sharp. She could see his anger in every line of his body, from his clenched jaw to his stiff shoulders. "Let's take the obvious first. When we turn on this tape, the first thing we hear is you setting everything up and walking away. Cara and I weren't hovering in the background so that we could whisper into the tape when you left the room."

She'd forgotten about hearing herself on the tape first.

"Second, you heard a piano? You told me you heard *thumping* at the back of the house. I would have felt a hell of a lot better if you'd told me that you heard a piano, because that was what I heard, too, and I've been wondering if I was going crazy. Apparently not. Only," he said, "you could have set up the piano trick. And the voices on the tape recorder. Did you?"

She stared at him. He'd heard the piano, too? He'd felt crazy?

She closed her eyes and rubbed her temples. Her head was starting to throb.

"Headache? Join the club. I started getting them right around the time that I met you."

He sounded awfully upset. He had a right to be. She'd accused him of being a con artist.

The cat, she realized, was watching them from the hallway.

"Here, kitty, kitty," she said.

He turned to look where she was looking.

"Here, kitty, kitty." The cat watched her, blinking, not moving.

"You see the cat in the hallway?" Mike asked.

"Yes. And I'm going to get him to come in here so you can see him, too."

"I can see into the hallway," Mike said. "You see the cat there right now?"

"Yes," she said through clenched teeth.

"Okay. Emma, I have twenty-twenty vision. I see in the dark really well. There's no cat in the hall."

"Come here, kitty, kitty," she pleaded.

The cat rose, picked up a mouse that had been pinned beneath his feet, and trotted toward her.

"You see him now?" she asked.

Mike didn't say anything. He was staring at the cat, though.

"Here, kitty, kitty," she said one last time, and waggled her fingers. The cat came over to her, and dropped his mouse. She reached out to pet him, but he moved out of the way. He was as solid as any cat could be, though. A big, rangy tomcat, elegant to look at, amiable of disposition, with an unfortunate taste in gifts.

Emma looked away from the cat, to Mike, and said, "You can dispose of the mouse he gave me this time," she said, and then she realized he was somewhere between green and ghost white, and he was staring at the cat.

"Emma, I swear, there was no cat in that hallway."

"You see him now?"

"Yes."

"He look like a cat to you?"

"Yes." Mike was still pale. "But he wasn't there." He stood up. "Emma, there's something wrong with this house. Maybe something dangerous." He paused. "When I was working here, the place felt scary. Like it was watching me, like it didn't want me here. When you moved in, that changed. It feels welcoming now, like home." He stopped cold and she watched his face redden all the way to the tips of his ears. "Forget I said that. It was a stupid thing to say."

She was nodding. "But I know what you mean. It felt like home to me the first time I drove by it. But . . . nothing strange happened to you while you were working on the place, right?"

He shook his head. "I sure as hell didn't hear any pianos. Or feet on the stairs, other than those of my crew. I didn't see any cats. I didn't hear any water dripping, or any voices, either. Why don't you stay in a hotel for a while? Have someone who studies paranormal occurrences come out and take a look at the place."

"I don't want to leave," Emma told him. "I wake up in the morning and I'm at home. I walk across the floors in my bare feet, and they say home to me. I look out the windows and see the old trees, and the old buildings, and the run-down garden, and the way the light falls at every hour of the day, and every bit of it is right. It's the way it's supposed to be, the way I knew it would be. It's like this place is a lock, and I'm the key."

He said, "That's a good analogy, though maybe not in a good way. You're the key. But I think you might have unlocked something more than the front door."

She had to consider that. She hadn't ever believed in the supernatural. However, she had been the last one to handle the tape and the tape recorder, she had been on it, sighing and walking away, and she knew she hadn't tampered with it. So the voices she and Mike heard so plainly were not of any origin she could comfortably explain.

She didn't want to think about it anymore.

Her head hurt. Her shoulders hurt. The tape recorder sat on the table, filled with voices she couldn't explain. She looked around to see if she could see the cat.

He was gone.

The mouse was still there, dead as anything, laid out on the kitchen floor. She rose, feeling scared and a little sick, and went to get a paper towel to use to pick it up.

Mike left around four. They weren't angry with each other anymore. They were a little strained, still, but not angry. Emma shut the door behind him and leaned against it.

She wanted to get her hands around the truth of her house, this place that had stood empty for so long before she moved into it. Other people had presumably looked at the place in the years that it had been for sale, starting back when it had stood empty for only weeks or months, rather than years. None of them had bought. She didn't know why. Maybe they had been like Mike—uncomfortable within the old walls. Maybe they had felt something wrong, and had turned away, deciding that other houses would feel more like home.

She did not understand why her house, still The House to her, had drawn her in so completely. She could not explain why she had done something so spur of the moment that was at the same time so life-changing. People didn't drive into towns they'd never seen before and buy houses without finding out how they liked the area, how it met their needs, how they fit into the community. They didn't just walk into the office of the first real estate agent they found and say, "I want to buy that house."

Did they?

She had, but the woman who helped her buy the place had been pretty certain from the very start that Emma was a few chips short of the bag. She'd been nice about it, especially when Emma was in the position to buy the place outright. Customers like that didn't come along every day.

But she said several times that she would never be so brave. Which was the polite way of saying she would never be so crazy.

It kept coming back to crazy, didn't it? To Emma and her crazy mother, to the crazy things Emma did when she came to Benina, to the crazy obsession she'd had all her life with a house she'd never seen, and that she had to possess the moment she found it.

And to the crazy way she felt around Mike, which not only didn't make sense, but which, in a world where people got horrible diseases from being careless about who they slept with, fell in love with, or trusted, was dangerous. Maybe even suicidal.

Crazy.

She walked through the rooms, and each of them spoke to her. Of warmth, of family, of belonging. She hadn't been exaggerating when she told him that she felt like she belonged there. She watched the light filter through a keyhole-sized piece of red glass in one of the leaded transom windows, to reflect on a corner of a door across the room. The red main reflection was surrounded by a rainbow from the prismed edges of the glass. And she knew that she could watch it march the rest of the way up the doorframe until it disappeared with sunset. It marched up the doorframe only in winter, though, and just for a short time. This time. A thing she was sure of, though she had no way to know it was true.

She could deduce that logically, of course, from the movement of the sun through the sky during the year. But her heart didn't know the movement of that little rainbow of light because of logic. It knew because . . . because it knew. Because somehow, she fit in the house, and belonged to every homey detail of it. She knew because she was home.

And how could she hope to explain that?

The phone rang, and she had to remember which room she'd hooked it up in. She had outlets in every room, but she had only the one telephone.

Living room? Kitchen. Yes, she'd plugged it into the kitchen.

She ran for it, grabbed it. "Hello?"

"Is this Emma Beck?" The voice was familiar, though strained by excitement.

"Gwen?" she asked.

"I found someone else who knew Maris," Gwen said. "I'm with her right now. She's very nervous about talking to anyone. She says there was something wrong with Maris's death, and she needs to know why you want to know about it before she'll talk to you. If you're just curious, she says you'll have to stay curious."

"Do you think she knows anything that would matter to me?"

Gwen said, "I don't know what would matter, Emma. I've been pursuing this because it appealed to the library scientist in me. This is what I do—dig down and find things out. But I've hit a point where I can't do any more research unless I have more details about what it is that I'm researching. I need to know why you need to know the information you're looking for."

Emma took a slow, careful breath. She didn't know why she was so afraid to tell anyone the truth. Maybe for fear that she would be judged. Her mother had been—maybe, probably—crazy. She'd possibly killed herself, and in a particularly ugly way. If people knew that Maris was her mother, perhaps they would look at Emma as potentially crazy, and dangerous, and deadly, too.

Perhaps.

Emma was afraid to tell the truth. And she was afraid not to. This might be her only chance to find out who her mother had been. Maybe she could find someone on her own who knew her mother well and was willing to talk about her. But probably not.

She said, "I'm Maris's daughter."

On the other end of the phone, a long silence. Then Gwen said, "Maris's baby died at birth. It was one of the things that just about destroyed Maris's mother—that she lost her daughter and her grandbaby, too."

Emma said, "I was adopted almost immediately after birth. The detective who did the background for my parents tracked me back to Maris, and to the nurse who delivered me. The nurse's name was Marjorie Salley. She was the contact for my parents, too. The detective said that after she gave me to them, she took the money they paid her and disappeared. My parents thought my adoption was legal—there was a lawyer involved who made them think it was legitimate. But they were uncertain enough that some years later they started asking questions."

"Oh, my God," Gwen said.

"You can't tell anyone about this, Gwen," Emma told her. "As far as I can tell, everyone who was involved in what happened is either dead or long gone now, and I'm the only person who could still be considered an injured party. And I'm not going to make trouble, or raise a fuss. I just want to find out more about the woman . . . well, girl . . . who gave birth to me. I need to know where I came from."

"I wouldn't think of telling anyone," Gwen said. "Except for . . . my informant, and only because she won't talk to you if I don't."

Emma leaned against the wall and closed her eyes. "Thank you for helping me with this, Gwen. I'm afraid to find out too much. But I'm afraid not to, too. Tell her."

Emma heard nothing as a hand muffled the phone. But a moment later, Gwen said, "She says she wants to think about it. She'll call you."

Less than two hours later, Emma was standing in the Harris Teeter, holding a package of Oreos and shivering as the mister in the fresh vegetables section went off. She checked her watch. Six p.m.

The whole thing should have felt ludicrously funny, a sort of James-Bond-gone-wrong business, where the woman had called her home an hour earlier—from a pay phone, no less—and told Emma that if she wanted to know about Maris, she was to go to the Harris Teeter at five forty-five p.m. and stand in the fresh vegetables section next to the cucumbers, holding a package of Oreos.

Emma had started feeling conspicuous at five forty-six.

Now, with her secret contact a full fifteen minutes late, she was almost certain that she'd been stood up, and that she was going to have to buy the damned Oreos and a bag of cukes just so she could give some plausible excuse for lurking in the section for so long.

"Put down the cookies and come with me," a woman's voice said from directly behind her.

Emma put the cookies into her shopping cart, which was otherwise empty, and turned to find a woman with her hair wrapped in a scarf, with dark sunglasses on, wearing a sad, vaguely green polyester coat that had seen better days back in about 1970, and jeans and work boots. When Emma nodded, the woman turned and walked away.

Emma followed, a few steps behind her, and the woman led her out of the store, and into the Subway right next to it. The woman ordered a soft drink and chips, and Emma followed suit.

They sat together. The woman did not remove her sunglasses or her jacket, or even her scarf. Emma could tell that she was in her late thirties or early forties.

"You don't want to make any public noise about this," the woman told Emma. Those were the first words out of her mouth since the grocery store, and Emma felt her gut knot. The whole thing should have felt silly or overblown. But it didn't.

"Don't think I'm being dramatic, you"—the woman snapped—"you weren't here when Maris ended up in the loony bin, with no one who cared about her allowed to see her. You weren't here when she died, and no one could give a reasonable explanation for why she'd died.

You weren't here when the story was that her baby had died, and she'd killed herself right after, but nobody could produce the baby—and then all of a sudden, Maris's mother killed herself, too. And then Maris's best friend and her family picked up and moved, and nobody knew where, or why. One night they were right in the middle of everything, and the next, their house was empty with a FOR SALE sign on it, and no one knew anything. We've never heard from any of them since."

"Don't you think those are just coincidences?" Emma asked. "Why would anyone care about some crazy pregnant girl who died twenty-five years ago? The whole idea of there being some conspiracy about her death seems insane."

"And yet you've discovered that you were her daughter, and that your parents didn't adopt you legally. That you were, in fact, kidnapped at birth and sold."

"It wasn't anything that dramatic," Emma said. But in fact, what the woman said had summed up the circumstances of her birth pretty clearly.

"Right. And Aileen Wilkes's death was just one of those things, and never mind that we haven't had a murder in this town in ages, and probably wouldn't have if you hadn't stirred things up."

"You're saying her death was because of me?"

"Gwen told me she'd sent you to see Aileen the day she died. She might have mentioned your pending visit to someone. Or Aileen might have. That woman could talk the ears off a statue. Gwen thought Aileen's death was a strange coincidence. I don't."

"What do you know about my mother that would make sense of all these people dying?"

"I know that she was a poor girl in love with a rich

boy, and she refused to get an abortion when he told her
to."

"What?" Emma inhaled sharply, her heart suddenly
pounding. "Who was he?"

"That I don't know. She would never say. She told me
he was in college already when she started seeing him,
and she'd tell me how wonderful he was. But she would
not ever, for any reason, tell me who he was. And when
she got pregnant, she talked to me a little, when she
wasn't talking to Amy Kirkbride, who was her best
friend back then. She loved him. So she didn't think his
refusal to marry her as soon as she turned sixteen, or to
come to meet her mother, or in any way to make her a
public part of his life, was creepy or dangerous. She
kept thinking that he was going to claim her and marry
her before the baby was born."

"Some college boy?"

"Some college boy from this town, or maybe Anderson, who had rich parents. Wouldn't be the first time
some boy from Anderson came sniffing around for
naive young girls. My guess is that the rich parents
pulled some strings, and paid her doctor to lock her up.
Maybe even paid him to kill her, though when the doctor got rid of her baby, she might have killed herself.
She wanted that baby more than anything."

Emma considered that. The business about the doctor
taking money to kill her mother sounded completely
outside the realm of possibility. But suicide? She
thought about the fact that *she* was that baby, and the
thought suddenly occurred to her that her disappearance
might have driven her mother to suicide. It wasn't a
thought that sat well.

"You have any idea who my father might be?"

"Yes. There are a couple of possibilities, and honestly, I don't think any of them are from Anderson. The one I'm pretty sure about followed his father into practice. He's the town's *important* lawyer, the one who works for the other rich families. You might have met him when you bought your house—not sure who did your paperwork."

Emma felt like she was going to sink into the floor. The town's *important* lawyer. "David Halifax?"

"That would be the one."

Emma shivered, in spite of the fact that the Subway was several degrees too warm.

She thought of how she had felt sitting close to David Halifax—how his clear distaste, and amusement . . . and something more, had left her feeling dirty. And scared.

If she was his illegitimate daughter, and he or his parents had sold her to strangers to get rid of her—and then she came back anyway—she could suddenly understand where those looks had come from. His father could have handled the adoption work. David could have known all along where she was. Who she was.

In fact, his response to her then became not just understandable, but to be expected. If his parents (or he, she realized), had killed people to keep her existence and his affair with an underage girl a secret, and they had succeeded in keeping the secret for twenty-five years, her return, and her asking precisely the questions she was asking, could have caused Aileen Wilkes's death.

If he were her father.

That wasn't proven. He could also have been cold and creepy because that was simply who he was.

She couldn't jump to conclusions.

Emma needed to think more about him. But the woman in front of her had actually known her birth mother. Emma had a thousand questions about Maris, and perhaps only this one chance to ask them.

"What was she like?" Emma asked.

Her informant dug through her bag of chips, and ate one before answering. "She wasn't crazy, that's for damn sure. Not a single minute of a single day of her life. She was the most sane, focused person I have ever known, except for her belief in the boy who fathered you. But even that was just idealism and hope and love."

"How can you know she wasn't crazy?" Emma said. She dared to hope, but not too much.

"Because I knew her. I'd known her for years. We lived next door to each other, and we weren't best friends, but we were friends. She was creative—she did beadwork and macramé and crochet, and she knitted. She liked to draw, and she was pretty good. She sang in the school choir and the church choir, and she played clarinet in the band—she always had to use one of the cruddy band instruments because her mother was a widow and didn't have the money to rent a good one. And even with not-very-good instruments, she was always first chair." The woman across the table from Emma glared into the chip bag as if it had tried to do her harm. "She was kind. She had this determination about her, that she was going to be someone someday. I could always see how some lawyer's son could meet her and fall in love with her and think she was perfect."

"But her mother was a widow."

"A widow, and poor, and Maris's father hadn't been

worth anything while he'd been alive. He drank and gambled, and if he ever did anything else, I never heard of it."

Her grandfather. She couldn't be too excited about that part of her family tree, but her mother sounded like someone who would have been wonderful to know.

"And she loved you. She had names picked out for you, the last time I talked to her. They were so outlandish—I could never forget them."

Emma felt her heart slowly breaking. "What were they?"

"The boy would have been the good-looking Musketeer in *The Three Musketeers.* Dart-something."

"D'Artagnan?"

The woman managed a thin smile. "That was it. The girl—you, I guess—was going to be Rosalinda-Claire."

"Oh, God. All of that? Where did she come up with that?"

"I have no idea. Well, Claire was her mother's name. But she thought Rosalinda was the most beautiful name she had ever heard."

"How in the world could you have remembered that?"

The older woman laughed. "I was young once. And I kept a diary. The fact that a friend of mine was going to have a baby was big news to me, and the names she came up with were . . . I don't know. Special. I wrote them down, just because it seemed important." She crumpled the chip bag into a ball. "I dug out that old diary before I came to talk with you, just to make sure I remembered the important things. I thought you might think the names were important."

"I do," Emma assured her. She wondered if Rosalinda might have been the name of her father's mother.

Or if, like D'Artagnan, it was something she'd read somewhere. "What else can you tell me about her?"

The woman shrugged. "She was a good girl. I'm not sure how the boy she fell in love with got past that so that she ended up pregnant, but I do know right up until the last time I saw her, she still believed that he was going to take care of her, and eventually marry her, and that somehow everything was going to be all right."

Emma was quiet for a while after that.

"It wasn't, of course," the woman said. "It wasn't, and a lot of people got hurt a lot of different ways."

"Yes," Emma said, feeling the weight of the past and other people's pain descending on her. "Yes. They did."

The other woman rose, and picked up her drink and her chip bag. "I've spent long enough sitting here. I don't want to accidentally run into anyone who shouldn't see me with you."

"Who would that be?" Emma asked. The woman's conviction that a murderous band of conspirators was waiting to slaughter her if ever they found out that she had told Emma about her mother had an odd sort of weight to it.

"I don't know," the woman said. "That's why I don't know whom to watch out for."

"You really think David Halifax is my father?"

"For your sake, I hope he's not." The woman shrugged. "There were three or four other boys who were from town, who were off at college, and who had the sort of parents who would have never let them marry her. But none of them seemed like the sort of boys who would fool around with a fifteen-year-old girl. She wasn't grown-up looking. She was skinny and pretty flat—she was still a kid."

Emma rose and followed her. "Is there anyone else I could talk to? Maybe to find out more about the nurse, or about how my mother ended up in the hospital?"

"Her doctor died quite a few years ago. He knew, I'm sure, since he was the one who put her in the hospital. The records for that have to be around somewhere, though. There are a lot of people alive who were his patients, and I don't think hospitals or doctors' offices can simply toss out old medical records. I'm not sure how you would manage to get in to see them, though. Your adoption papers and your claim that you were Maris's daughter aren't going to be good enough for a lot of people."

"Why was it good enough for you?" Emma asked.

"Because I stood watching you for about ten minutes before I came over," the woman said softly. "You look just like her, Emma. I could never have doubted who you were."

They walked across the parking lot in their separate directions. Emma got in her truck, and saw the woman get into an old Firebird, bright red with Bondo fenders, and drive off.

She waited a few minutes, sitting in the parking lot and staring out at the store, and the cars all around her, and the street in front of the little shopping center.

There might still be people in this town who actually knew what had happened to her mother. There might still be people in this town who had been *involved* in what had happened to her mother. And her. She had to remember to put herself into the equation, because what had happened to her mother had happened to her, too. She'd been sold.

She loved her adoptive parents. They'd been wonderful, they'd been loving, and they had given her a good upbringing grounded in honesty and faith. They had *also* been the people who had bought her in a black-market deal that her father, at least, had considered shady enough that he'd eventually hired a detective to backtrack her past as far as he could take it.

How did she reconcile the people who had bought her with the people who had raised her? How did she locate the people who had stolen her and sold her?

And how did she know whom to trust? She had to admit that if someone had been involved in selling a child, and perhaps in killing people who might have discovered what he had done, that it was entirely possible that she could be in danger if she stirred things up.

She started the car, and drove off toward her home. She had to be certain that knowing the truth would be worthwhile before she risked her life to pursue it further. She tried to convince herself that her terrified informant had given her enough information—she knew that her mother had loved her and wanted her, and she was pretty sure Maris had not been crazy. She wanted to be able to take that with her, and hang on to it, and have it be enough that she never had to mention what she'd discovered to anyone else, ever again.

Because if she started digging, she was going to have to find out if her father was still alive. If he'd had a hand in the death of her mother, and perhaps her grandmother. If the people who had sold her may still be brought to justice.

If. If. If.

Chapter 7

THE SEVENTH DAY—Friday

Emma had just finished breakfast when she heard a car pull up out front and a car door slam. She hurried to the front door to find Cara starting across the drive.

Emma was puzzled by Cara. She felt like they knew each other, which made no sense. She'd liked Cara instantly, and she found a smile on her face as she stepped out onto the porch.

Cara jogged across the yard. "I told Drew to let the part-timer handle the office today. I said I needed a break."

Emma grinned. "You don't get too many breaks?"

"The office is always busy, and I have to pull a lot of charts, and make appointments, and do the billing, and a list of other things as long as your arm. I have a horrible problem getting any free time on the days the office is open. Mostly I don't mind. But I wanted to come out and see you. It sounds silly, I know. I have a lot of friends in town, but, well, Mike is crazy about you—and you can't tell him I told you that—you and I hit it off so well, and I figured you don't seem like you know anyone here—"

"I don't," Emma agreed.

"You're so brave. I can't imagine moving someplace where I didn't know anyone. I mean, I guess you did it for your work and all. For inspiration?"

Emma laughed. "I couldn't begin to tell you why I did it. I have no clue. I saw this house, and I had to have it, and then I had to live in it. It doesn't make any sense to me now, it didn't make any sense to me then, but there you have it."

Cara said, "I understand about the house. I love this place. Always have. I mean, it makes me sad when I drive by it. It seems so tragic. But at the same time, with the trees planted along the drive, and the way the porch welcomes you, and . . ." She looked sidelong at Emma and grinned. "Some houses are just like that, I guess."

"This one more than any I've ever run across before," Emma said. "Come on in."

Cara grinned. "I had an ulterior motive, actually. I was looking around this place when I was in here before, and I was wondering what you were going to do with it. Mike said you said you have very specific plans, but I was hoping you could actually show me around. Give me the tour. And we could talk decorator for a while."

"You're into decorating?"

"I would be, given the opportunity. Drew had his place done professionally before we became a couple. It's really old-fashioned, but expensive and very professionally done, and nothing I could do to it would improve it. So I have dreams about starting with a blank slate, but . . ." She grinned and shrugged. "We have a little place at the beach that we almost never get to go to. I got to do some of the decorating there."

Emma laughed. "I have to admit, I've been dying to take a day off and really get to work on my plans. I've been wrapping up a deadline, but I have the painting finished now, so I have a genuine excuse to take a day off."

She looked at Cara's blue jeans, sneakers, and heavy sweater, and said, "You dressed right."

"I had hopes."

Cara hung her purse and jacket on the pegs in the corner. Emma said, "Then let me show you around."

They started with the downstairs. Cara loved the old formal dining room, and thought the pantry was fantastic. It was huge—something Emma loved, too. "You could have enough food in there for three months," Cara said.

"More than that," Emma told her. "There's only one of me, and I eat pretty well, but still—there's only one of me. If I bought the right sorts of things, I could probably be stocked for six months."

"Oh, wow. I have this fantasy," Cara told her, "of being on a remote island, with no one around, with just me and books and knitting and enough food so that I didn't have to do anything but read, and knit, and go for runs around the beach. Which would, of course, be exactly two miles around, so that I could go out my front door, do one loop, and be done for the day."

Emma glanced at her. "You run two miles a day? I have never been able to get myself to commit to exercise that way."

Cara laughed. "Neither have I. But I tell myself that if I had a beach with an exact two mile circumference, and I didn't have any distractions, and enough food to keep me going without having to shop, I would."

"How about the reading and the knitting?"

"Those I do. And love. I never have as much time for either as I'd like, though."

"I'm a reader, too," Emma said. "I've already made my first forays into the library, but I have to get a local driver's license before I can get a library card."

"You've met Gwen, then."

"She's wonderful."

Cara said, "She'll track down anything for you. She's relentless. Best librarian ever."

Emma grinned and did not comment on how true she had found that to be. They walked from the kitchen into the dining room, and she changed the subject. "I can see this with period furniture, with walls done in a rich burgundy to bring out the gorgeous wood details." She pointed to the carved dentil molding that ran along the high ceiling, and the broad, detailed trim around the windows and doors.

"You'll leave the woodwork white?"

Emma shook her head. "I want to strip it back to bare wood, maybe stain it, and give it a tung oil finish."

"You're a masochist, then."

"Since childhood," Emma agreed. "Never go the easy route if a really difficult one exists; that's my motto."

Cara laughed.

They went through the living room, the downstairs bathroom, and even the utility room, and started toward the stairs.

"This is a gorgeous staircase," Cara told her.

"It will be better once I've had the chance to strip it and refinish it. And replace the missing balustrades. The stairs themselves are pretty sturdy."

"You have a lot of space under the staircase," Cara noted. "You thinking about putting anything in there?"

"You mean like flowers, or a table or something?"

"A little chair with a book table beside it, and a tiny light? Like a secret book nook?"

Emma sighed. "I hate to admit it, but that space feels a little . . . creepy to me. It isn't the sort of place I'd want to sit and read. I don't exactly get shivers walking past it, you know. But, well . . ."

"Not the place you want to curl up with anything scary. Got it." They headed up the stairs. Cara looked around the upper hallway, balcony, and overlook from the landing. "This is nice. You have great vertical elements here. I would never have realized from the outside that the window in the center gable wasn't for an upstairs room.

"The house has a few places where the windows don't seem to match up. But the layout gives lots of light," Emma said. "And good movement."

She looked at the door to the first room to her right, and thought, *I don't want to go in there.*

And then she opened the door anyway. Cara walked in. A look crossed her face, an unreadable expression that startled Emma, and she backed out. "Small," she said.

"Wait," Emma said. She stepped out of the room too, and as soon as the door was closed, felt better. "You didn't like that room."

"I can't say that. It felt very familiar to me. Homey, and . . . I don't know, Emma. I walked in and suddenly I didn't want to be in there anymore. I thought if I stayed another second, I was going to cry."

Emma looked at her, curious. "But you weren't afraid?"

"No. Terribly, terribly sad. But not afraid."

"That room scared me to death once," Emma told her. "I have no reason I can even guess about why. No explanation. But walking in there with you just now was the first time I've gone in there since the day I moved in. I was just as terrified this time as I was the time before. But the feeling goes away the second I walk out of the room and close the door."

Cara looked thoughtful. "Mike hated working out here. He supervised the crew, but he stayed out on the grounds as much as possible. Maybe you've both been feeling echoes."

Emma led her to the other rooms, which didn't hold any dread for her. "Echoes," she said. "Yes. This place is full of them. For me, the strongest ones are in the rose garden."

They finished the upstairs tour, and Cara said, "What's this door? Closet?"

"No," Emma told her. "That goes up to the attic."

A huge grin spread across Cara's face. "An attic with stairs? God, I love attics."

Emma laughed. "It's huge, and it's full of old stuff. I keep telling myself I should go through everything, but I haven't even gotten started on the downstairs yet. And I've only been up there once, but the room itself has a lot of possibilities. It could be an extra room, maybe, something kind of dramatic, with great sloped ceilings and a sort of cozy feel. Not that it's anything like that now, mind you." She started up the narrow stairs. "It's dirty and cold and dark and it has this weird half wall that messes up the flow."

"You have a flashlight?"

"Mike put a light in for me."

She switched it on, and the room lit feebly from the

center, with long shadows thrown into dark corners. The dust and cobwebs gave the place the sort of creepy aura that would have been right at home in a horror movie. But neither Emma nor Cara were put off.

"You're right," Cara said. "This place would be perfect for a master bedroom, or a recreation room. TV room, maybe. The angles are fantastic, and it's so big."

"I have a huge amount of floor space in this place," Emma agreed. "If I count in the attic, I'm over five thousand square feet." They walked the length of the attic, and turned into the el.

"This would be a wonderful playroom," Cara said, "if you had kids. I could just imagine sitting up here, away from everything, with it quiet and nobody bothering you. Playing jacks, maybe, or drawing. Or reading a book."

As she said that, she was walking toward one of the edges, where the ceiling sloped down to meet the floor. She had a little frown on her face, Emma realized, as if she were concentrating. She got down on her hands and knees, in the midst of the grime, and lifted a disgusting, dust-covered, folded blanket, and from beneath it pulled out an old doll.

"Or play with my doll," she whispered.

Emma shivered. "Perfect place for a child to play," she said.

Cara was staring at the doll. It had a porcelain face, a cloth body, and a dress with a tight bodice and a long, full skirt. The hair was long, and had been carefully braided, with the braid tied in place with a childish yarn bow.

Emma watched Cara, and saw tears start down her cheeks. Her own throat tightened, staring at that doll.

She felt like she was standing on the edge of a precipice. Feeling as if she might ask the wrong question, and in getting the answer suddenly understand what that doll meant. Knowing that if she understood, she would fall over the edge, and nothing could save her.

It was just a doll, she told herself. An old toy abandoned in an attic. Meaningless. She had to get hold of herself. "What's wrong?" she asked.

"It's just so sad."

Emma waited.

"The little girl who loved her put her down there one day. And then she never came back. Why didn't she ever come back?"

"Maybe because she grew up."

Cara shook her head. She was crying harder. "It's all . . . a tragedy. Sadness, and loss. The little girl is dead, and has been for a long time, and the doll is still here."

Emma could feel the truth in Cara's words. In her mind's eye, she could *see*. The child, tucking her doll away for sleep, and being called away. And never coming back. She didn't want to see. She didn't want to *know*. So she said, "Our things outlast us. We touch them, we love them, and then we're gone and they're still there. Maybe for someone else to touch, or love." She looked at Cara holding the doll, and she felt the tragedy that Cara spoke of. The doll looked old. It looked like it had been lying there for a very long time.

"You should have her," Emma told Cara. "You should take her home, clean her up . . . maybe take her to a doll restorer. She looks like she could be worth a lot of money"—but it wasn't about the money, and she knew that the second she'd said the words—"never mind. But you should still have her."

Cara said, "I want her to stay here. I'll take her to someone who can make her new again, but this was her home. She was waiting for her little girl to come back. Maybe someday she will."

Emma thought of the whispers on the tape, of the inexplicable things that were happening around her, and a chilling thought occurred to her. Maybe the little girl had never left.

She watched Cara leave with regret. She'd enjoyed the company, even if the whole situation with the doll made her shiver. She couldn't imagine why either she or Cara had reacted that way; with Cara and the doll gone, it seemed completely irrational.

But perhaps that was part of the appeal of old houses; they had stories already built in, little mysteries to discover. The little girl leaving her doll was probably nothing tragic at all. She'd forgotten her, gotten a new doll, moved on to a fascination with a neighbor boy, got married and moved away and had children of her own.

Emma watched the shadows shift outside. She guessed it was about noon. She sank onto her futon, still tired. Still sore. She had so much to think about with what she'd discovered about her mother, and the questions about her birth, and her possible birth father. The house occupied much of her mind, too.

And the exhaustion that followed her from the time she got up in the morning to the time she went to bed was slowing everything down. She couldn't focus well on anything, because she was too weary.

She put on a jacket and walked outside to look at the rose garden again. She didn't know why, but after finding the doll, she'd wanted to go out there and sit.

She settled onto the stone bench, and looked at the broken fountain, which, as she studied it, ruined the symmetry of the place. Everything else belonged, but the fountain was ugly and foreign. It would have to go. Something else belonged there, though she wasn't sure what would fit.

She imagined the place when it had been kept up, and certainly beautiful. She could feel the warmth of it, the light shining on a thicket of sweet-smelling roses every summer morning. She could hear the fall of water, so certainly some sort of fountain belonged in the garden. Just not that one, and not there.

She could imagine the singing of the birds. She could see a mother and her small daughter, both dressed in the fashion of an earlier century, their skirts almost to the ground, their waists nipped in by corsets. They were delicate and pretty, and they seemed so happy, coming into the garden and watching hummingbirds dip to taste the nectar from the flowers.

She could hear their voices, talking and laughing as mothers and daughters did. They were warm and beautiful together, close, delighted with each other's company.

She opened her eyes, realizing that she was crying again. She'd managed to live twenty-five years without crying about much of anything except for her mother's and father's deaths. Since finding her house—The House—she was beginning to think crying was all she did.

"For Pete's sake," she muttered, "I'm going to have to get some sleep before I fall apart."

She headed back into the house, to the promise of a nice cup of hot chocolate and a nap on the couch.

The house enveloped her, embraced her, as she went through the door. The smells were right, oddly redolent of fresh-baked bread and simmering stew, though she was cooking neither. The light and shadow fit, and all she could think of was how much she belonged right where she was.

She went into the kitchen and watched the cat loping across the floor from the windowsill where he'd apparently been sitting and watching her. He gave her that silent meow as he trotted past—his acknowledgment of her presence—before he disappeared in the direction of the front door.

She rubbed her eyes. A nap sounded like an even better idea than hot chocolate. After her nap, she could think about whether she wanted to pursue finding information on her mother, or whether she wanted to drop the whole thing. She wasn't sure how much she wanted to know. She was relieved to learn her mother hadn't been crazy or schizophrenic, because then perhaps she could stop worrying about losing her mind. But that thought was terrifying, too. Because then she had to consider that if her mother had been a healthy, sane sixteen-year-old girl when she'd given birth, someone had been able to get her locked up in a mental health ward in spite of that, and had then either driven her to suicide, or perhaps murdered her outright. And it meant she wasn't imagining what was going on in her house.

Emma could find nothing but fear in any of that. She didn't know how to think about what she'd already learned. It all seemed so far away from her. Maybe it shouldn't. Maybe . . .

She yawned. There was no way she was going to be able to stay awake long enough to make hot chocolate.

She was too tired even to go upstairs to sleep on her bed. She checked to make sure all her doors were locked, then curled up on her futon, and fell asleep almost as soon as her eyes closed.

Mike had the crawling feeling in his gut that something was wrong, and when he closed his eyes, he saw Emma's face. He was in the middle of a job, he and his men were framing in a sunroom for the Strouds, and he was up to his elbows in wood and nails and loud, sweaty guys. And all of a sudden he had to call her. He had to know that something hadn't gone wrong out at that house of hers, the house that felt right and good and homey when he was in it with her, and like death waiting to happen the instant he was away from her.

He walked out to his truck so that he could look like he was going through his toolbox, because he didn't feel like taking any shit from the nosy guys in his crew about being on a leash, or anything else. He called the house.

He let it ring a good long time, and got no answer. So, he figured, she was out, and he tried her cell phone.

Again, no answer, but her voice mailbox came up. She could be out of cell range, he thought. She could have the ringer turned off because she was at a movie. She could have a million different explanations for why she was not answering her phone, all of them good, and none of them would put her in any danger.

But his gut said something was wrong, and because it so rarely suggested anything with more depth to it than that he was hungry, he felt this once he ought to listen.

So he made another quick excuse about getting a call and needing to go out and check on something on their last job. He took off for her house, which was on the other side of town. He was going to kick himself for this. He knew he was. It was insane. Emma was fine.

He knew she was fine—logically, rationally.

And he just kept driving.

Beneath her hands, a stark picture emerged, done in bloody reds, dull blues, and shades of gray: two men struggling. One held a knife, the other a revolver. Both wore clothing appropriate to the time around the War Between the States and the gold rush. Both were men with long, lean frames and the merest suggestion of faces. But the suggestion carried the full freight of fury, hatred, rage, and madness.

Emma put the knife down, ripped the palette paper away, and carried it and the canvas board to the hidden room under the stairs.

Her truck was there, so he rang the bell, but she wasn't answering. He peeked through the sidelights. No Emma.

He could imagine something horrible happening to her in the old carriage house—the image was so clear and stark it damned near knocked the wind out of him. So he trotted back that way, looking for any sign of breaking and entering in the house, sniffing for fire, looking for anything that might indicate the cause of the worsening tightness in his belly.

He stepped into the gloom of the carriage house, and for an instant he could see her body, curled in a fetal position, bloodied and battered, dumped against the back wall.

He ran forward, heart racing, to help her.

But nothing was back there but gunny sacks and a

pile of old baling twine. Barely breathing, he called out, "Emma? Emma?"

Nothing but the thudding of his heartbeat in his ears answered him. He did a quick check through the building.

His logical mind was screaming at him that he was acting like a lunatic, that he was completely over the top, but fear just kept ratcheting the knots in his gut tighter and tighter and tighter.

He looked into the shed, and she wasn't in there, either. He ran back to the house, knowing that if he started banging on the door and screaming her name and she was fine, she was going to think he was crazy, and maybe dangerous.

Maybe, he thought, he was. He knew his behavior made no sense, but knowing didn't stop him from acting like a fool.

He stepped onto the porch, and raised his hand, ready to bang on the door like the craziest of the crazed, and caught movement in the foyer through the sidelight.

Emma was there, she was upright, she was walking, but something about the way she was doing it made his skin crawl. She was heading from the stairs toward the living room, and as she disappeared from view, he shifted left and watched her stepping into the other room and moving toward her little couch, and toward him.

The hair stood up on the back of his neck, and he froze, staring at her with sick dread.

Her eyes were almost closed, and he could tell that she wasn't there. She didn't look like someone sleep-walking—his sister had done that on occasion when she was a kid, and her eyes had been wide open. Emma looked like she was asleep and something else was dragging her upright body around on marionette strings. Her muscles were bunched, her whole body tensed and rigid. She'd mentioned being sore, having all her muscles aching. Watching her moving, he suddenly understood how they'd gotten that way.

Watching her, he wanted to scream.

She lay down on her couch, and her eyes closed the last little sliver, and her body relaxed in a sudden slump; the puppet master had cut her strings.

He backed away from the window, heart skipping beats, mouth dry with fear.

What the hell had that been? He debated just leaving. She was clearly physically fine, and he didn't want to discover that she was doing drugs, or . . . anything else even less pleasant than that.

But he wanted to know that she was all right. He tapped on her front window, and she opened her eyes, and the grin of pleasure that crossed her face when she recognized him damned near broke his heart.

She yawned and stretched, and rolled off the couch, and came to the door.

"Hi," she told him. "I wasn't expecting to see you." The sweetness of her smile told him she was glad that he was there, though.

"I wasn't expecting to drop by. But I was on my way back to a job from getting supplies, and I saw your car here, and I just wanted to see you." It was a lie, but he didn't care. He didn't want to tell her about the crazy fear that had consumed him.

"Come on in," she told him, and he walked through the door. And suddenly everything felt okay. No. Not okay. Good. Cozy, cheerful, wonderful, as if he'd never been acting like the madman in the yard.

He could still see that image of her lying in the barn, though, battered and lifeless, and without knowing he was going to do it, he scooped her into his arms and started kissing her.

She kissed him back like she'd been starved for the taste of him, and he said, "I missed you."

"I missed you, too," she whispered. He shut the door behind himself and locked it with one hand, and pulled her tight against him with the other hand. "I couldn't get you out of my mind."

She made a sweet, soft purr in the back of her throat, and slid her hand across his chest. "I'm so glad you're here. The whole world feels better when you're here."

And then her lips met his, and their kiss deepened. Her hands slid under his shirt, his hands undid the buttons on her blouse, she unzipped his pants, he undid hers and gripped the rounded cheeks of her ass and lifted her up as her legs twined around his waist.

"Upstairs," she gasped, and he carried her like that, up the stairs, down the hall, to the back bedroom, the master bedroom. He knew his way. Knew it like he'd done this with her a thousand times, but at the same time, he thrilled to the newness of this.

She had a bed in there. Big. Fancy. It felt right, though. It suited the room, and her. And he pulled her clothes off of her with the impatience and enthusiasm of a man who'd never had the privilege of getting naked with a woman before. She had him out of his clothes just as quickly, and he pushed her back on the bed, and for a moment just stood looking at her, sprawled, waiting, welcoming.

"Come here," she told him, her voice husky.

He didn't say anything, but when he moved within

reach, her legs wrapped around him again, and she pulled him to her, and onto her, and into her, in a movement so strong and wonderful it felt like the two of them had practiced it forever.

"Oh, God," she moaned.

His sane, rational self protested the impossibility of what they were doing for only an instant, and then, like a drowning man going under for the last time, it shut up, and she consumed him. He moved in her, and felt her arch against him. He lost himself in skin on skin, heat and wetness, the sharp bites of her nails digging into his back and buttocks, the weight of her heels against the small of his back, the strength of her as with a deft move, she flipped him over and came up on top, riding him.

He groaned and gritted his teeth, and she lifted high above him, never completely pulling away from him, and then drove down onto him, until he was sure he was going to lose his mind. Her eyes were heavy lidded, but she looked into his eyes and the faintest of smiles curled at the corners of her lips as she impaled herself again and again. Her fingers brushed over his hair, her breasts fell heavy and soft on his chest, and the palms of his hands traced and retraced the curves of her hips, the fullness that slid in to the narrow waist, the strong, slender back, up and down as she moved over him.

When he couldn't stand it anymore, when he was sure he was losing control, he grabbed her hard and pulled her tight against his chest and rolled them both over.

Standing on the floor again, he draped her ankles over his shoulders and leaned into her. Her legs tightened around his neck, and her eyes closed, and he watched her hands dig into the covers, watched her head thrash from side to side, heard her scream his name again and again as he pounded into her, and as they rode to the crest of their passion and he spent himself within her.

Exhausted, lost outside of time, drained, he slid against her and pulled the two of them all the way onto the bed, and wrapped her in his arms.

Emma woke feeling well rested and completely relaxed for the first time since she'd moved into the house. Mike's arms were around her, and, from somewhere that seemed like a million miles away, something chirped incessantly.

She tried to put the pieces of this whole situation together in a way that made sense.

She was naked, and she remembered, both suddenly and vividly, how she'd gotten that way.

"Oh, boy," she whispered, and sat up.

She and Mike had gotten lost in the lust that consumed them every time they got within touching distance of each other, and they had ended up in bed together—

Her mind took a few moments to replay that whole episode, and to marvel at it. It had been like Sex: The Good Parts Version, and she wondered if anything could ever or would ever feel that good again. She stared at him, sleeping beside her, his arm now draped over her thighs. Asleep, naked, lying sideways on her big bed with nothing hidden, he was the most perfect and most beautiful thing she'd ever seen.

She traced the veins of his hand, noted how big it was compared to hers, and how fine and strong his wrists were, and how muscular his arms. His fingers and palms were callused by hard work, his body was bruised and scarred, the flat muscles showing the effects of both hard work and a job where he got hurt from time to time.

Mine, she thought.

And her haze of euphoria slipped a little.

They hadn't used a condom. She'd had sex with only one other man, and then only when she'd been sure that the two of them were going to end up together, and they had never had sex without a condom, plus other birth control.

This was her first time. She did numbers in her head, and realized that she was anything but safe; she could very well end up pregnant.

The chirping started again, and she realized it was coming from Mike's pants, lying on her floor.

Regretfully, she put a hand on his shoulder and shook him lightly. "Mike? I think it's your phone."

He roused from sleep to bewildered wakefulness, and then looked at her with realization marked on his face. "Wow," he said, and then, "Gimme a minute."

He grabbed his pants, pulled out his phone, and said, "Yeah."

He didn't say anything for a moment; she could catch someone on the other end sounding a little agitated, and then laughing.

"No," he said. "I got tied up with something. I'm not going to be back out to the site today. Make sure you stow the tools before you clear out; I don't want another circular saw walking off the job." A long pause. "I'm not blaming you. But you're in charge today—I'll get there first thing in the morning and go over everything, and then we'll pick up with her changes." He said, "No, I'll see you tomorrow. I have to go." And hung up.

And then he looked at her again. "I . . . oh, Emma. I don't know what to say. I can't say I regret that—that was the most amazing experience of my life. But I feel like I owe you an apology. That wasn't . . . *me* . . . I'm not that way with women, and I . . . that was completely out of control." He turned to face her, and leaned forward and looked into her eyes. "Are you okay?"

She said, "I feel better than I ever have in my entire life," she told him. "And a hell of a lot better than I have since I moved here. I feel like I own the world." She shook her head. "But that wasn't me, either. There's only ever been one other man, and we were engaged."

"Really?"

"Yeah. I didn't want a long string of regrets and bad experiences behind me. I wanted sex to matter. To mean something. So I abstained from all the times when it wouldn't have mattered."

He nodded. "That fits. Your personality, your character. You." He gave her a wobbly smile. "But, ah. Whether we were acting in character or out of it, we missed the condom there. Any chance you're on birth control? I'm guessing not much, unless the fiancé was recent."

"He was three years ago. And my chances of being on birth control?" she said. "None whatsoever."

"Oh, boy."

They sat looking at each other, measuring each other, trying to figure out what the other would think about the one unasked question that hung between them.

Finally Emma cleared her throat. "I won't have an abortion if I'm pregnant," she told him.

And Mike whispered, "Oh, thank God. It would break my heart to think of my kid being aborted." He took her hand. "Emma, if you become pregnant, I'll be right with you all the way, with any support you want, whether you decide you want me to be a part of your life or not." He paused. "I'd want to be a part of my kid's life, though, no matter what."

She nodded. "Kids need their dads."

They sat on the bed a while longer, looking at each other, still naked, still open. "I'm not sure where we go from here," Mike said.

Emma smiled a little. "Clean up? Get something to eat? Talk?"

"Not going to kick me out?"

"No."

He got off the bed, turned to her, and said, "By the way, has anyone ever told you that you sleepwalked before?"

She laughed. "Me? I'm the world's deepest sleeper. I go to bed, and most times I'm still in the same position when I get up." She tilted her head, puzzled, and asked him, "Why do you ask?"

"Because I stopped by when I saw your car here, and rang your bell, and when you didn't answer, I went out back, thinking you might have been in the yard or one of the outbuildings. You weren't there, so I came back to the porch—I was going to knock again, on the chance that you hadn't been able to come to the door before. And as I was pushing your doorbell, I saw you walking across the foyer from the stairs. You crossed into the living room and went to your futon and laid down on it. The whole time you were walking, your eyes were almost completely closed, and your movements were . . .

well . . . strange. You looked a little like a badly done stop-motion video character, like your arms and legs were being moved by someone who didn't know how they were supposed to work."

She sat staring at him. She was tempted to call him a liar, to say that there was no chance that she was sleep-walking. But she thought of her paint supplies tampered with, her palette paper covered with mixed paint tossed in the trash, her palette knife and paint knives left imperfectly cleaned, her paints used and in disarray.

Could she be going into her studio and messing around with her paints while she slept?

She could, she supposed. It made more sense than thinking someone else was breaking into her house to paint.

Sleepwalking might suggest why she was so sore and tired when she woke up in the morning.

It was the weirdest possibility she'd ever considered, though. Because if it were true, then what was she doing? She didn't seem to be doing paintings. There were no new sleep-painted paintings around. She hadn't—thank God—painted over her commissioned painting in progress. Was she just messing with her paint?

Or was there more to it than that?

A little itch started at the back of her neck. Was she getting a little crazier? Exhibiting multiple personalities? She'd read that people who had multiple personalities could live complete double lives without even being aware of it. If she was one of those people, was playing with paint the *only* thing she was doing? Might she be dangerous?

She looked at Mike, who felt like the other half of her, the part of her life that she'd only been able to imagine until he came into it. She didn't know him well enough to be in love with him; she barely knew him at all. And yet, he fit her. She couldn't explain him, she couldn't deny him.

But perhaps she could hurt him. If she were dangerous, walking around the house in her sleep or in some altered state, doing things that involved knives—even painting knives—it might be possible for her to hurt him a lot, when he was the most vulnerable, and never even know that she did it.

She closed her eyes and took a deep breath.

"Are you sure you're all right?" Mike asked her.

"Sleepwalking would explain a couple of things that I was having to put down to intruders or ghosts," she said, forcing a smile to her face. "I went to the police the other day because things in my workroom kept being rearranged between the times when I used them. Paints were out of place, tools were dirty, my palettes had been tampered with. It didn't make any sense, and the deputy, when he came out and checked the house to see if there were any signs that someone had been trying to break in, told me as much."

"The house was okay?"

She grinned at him. "Your locks were good, everything was fine, there were no signs at all that anyone had even thought about breaking in."

He didn't look reassured. "All right," he said slowly.

"Really. Nothing else was changed, nothing has gone missing. It was just my paints, and the reason I realized they had been messed with is because I'm picky about my tools. They have to be in their places when they're not in use, and they have to be in their places when they are. I'm funny that way."

"I'd know in a heartbeat if anyone but me had gotten into my toolbox," he told her. "I understand."

She scooted off the bed. "Dibs on the upstairs bathroom. I'll get us dinner when I'm done."

"If you don't mind telephone cooking, I'll take care of dinner." He grinned at her and gathered up his clothes.

"As long as telephone cooking includes neither telephones nor anchovies, I'm game."

He headed for the downstairs bathroom. She walked across the hall and into the upstairs one. She stood in front of the mirror for a long time, staring into her eyes, looking for signs of something amiss. "What have you been up to while I've been sleeping?" she whispered at last.

They avoided the topics of sleepwalking, voices caught on tape recorders, the cat (that had been conspicuously absent), and anything else that left them dealing in uncertainties.

They talked instead about their childhoods. Emma found herself laughing over and over at Mike's tales of childhood misbehavior; he had a lot of them, and he told them well. From swinging out over the swimming hole and spotting the alligator just as he was getting ready to let go and drop in; to going with the other boys to streak across the golf course during the middle of the tournament, only to discover when he was halfway across the fairway that his companions had, to a one, chickened out and faded back into the azalea bushes; to pranks pulled on Driscoll Cavanaugh, the chief of police. He left her sides aching.

She in turn found him to be a receptive audience for

her tales of trying to ride cows and herd them with her horse, of kayaking and fishing and swimming, of summer camp and five a.m. chores.

After dinner—a not-terrible pizza and some garlic bread and sodas from the town's only pizza place—she and Mike went up to the attic so that she could show him what she and Cara had talked about, renovation-wise.

"It's going to take a fair amount of insulation to make this place livable," he told her as they were climbing the stairs to the attic. "These old houses were built with high ceilings and steep roofs to give all the awful summer heat a place to rise into. If you're going to be up here, you're not going to make it on ceiling fans and vents. We'll have to install central air and run ducts and insulate everything."

She flipped on the light switch. "I haven't actually been here in the summer."

"And you're from up north." He shook his head. "It's not a treat, let me tell you. A southern summer melts the starch right out of those of us who were born and raised here, but it fries tender Yankees into crispy, crumbly little nubs."

She sighed. "I'm afraid the concept of summer in the south never crossed my mind when I bought the place. I'd like to think I'm tough, but I wilt in the heat. Maybe we ought to talk about putting in central air anyway."

They reached the top of the stairs and she turned on the attic light.

"I wanted to see what you thought about making this into an open L-shaped room. I'm not sure what I'd want to use it for yet, but I don't have that much stuff; I don't need it as storage."

"You might be the only woman in the country who isn't begging for more storage space."

Emma laughed. "I might. I can just see this, though— a good hardwood floor, maybe some pretty rugs to sink your toes in, the angled walls painted a dark blue down at floor level that gets lighter as you go toward the ceiling. Recessed lighting along a little white strip of ceiling in the center, maybe two or three feet wide. Nooks and shelves at the end around the corner . . ."

He nodded. "Sounds good. I can see it; the way you describe it, I'm seeing something a lot more modern than the rest of the house."

"Yes," she said. "I want to restore the rest of the place as close to its original state as I can get. But this wasn't a space anyone ever used before"—as she said that, she thought of the child's doll left in the corner, dropped and never retrieved, and she knew that wasn't completely true—"at least, not in any formal way," she amended. "They mostly just put junk up here. So I don't feel like I'm doing the house any disservice by turning this into a room that isn't a restoration."

"Still classy, though," he said.

"Right. It has to feel like it's part of the rest of the house."

"This wall is going to have to go," he said, his hand hitting the half wall that created a traffic obstruction between the front and back halves of the long leg of the attic.

Something bonged inside the wall.

Mike froze, his hand stopped in midair. Emma said, "What was that?"

Mike tapped the same spot with his knuckles. Again, from inside the wall, Emma could hear the metallic sound.

"I don't know what that is," he told her. He dropped to one knee and started tapping all along the wall. Some parts of it sounded solid, but some parts were hollow, and in places, things rattled or rang or even chimed.

"I have my tools down on the back of my truck," he said, turning to her. "If you wouldn't mind helping me bring stuff up here, we can be into this wall and find out what's in there in just a few minutes."

"Let's do that," she said.

They carried up mallets and a couple of small hand jigsaws and some bigger tools of demolition.

Mike tapped around and found one of the hollow spaces. "Houses built before the Civil War—like this one—sometimes have valuables hidden in false walls and floor joists. People were trying to hang on to their belongings when raiders came through. Mostly," he said, frowning, "they got them out after the danger had passed. If something went wrong, though, the knowledge of what they'd hidden—and where—died with them. I don't want to discover that someone hid rare bone china in here by smacking it with a sledgehammer. So before we start swinging, hand me the jigsaw and let me cut into this and see what's here."

He went through a layer of plaster and lathe, carefully cutting out a square. The plaster dust got thick quickly, and Emma ended up putting on a mask and handing him one. They both donned protective eyewear.

She caught a glimpse of something bright glimmering in the shadowed recess. As bits of plaster and lathe fell away, she could see more.

Finally, Mike brushed off the edges of the square he'd cut, flicked on a flashlight, and shined it into the recess.

"Well, I don't think you're a millionaire," he told her. "But you're a little richer than you were a minute ago." He pulled out a handful of gold coins and a small pile of paper money. He handed her the gold and riffled through the paper. "How about that. Usually when you find stacks of bills hidden in these old places, it's Confederate, and about useless for anything but making conversation-piece wallpaper. These are *Union* bills, though. Hmm." He handed them to her and grunted, and started fishing around inside the hole he'd made. "Date on them is post-war. That's odd. And that's all for this spot."

She was staring at the gold coins and the bills. They were both exciting and unsettling. She had the feeling there was something wrong with them; that they were part of something bad. Ugly.

Frightening.

Mike had tapped down the wall to the place where he'd heard the soft "bong." He started in with the jigsaw again, hit something the first time the saw went all the way through the lathe, and backed off. It took him a lot longer to make a hole at that location, because he was having to saw very shallowly to keep from hitting whatever was hidden there.

"What do you think it is?" Emma asked him.

"No clue," he told her. His voice was muffled by the mask he wore, and distorted by his heavy breathing.

"You need any help?"

"I'm good. I'll be through this in a few more minutes, and then we'll find out."

He kept sawing. She dug around the attic, found an empty box, and put the cash and the coins in it. When she rejoined him, he was getting ready to tear out the last bits of the second hole.

She held her breath. It was exciting watching things come to light, but she couldn't even begin to guess what it was he'd found the second time.

"Weird," he said. He started pulling away bits of wall with his fingers. Eventually he got a claw hammer and started carefully ripping downward on the lathe with it.

"What is that?"

"Matched statues?" he said. "I'm not sure."

She closed her eyes, and a wave of nausea rolled over her. She could imagine what was hidden. She could almost see them. "Two silver candlesticks," she said under her breath. "A figurine of a Colonial man worked on one, and a Colonial woman worked on the other."

The more she thought about them, the more clearly she could see them. Her head started to hurt.

And she hoped with all her heart that Mike pulled a pair of plain candlesticks out of the hole he was enlarging. Or a dancing couple. Or two southern belles in big hoop skirts.

"Did you just say it was . . . candlesticks?" he asked her.

"Yes."

He pulled them out. They were tarnished—almost black, and in her mind's eye, she had seen them bright silver, recently polished. But they featured figurines of a Colonial man and a Colonial woman. Just as she'd imagined.

Mike held his flashlight to the base, and stared at it. "This is amazing. How did you know that?" He held one up for her to take—to see more closely.

She recoiled. The sickness in her belly sharpened. The throb in her head became fierce. She stood there, confronted with something that she knew intimately, though she had never seen it before in her life. Places on the tarnished metal glimmered in the light of Mike's flashlight.

A woman's voice whispered in her ear, "Those are mine. And he . . . hit me."

Emma remembered. She *knew*, she *understood*, she felt the horror of it. That candlestick swinging in an arc, the rounded base hitting . . .

Hitting . . .

Hitting . . .

Mike almost didn't move quickly enough to catch her.

He saw her knees start to buckle, and it took him an instant to realize that she was fainting. He hadn't seen anyone faint since band camp in high school, and it was everything he could do to toss the statue to the floor and fling himself forward in time.

She went down in a rush, but at least he kept her head from hitting the ground.

He felt her pulse. It was too fast, and fluttery. Her breathing was rapid, her skin was clammy.

"What the hell?" he whispered.

The stuff inside that false wall was more than a century old; he'd bet anything on it. It hadn't been tampered with. How had Emma known about the candlesticks? And why had she reacted so strangely?

"Emma?" he said. "Emma? Wake up?" He found a box of junk, dragged it over, and rested her feet on it. He watched her closely—her body was relaxed, she didn't appear to be having seizures of any sort, her breathing was okay, her heart was beating just fine, if still too quickly. . . .

He rubbed his knuckles over her sternum, but she didn't respond.

"Emma?"

The candlesticks made his skin crawl. They were affecting him, too. They were oddly familiar, and his hands felt contaminated from having touched them. Something inside of him was furious. Mike wanted to lash out, hit someone, crush the person who had last touched them, but his anger had no place to go. He didn't know why touching them filled him with such rage.

Emma moaned.

He held her hand and said, "Emma? You with me yet?"

Her eyes opened. She looked around the room, and then at him, and she said, "I . . . fainted?"

"You did. Over candlesticks."

"Right." She put her hands to her head. "I don't know what happened to me. I was watching you show me one of them. I was looking at it. And then . . . well . . . here I am." She sat up. "And I'm embarrassed. I hate for you to think that I'm a fainter. I'm not."

"Those candlesticks feel . . . slimy to me. Nasty. When I look at them, I don't feel like fainting, but I do feel sick. And angry."

"Farm girls don't faint at candlesticks," she told him. "But I *hate* those things." She nodded, thoughtful and pretty and delicate-looking. "So maybe I'll clean them up and sell them, and fund some of the attic refurb from the proceeds. They look valuable."

He couldn't see her being a tough farm girl right then. She simply didn't look the part. "That sounds incredibly practical of you."

"How long do you think they've been in there?" she asked him.

"Since around 1866. Not before, but maybe a little after."

"That's pretty specific." She looked startled.

"It's the most recent date on any of the money I found in the wall."

"That's a long time." Emma sat up and looked at him. "We can't stop now, you know."

"I think maybe we can."

"No." She grinned at him. "I had a bad-movie-heroine moment, but trust me. I *really* am not a fainter. And I'll never get to sleep if I don't know what else is in this wall."

He said, "All right." He looked at her with concern, and she burst out laughing. "What's funny?" he asked.

"The expression on your face. Please, don't worry. I promise I'll sit beside you so if I faint again, it won't be such a drop."

He told her, "That's more of a consideration than you might think. I almost didn't catch you last time."

But in the end, he was curious, too. What else was in there? More money? Something that would give him hints about the sick feeling in his gut when he looked at those candlesticks?

He got his crowbar and started ripping off the plaster and lathe, working from top to bottom and left to right, in toward the slanting ceiling. Emma proved to be surprisingly sturdy help. She moved nails and debris out of the way, and carefully set aside each item that the two of them uncovered, not bothering to examine any of their finds until at last the whole front face of the false wall was gone.

They sat down beside each other, and Mike marveled

at how right it felt to be with her in her attic, at night, just the two of them. If they were uncovering an old crime scene, it seemed to him that they were precisely the people to do it.

He knew that they should call in the police. She knew it, too. But they didn't.

Instead, when they were done, they took the entire box full of their finds down to her kitchen, except for the candlesticks, and spread them out on the table.

They'd found a pair of men's shoes, of a style popular around the time of the Civil War, worn almost through at the soles, and a gray Confederate uniform that was beyond threadbare. They'd found a diary and a small metal box, locked but with the key still in the lock. They'd found a ledger, the handwriting in it fine and elegant and careful, the handiwork of another time.

They'd found the money, and a man's wallet, and a bunch of dried-out roses, and a little girl's fancy dress. And a woman's wedding band, of a size to fit a small, delicate hand.

Emma had placed all their finds out in neat order. Mike sat beside her at the table, staring at them.

Emma, having set out everything for display, seemed reluctant to touch anything.

"You want to open the locked box, or maybe the diary?" he asked her.

"Not really," she said. "Everything here seems so personal. And it seems somehow personal to me. I know that doesn't make sense. I do. But . . . Mike. I knew what those candlesticks were going to look like. I knew it before I could see them."

"I'm thinking about the voices we heard on the tape," he told her.

He watched her lips tighten. "I know." She shivered. "And the roses. The rose garden. I keep feeling that they mean something. But I don't know what. And I'm afraid to find out."

"This stuff feels tragic. But"—he put an arm around her and pulled her closer—"I'm here. With you." He didn't know why that would make the mystery they'd uncovered any better. It seemed to him that it did, though.

She rested her head on his shoulder. "I feel like I'm a part of this," she told him. "And like you are."

"Like the house is," he added.

"Yes."

He remembered thinking he'd find her in the carriage house, dead and bloody against the back wall. But when he closed his eyes and tried to re-create the scene he'd been sure he was going to find, he realized that the woman he'd been expecting to find there wasn't Emma at all. He sat holding Emma close, and let his mind relax while he tried to bring back the details he'd thought he'd seen, before his mind sorted out burlap sacks and baling twine.

Pale, small face; dark, long-skirted dress; voluptuous curves; gold-blond hair.

Not Emma.

But still, somehow, Emma.

He would have been willing to write the whole thing off to incipient madness, except that they had uncovered hidden secrets. The house was full of them, and his gut insisted more mysteries remained.

"We have to read the diary," he told her. "We have to open the box. Maybe we'll find out who hid these things away, and why."

"I'm afraid we will."

"Don't you want to know?"

"Of course I do. But I'm scared, too." She pulled away from him and stood up. "I'm not ready to deal with this tonight," she told him. "I'm tired, and I want to take a shower, and I need to get some sleep. I feel—strange."

"Right," he said. He stood, too. "You want me to go home?"

She stood there with her head cocked to one side, looking up at him, and his heart thudded hard in his chest. His body, his mind, and his soul all insisted that they knew her. That she had been the reason he was born, the reason he had never been able to commit to anyone else. Some part of him had always known Emma was out there, waiting.

She had been waiting, too, and now she was with him.

They were together, and he had to believe that they were going to be together for the rest of their lives, whether she knew it yet or not.

"Go home?" she repeated. "Not so much. But I don't know how you'd feel about staying."

"I don't want to leave you here alone. I *want* to stay. I'll be fine. I'll set my alarm," he told her. "I'll head home tomorrow morning to get a change of clothes. Go in to work." He winked at her. "Pretend my whole life hasn't just been turned upside down."

She smiled that sweet impish smile, and he stepped forward and pulled her into his arms and kissed her.

Emma led Mike upstairs. The two of them showered together. She knew it wasn't the best of ideas, she knew that she should chastely keep her distance, at least until the two of them had purchased birth control, but she couldn't keep her hands off of him. They washed the attic dirt off of each other, laughing, but the laughter turned serious quickly.

The playful kisses deepened, and she stopped pretending that the two of them were simply going to shower. When he leaned her against the wall, she felt how hard he was. His fingers slid between her legs, into her, and she whimpered at the pleasure of his touch.

She clamped around him, and heard the soft chuckle at the back of his throat. She moved against his hand, her own hands caressing his shaft. She dropped to her knees, and licked and nibbled and sucked until he moaned and pulled her back to her feet. "No more," he whispered. "You'll wreck everything I've planned."

She laughed.

The water from the shower poured over the two of them, hard enough that she could not lift her face up to his. Instead, she sheltered behind the flat, hard muscles of his chest.

"God, you're beautiful," he whispered.

"I want you," she told him. "Take me. Now."

"Already?"

"Yes."

She guided him into her, feeling him fill her, stretch her, push deeper and deeper into her. He moved slowly, and she groaned and shuddered, beginning to lose herself in the feel of the two of them. Their wet bodies slid against each other, slick and hot. And he pushed into her until she didn't think she could take any more. Then he pushed again, deeper, and she cried out.

Her hands clung to his shoulders, her legs fought for

purchase against the lean lines of his hips. Her back slid against the cool tiles, with his fingers hanging on to her ass.

"Faster," she told him.

"No," he said, and laughed. "Slower."

And he started to withdraw from her, agonizingly slowly, while she squirmed against him, tightening and relaxing, trying to hang on.

"You're too impatient, and this time I want to take my time."

Still inside her, he reached behind himself and turned the shower off. He grabbed the towel hanging on the closest rack and pulled her forward and wrapped it around her shoulders. Then, with her wrapped in a towel, he pulled her against his chest and, stepping carefully, carried her out of the shower, and across the hall, and into her bedroom.

Where he put her on her bed. He'd stayed inside of her the whole time, and the feel of him as they'd moved drove her to the edge of her control.

She lay facing him, atop her towel, sideways on the bed. She looked up at him, at the way lights outside gleamed off his wet skin in the darkness. She wanted more. She wanted all of him, but for always. She never wanted to have a last time between them. In the back of her mind, the thought, *I've waited forever for this*, stirred to life.

He leaned down and kissed her, and began to move inside her again, slowly, so very slowly. While he did, his hands explored her breasts, rubbing against her nipples, tugging them, massaging and caressing.

Emma tried to pull him down on top of her, but he resisted. Instead, he grasped one of her ankles, lifted her leg, and moved it across his chest, turning her onto her belly. The feel of him in her as she turned brought her to a quick, hard climax, to mindlessness and screaming pleasure.

"Oh my God, look at you," he whispered.

His hands stroked her back, her waist, her hips and buttocks, his thumbs describing small circles over her skin as he climbed onto the bed behind her, pushing her forward.

Now he moved faster, driving into her hard and steady, with his legs bunching and relaxing inside her spread thighs. She pulled her knees to her chest and pushed against him, and was rewarded with a moan from him. "God, Emma," he said.

"Harder," she gasped.

This time he didn't argue. He tangled one hand in her hair and pulled her up to hands and knees, and drove into her while she rocked against him. They crashed together, wild, wanton, desperate, voracious as starving people at a banquet, unable to get enough of each other.

Emma lost herself, lost time and place, lost her name in the moment, in the passion, in the power of their bodies moving together. In the throes of her ecstasy, at the moment when they both exploded together, she cried out "Sam!" and heard him shout "Mattie!" and she knew that it was right. That they were right.

That love lasted. They had lasted.

They would never die.

Mike was sound asleep, but at some point he had rolled away from Emma, so that she lay alone in the bed.

Her eyes were still closed when she slid out from

under the covers, and, still naked, moved silently through the bedroom. Her movements were jerky and foreign as she slipped out the door, and down the long hallway, and then down the stairs.

Mike, always a light sleeper, lay behind her in the bed, caught in a dream he had not conjured, held transfixed by something deeper than sleep. From the top of the dresser in the corner of the room, the cat watched him, still as a sphinx.

It made no sound. It neither twitched nor flicked its ears to follow sounds from below.

And when a car passed on the road in front of the house, and its headlights reflected into the room, it cast no shadow.

Chapter 8

Gwen Carlston stepped out her front door before the sun had a chance to rise. A patron had donated over five hundred books to the library the day before, delivered in boxes that mixed fiction with nonfiction, and rare and antique books with current paperback thrillers. Gwen had given the collection just a cursory glance, and had been excited. The books were stored in the back rooms, and if she got in early, she figured she could have several hours of fun cataloguing and shelving new acquisitions, and marking others for the library fund-raiser book sale, before she had to open the doors.

She decided to walk. She lived only two blocks from the library, the morning was cool and crisp, and she felt wonderful. A brisk morning walk could do only good things.

She set off down the driveway, and spotted an old friend coming around the corner of the rhododendrons that crowded her front yard.

"You're up early," she said.

Her friend smiled. "Things are busy. If I don't get out for my walk now, I won't get out at all today."

She laughed. "I understand. I have enough work waiting for me to keep me busy for a month." She turned and gestured toward the library. "We just got in boxes—"

Something heavy hit her on the back of the head, hard enough to make her knees buckle. She started to cry out, and a gloved hand wrapped around her nose and mouth, holding a cloth that reeked of something pungent.

Confusing.

Overwhelming.

Mike's alarm went off. Emma woke to it before he did, yawned and stretched and worked her way out from under his arm, and crawled over to his cell phone to turn it off.

She was sore. Again. Always. The same sort of soreness, the ache through the shoulders and the spine that would take half a day to work out. This morning, sore in other, better places.

"Hey, you," she said, and shook the sleeping Mike lightly. "Wake up. Your alarm went off."

"I'm taking the day off," he told her, "and so are you. Come back to bed, and we'll make each other feel good. And then we'll have breakfast. And then we'll go through the stuff we found and see if we can make sense of it."

"Are you sure?" she asked. "I mean, with your difficult client who wants to change everything, and your crew waiting, and . . ."

He wrapped his arms around her and pulled her down into the bed beside him. "I'm sure. How many times in your life have you ever made love until the sun came up, had a decadent breakfast, and then examined the mysterious treasures you'd discovered in an old house?"

"Well . . . never," she said.

"Me, either." He rolled over on top of her, and kissed her. "So this will be a first for both of us. I say we get started."

Mike watched Emma moving through the kitchen, putting a meal together that would be the envy of kings and paladins. She was beautiful. She wore tight jeans and a loose sweatshirt, her hair was back in a damp ponytail, and her feet were bare—and he couldn't help but think that, if she were the woman he got to keep forever, she could be barefoot in the kitchen—and maybe pregnant—and he wouldn't suffer a moment's doubt.

He thought about telling her that he loved her, but was kept quiet by the obsessive nature of that love, and the mystery of how the two of them had ended up in bed together the night before when he had intended nothing more by his visit than to make sure she was safe.

He hadn't known her long enough to be thinking of marriage. Of children. Of always. But he was thinking of all those things—hell, he was *believing* them—and he didn't even think it was stupid, or a bad idea. Sometimes, he mused, watching her scrambling eggs, the head and the heart got together and said, "That's the right one, for all the right reasons," and years of shared history didn't matter.

His phone rang. He considered blowing it off, but the guys would need some direction on the day's work. So he pulled it out of his pocket. The name on the screen was Cara's.

"What's up?" he asked her.

"If you're not sitting down, sit."

"I'm sitting." The sound of her voice scared him. "Mom and Dad are all right?"

"Fine. They're fine. But Gwen Carlston was murdered in her front yard this morning. Her next-door neighbor found her body when he left for work. She was half in his yard, and half in her own. He's the one who called the police, but they've still taken him in for questioning."

Mike sat staring at the phone. "Why in the hell," he said, "would anyone ever murder Gwen?"

"I don't know," Cara said.

"How did you find out?"

"Drew called me. He was doing morning rounds, and they called him into the ER to work on her. Apparently she was still breathing a little when the ambulance brought her in, but the back of her skull had been caved in by something big and heavy."

"Anyone found the murder weapon?" he asked, and became aware that Emma had stopped making breakfast. That she was, in fact, standing on the other side of the room in a state of frozen horror, her hands over her mouth, her whole body rigid, her skin white as death.

"No," Cara said. "There doesn't seem to be any motive yet."

Mike cut her off. "I have to go. Stuff going on here needs my immediate attention. But I'll call you back."

He hung up and said, "Emma? Honey? What's the matter?"

Her hands stayed over her mouth, and her eyes were wide and white-rimmed, giving her an almost comically childlike look. "Who?" she whispered. "Who was murdered?"

He got up from the kitchen table and walked over to her. He put his arms around her. "A very nice lady in town. Her name was Gwen Carlston."

"I knew Gwen," she told him. Her voice was so soft he could barely make out the words.

He was startled. "You'd been to the library already?"

She nodded. Her clear shock and dismay were heartbreaking. "She was helping me find out . . . something."

He looked at her. "That was what Gwen did."

"I think it might be my fault she's dead," Emma told him. "I think it might be my fault that the florist was murdered, too."

Mike felt his muscles tense.

He dragged her over to the kitchen table and sat her down. Then he sat down across from her. "Okay. I'd tell you that's impossible, that you couldn't ever do anything but bring good things into anyone's life, but I don't know as much about you as I should." He took both her hands in his. "I can't believe you could be the cause of this. So tell me what's going on, and then I'll see if I can make you see reason." He gave her a crooked smile, and she sniffed, and swallowed hard.

And then she told him a story that floored him. About having been born in Benina, about her birth mother's tragic death, about having been sold on the black market by a doctor long since dead and a nurse who had vanished right around the time of the doctor's death. About tracking her mother back, trying to find out how she'd died. And about how everyone she talked to about it kept dying.

When she was done, he sat there, stunned. "And there was a third woman?"

Emma nodded. "I don't know her name. I don't know

anything about her. She wore a disguise when she met with me, and told me she was leaving town after talking to me—so I can't even hope that she could tell her story to the police and help them find the person who is doing this."

"She had an idea?"

Emma stared down at the floor for a long moment. Then, reluctantly, she named Drew's cousin David as the man her secret source had suggested was her father.

Mike could see that. He knew and disliked David Halifax. The guy was creepy. He'd heard rumors that David had negotiable ethics. He suspected that David had a few skeletons in his closet besides the golf handicap he routinely fudged. Discovering that one of them was a fifteen-year-old girl that he'd impregnated when he was in his early twenties wouldn't surprise Mike at all.

"But you don't look anything like Halifax," he said.

"Apparently, according to the women who knew my mother, I look just like her."

"Ah. Have you considered requesting DNA testing?"

"With people dying? No. I'm considering running away."

He thought about her gone, and sudden fear reached up out of hell and slashed through his heart. His fingers tightened on his knees, and for a minute he couldn't breathe.

Irrational. He was being irrational. But inside him, the man who loved Emma screamed NO! at the top of his lungs, a visceral animal howl far, far away from the realm of sane words and good decisions.

NO.

She wasn't going to leave. She wasn't going to walk out of his life with as little ado as she'd walked into it. She wasn't going to leave, because having found her at last, having made love to her, having held her in the morning and at night, having eaten at the table with her, and watching her being afraid in the attic and calm and assured in that rose garden that made his skin crawl, all he could say with certainty was that he could not live without her again.

Not again.

Emma sat in Driscoll Cavanaugh's tiny office, her hands folded on her lap, the papers detailing her adoption and the detective's report of her origin and the identities of those who'd had a hand in her trip to Wisconsin folded into a large manila envelope in her lap.

The chief of police already had his hands full with two murders, and he didn't seem to be sure what to do with Emma.

"So you talked to one of them. Gwen Carlston. And Gwen had set up a meeting between you and Aileen Wilkes, but Aileen was already dead when you headed to the flower shop to meet her."

Emma nodded.

The cop ran his fingers through brushy hair and sighed. "It's circumstantial at best. You were going to talk to one, you had talked to the other. But, see . . . if I canvas Benina, I'm going to find a dozen men and women who had recently talked with both Gwen *and* Aileen, and right at this moment, I guarantee you they think they're somehow to blame for these killings, too." He leaned forward. "The mind looks for patterns. If patterns don't exist, it will create them."

"But the third woman told me that there were deaths surrounding my birth mother back when she died, too."

The chief studied her with narrowed eyes as she told

him about the third woman and her suspicions, and mentioned David Halifax, and gave a description of the woman that she knew wasn't very good. But she didn't want it to be very good. She wanted the woman to have her anonymity, because Benina was a small town, and even the chief of police might have a friend who wasn't quite who everyone believed him to be.

"I'll reopen your mother's and grandmother's cases," he said. "I'm not sure what good it will do. I don't feel a link here, but"—he sighed—"I don't have anything else that might tie my two current murders together. If there's a connection, I'd like to find it."

Emma nodded.

He looked out the window. "You have anything else I need to know about?"

Emma considered her haunted house, and was quite certain he would have been interested in knowing all about that. He would find it quite useful to be able to file her under "crazy" and ignore everything she'd said.

She made a command decision. She'd lie. "No," she told him.

She hated talking with the chief, though.

She was afraid she might end up in a spotlight. Like her final contact, who had done everything possible to keep her identity secret, she was terrified to be publicly connected with anything that was going on.

If David Halifax was killing people who were looking into or talking about the circumstances surrounding her mother's and grandmother's deaths, Emma was already on his radar. But in no way had she been publicly connected to him.

That, she thought, was important. It might be the factor that kept her alive.

She hoped he wasn't her father. She decided she wouldn't pursue the information about her mother anymore, because she remembered his cold, pale eyes assessing her while she signed the paperwork, and she could imagine without any difficulty him walking up to her and bludgeoning her to death if she ever looked like she might get in his way.

Cara was waiting for Emma when she got home. "Mike told me you were scared," she said. "He said you'd been to the police, and that there were things going on in Benina that might put you in danger. So I'm staying with you while he takes care of a few problems that came up at his job site. And then he'll be back, and he'll stay with you."

"What about the office?"

"I was glad to get out of there," Cara said. "Drew's in a terrible mood. Gwen was a friend of ours, but even more his than mine. She and her late husband had been close friends with him and Hannah—she was his first wife. When Hannah died, Drew and Gwen each found a lot of comfort in being able to talk with someone who was intelligent and focused, and who had a lot of interests in common. He said it never got romantic between them, and I suppose I believe that. It never mattered to me anyway. I was a child back then."

Cara sighed. "Anyway, he's in a mood. He's canceled his afternoon appointments and retreated to his study, and I won't be able to get a word out of him until tomorrow. He took Gwen's death hard—that someone had hurt her so horribly, first, but even more than that, that he had the chance to save her, and he couldn't."

Emma was thinking of David Halifax, and wondering

if Drew had ever suspected David of the sorts of evils she suspected. He had to have. He'd lived in Benina all his life, he knew Gwen, he might even have known Emma's birth mother. She said, "That would be hell," but she was wondering if David had been able to use Drew, to pump him for information about his patients—or other doctors' patients—without Drew ever suspecting what he was doing.

"I wouldn't want his job," Cara was saying. "It consumes his life. He's done a free clinic for the indigent kids in the area for years. He and one other doctor used to do it together, but then the other doctor said he couldn't afford to keep paying for everything out of his own pocket. So now Drew does it alone. Besides that, he's available almost all the time, and his patients call him at all hours, and stop him in the street or when we're going out to dinner. It's to the point now where he delivered two generations of patients. Now he's delivering his first patients' grandkids. They all think of each other as family, in a way."

"Isn't that hard on you?"

"I knew how he was when I married him. It was part of what made me fall in love with him." Cara smiled a little. "Good enough is never good enough with him, you know? He's always reading about a new technique, or studying up on a new drug, or working on obtaining a new certification." She smiled a little. "I worry that he won't hold up. I'm afraid one day he'll give so much of himself that there will be nothing left of him, and his heart will just give out."

Emma sat watching her. "You love him so much."

"I do. It was like a miracle to me that he even noticed me. He was *my* doctor when I was a kid. I managed to hurt myself pretty badly when I was eleven, and my parents were gone. Which was why I was acting like an idiot in the first place, of course. The babysitter had her hands full with my brother, so Drew tossed me into his own car and dragged me to the hospital and while he was stabilizing me, he managed to have the nurses get in touch with my parents. My folks got to the hospital in time to sign the consents, but he would have taken me in without them, I think, and risked his career to save my life. He wasn't going to let me die."

Emma stared at her. "You could have died? What happened?"

"I fell out of a tree that branched out over the road in front of our house, and got hit by an oncoming car. It was a case of massive stupidity on my part."

"How did your doctor end up driving you to the hospital."

"It was summer. A Tuesday. He was getting ready to go play golf with his cousin. And my folks lived across the street from him. Drew was putting his golf clubs in the car, and he saw me fall. My angels were watching out for me that day, I guess."

"Wow."

Cara said, "And then, after Hannah died, he lived for his work, he mourned his wife quietly, and he raised their two kids. Ungrateful little monsters. The kids moved away and never looked back, and he was all alone. And he just worked more, and more." She kicked her shoes off, and pulled her knees up and tucked her feet under her. "It hurt me so much to see him so alone. So when I came home from college, I went out of my way to spend time with him. I got a job working in his office, and then started helping him with the business side of his practice. And then I wheedled my way into the rest of his life. I was shameless, and a lot of the town was horrified that I was making my move on their sainted doctor."

She sighed. "They didn't see what they were doing to him, how they were wearing him down to nothing. I saw it, and I made myself the barrier between all their constant demands and him. I cooked real meals for him, I made sure he took a day off every week that was just for him, I took over all the business aspects of the office so that he could concentrate on the part he loved. The medicine."

She glanced over at Emma. "I sound a little scary there, don't I?"

Emma said, "You sound like someone who is sacrificing as much as he is." She smiled. "And you sound like someone who loves him very much. Did the town ever see you as the good guy? Do his kids?"

"His kids were pampered, selfish little bastards. They took their expensive educations and their trust funds and moved to the other side of the country, or to the other side of the world, depending on which one you're talking about. They don't call him, they don't write. If he calls them, about ninety percent of the time they won't pick up the phone. It breaks his heart." Her face had turned a dull shade of red. "And watching how it hurts him breaks my heart."

And then Cara closed her eyes and took a deep breath, and shook out her hands. Emma could see her forcing herself to relax.

"Sorry about that," she said. "His kids are about my age. We lived in the same neighborhood, but they went to private boarding schools. In the summers when they

were home, they were pompous asses. I hated them
when I was a kid, and I'm not much better about them
now."

Emma grinned. "Oh. Wow. And now you're their
stepmom."

"Drew says no. He married me after they were already gone. He says I do not owe anything to his kids.
We are us, he says. We get to be good for each other, and
not worry about his heinous, spoiled offspring."

Cara turned and studied Emma, her face suddenly serious and intent. "So. Are you going to tell me what happened to you? What's going on that makes Mike think
that you're in danger, and that you're somehow involved with the two women who were killed?"

Emma bit her bottom lip. "I should, shouldn't I? But
what if I tell you, and my telling you puts you in danger, too. If I am part of the reason someone killed Aileen
and Gwen, then you don't want to be too closely asso-
ciated with me."

"I suppose not," Cara said. She pulled her knees back
up to her chest, and leaned forward and rested her chin
on them. "But I still want to know." She flashed Emma
a sudden grin. "And I want to know what's going on
with you and Mike. He won't say a word to me, but I've
never seen him like this before."

Emma sighed. "I'm not sure what's going on with the
two of us. Something. Something that to me seems
good, and wonderful. But . . . I don't want to say anything too soon."

"God, you sound just like him."

Emma sat on the other end of her futon, wondering
what she could say. And she remembered the box full of
little treasures from someone else's past.

"Did Mike tell you what we found up in the attic last night?" she asked.

Cara said, "That would imply that he had imparted information of any sort, honey. He is not giving out the information. He's being a total pain in the ass."

"Stay here," Emma said. She went into the kitchen, and carried the box out to show Cara.

Cara stared at the contents as Emma started rummaging through them. "Where did you two find all this?"

Emma said, "You know the half wall in the attic that was in the wrong place to serve any purpose?"

"Yes."

"Its purpose was to hold all of this stuff." She sat back and watched as Cara started to touch the various items—and then as she pulled her hands back, as if they'd been burned.

"What's wrong?"

"I don't know. I . . . don't want to touch those things. I just had this feeling—"

"Kind of sick? Kind of scared?"

"Yes. Like I wanted to cry again. Like there was a . . . tragedy." She looked over at Emma. "It's stupid. I know it's stupid. But . . . *ugh*!"

"I fainted," Emma said. "I have never before fainted in my entire life, though I did have to put my head between my knees after running track once when I was in high school. But last night, Mike pulled one of those candlesticks out of the wall and tried to hand it to me, and I saw it, and everything started spinning, and I just plain passed out."

"Good Lord."

"I was pretty impressed, too," Emma told her. "I mean, you want to end up feeling like a total wimp *and* a complete idiot, then that's just the way to do it, isn't it? Who faints anymore?"

"Guys," Cara told her. "When you draw blood from them, and they see it coming out into your tubes. That's about it. No. Not quite. Some of them, when they see their kids being born, and get their first look at the placenta. That will drop 'em like rocks in a pond sometimes."

Emma tried not to laugh, but she did anyway. "So I'm in good company."

Cara was nodding. "There's a box in there with a key in it. What's in the box?"

"I don't know," Emma told her. "I haven't had the guts to open it yet."

"Let's do it now."

"You don't even want to touch the things in the box."

"I don't. But I want to know what's in the locked box."

Emma did too, actually. But she'd thought she ought to wait for Mike. He'd been the reason she found the items in her house in the first place.

"You want to wait?"

"I think I should."

Cara pulled her cell phone out of her purse and pushed buttons. After a moment, she said, "What's taking you so long? She has this box with a key in it, and she won't open it until you're here." A pause. "Yes, I want to know what's in it. I'm simply wild with desire." A longer pause. "So tell them where to put their porch, and get back here. You're needed. And no, we haven't seen anyone suspicious out here. We haven't seen anyone out here at all but the two of us."

She hung up. "He said he'll be here in ten minutes.

Apparently his client is having porch issues, and wants to be a pain in the ass, pardon my French."

Emma laughed.

And glanced over at the window. The cat sat in the sill, watching her. Emma froze. "Do me a favor," she whispered. "Don't move your head, but look over at the window directly to your right, and tell me what you see."

She watched Cara's eyes track to the right. Cara said, "Porch, field, car coming up the road. Cat on the sill. Nothing else. Did you see someone, Emma. God, Mike will go off the deep end if he thinks someone has come out here to hurt you."

Emma breathed a sigh of relief. "No, it was nothing like that. I—" She couldn't say she wanted Cara to identify the cat, because what kind of idiot would say, "I thought you might not be able to see the cat?"

Because then the person looking at what was clearly a big old cat on a windowsill would be required to either say, or think, "Why wouldn't I see it? Is it a magic cat? Are you a freakin' idiot?"

The truth would raise questions Emma did not want to deal with. "I thought I recognized the car coming down the road. But it was one of those stupid things. I didn't."

"Right. Cars do that to me, too."

They sat looking at each other.

"Why does it seem like I know you so well?" Cara asked.

Emma leaned her head back on the futon and laughed. "I have no clue. I feel the same way about you. I feel the same way about Mike. Mike feels the same way about me. It's the sort of goofy thing that people talk about—they met someone they were sure they knew. Only they didn't." She shrugged. "That's us, as best I can figure."

Cara said, "I had a dream about the doll in your attic last night. It scared me to death."

Emma sat up. "Really?"

"You were in the dream, and so was I, and so was the doll. And a man I'm sure I knew, only . . . only I couldn't see his face, and in the dream, I couldn't hear his voice."

"What happened?"

"It's all foggy now. I was in the attic playing with the doll, and the man came up the stairs and grabbed me. And dragged me . . . somewhere. I don't know where. Someplace dark. And you were there. And then he started hitting me with something big. Something awful. And I woke up. I woke myself up trying to scream, actually."

Emma considered that. "I don't think I've had a dream since I've been here. I go to sleep. I wake up. I'm sore and I'm tired." She glanced over at Cara. "Mike said he saw me sleepwalking. I've always been a good sleeper, but I think he actually might have. That I might have been doing that." She played with the bottom hem of her shirt, absently. "But I don't dream. That dream— that dream sounds like it would have terrified me."

"It was so real," Cara said.

Emma looked out the window. "Mike's here," she said.

She glanced over to the other window, the one where the cat had been stretched out, and realized the cat was gone.

But Cara had seen him.

She pushed the cat out of her mind.

Mike loped up the stairs and across the porch, and Emma had the door open by the time he got to it.

He picked her up and swung her around, and kissed her, and in the background, Emma could hear Cara laugh. "I knew it!"

"She's still here?" Mike said. "I should warn you about the company you keep."

Cara said, "Which was what I was thinking I should say about you."

Brother and sister grinned at each other, and Mike put Emma down. "I'm glad you're safe," he said. "It's been rough. My clients were impossible to deal with, and I've been worried sick about you."

"I've been fine," Emma said. "Nothing is going to happen to me."

They went back to the kitchen and sat over the locked box. Emma's hands hovered over the key. Emma, Cara, and Mike exchanged glances, and finally Emma took the key in hand and turned it. The lock made a surprisingly loud click, and the lid of the box popped upward about an eighth of an inch.

Emma pushed it open.

It held photographs. Old ones, sepia tints and daguerreotypes, people sitting in formal poses.

She stared at the faces. She felt like she knew those faces. She knew the clothes they wore. She knew *them*.

Only of course she didn't.

The first one on top was of a little girl in black stockings and dark shoes, her face solemn, her long golden hair carefully curled into ringlets. She wore a neat, full-skirted dress that, had she been standing, would have

gone down to about her ankles. And she held a doll—
the doll Emma and Cara had found in the attic.

Emma felt her hands tightening into fists. She tried
not to think about the doll, but all she could feel was
tragedy.

Mike's face had gone grim. He pulled the picture out,
laid it faceup on the table, and so revealed the next picture. A solemn-eyed young man stood in front of an old-
fashioned tent. He was handsome, clean-shaven except
for a thick mustache, and he wore Confederate gray and
stood stiffly, holding a rifle at his side.

Emma didn't scream, but it was only because everything in the house and everything that had happened to
that point had prepared her for the sight of him.

She had thought the face of the man in her dreams
had looked a lot like Mike. It had. But this man . . . she
might as well have been working from a photograph.

The scar was missing. But that, she felt certain,
would come later. After he had been in battle, after his
uniform was no longer clean and pressed and neat and
new. She knew the man in the picture, she had dreamed
him, she had . . . loved him?

She had sought him out, certainly. Walking through a
crowded place, her eyes were always scanning faces.
Meeting new people, she had always sought the line of
his jaw, the shape of his eye, the curve of the smile that
the picture did not show.

In Mike, she realized, she had found the man that her
heart had accepted as the missing piece to the puzzle of
her dreams. But this man, long dead—he was the original.

She gripped her hands together tighter, so tightly she
felt her fingertips starting to tingle, and her wrists and
palms starting to ache.

"He looks a lot like you, Mike," Cara said.

Mike nodded.

Emma said, "I have something I want to show both of you. Stay here."

She ran to her studio, to the box, opened but still packed, that held her brag books—the books for which she had painted the cover art. Several of them held the face of the man in the photo, and one of them had been a time travel novel in which heroes from the future had gone back to the Civil War to correct something that had eventually led to World War III. The book had been mediocre, but the cover art was some of her best.

She rummaged through the paperbacks and pulled out several titles. Without looking at them, she carried the books down the stairs.

In the kitchen, she laid them out faceup on the table, one by one. "I did the first of these five years ago. The second and third and fourth three years ago. The fifth and sixth two years ago, and this one at the beginning of this year."

She watched both Cara and Mike look from one cover to the next, and the next, and the next, and she saw the increasing bewilderment in their faces.

"It's the same face," Cara said. "This one is even wearing the same uniform."

Mike looked up at her at last and said, "What is this? How did you do this?"

Emma looked down at the books, and the face of her dream man looked up at her. "I don't know," she admitted. "I painted the first draft of each of those paintings from a model, but the model's face didn't fit the image I was looking for. So I made up a face that I liked better. And that was the face I made up."

She turned to Mike. "The first time we met, I thought he was you. You look a lot like him. And we had that . . . connection. But there were differences. Enough to make me decide the similarities between you and my paintings were just coincidence." She stared at the photo. "How do I tell myself that's a coincidence?"

Neither Mike nor Cara answered her.

"Do we look at any more of them?" Emma asked at last.

"Do we dare?" Cara whispered.

Mike said, "We dare. Something strange is going on with this house, and with us." He rested his hand on Emma's arm and looked into her eyes. "Something inexplicable has happened with you and me. We have to try to understand it."

She nodded. And then she said, "I'm afraid, though."

"So am I," he said. "But finding you, and having you find me—that can't be a bad thing. The sort of magic that we've found doesn't happen to everyone, and it doesn't happen often. It has to be something good."

"So we'll keep looking. And we'll find . . . something good? Do you really think so?"

"Maybe not in the past," he said. "But now. Yes, I think we'll find something good now."

They lifted the next photo. The beautiful little girl with blond hair. A woman with ringlets framing her face, and with a heavy mass of long, curly, fair hair pulled back and pinned up into a knot. Her hand rested on the child's shoulder. She wore a plain, dark dress, the bodice tightly fitted, the skirt wide and long. She was pretty, with large, dark eyes full of a sadness that reached out from the old photograph.

Mother and daughter looked a great deal alike.

Mike glanced from Emma to the photo, and back to Emma. "I thought perhaps you'd look like her."

"I don't though."

"In the eyes, you do. Nothing else, but your eyes look like hers. Sad. Dark. Knowing."

"I always thought I had happy eyes," Emma said. She didn't see the resemblance.

Cara moved that photo. The next one was of the soldier, older, back from the war, with the woman and child. It looked like it had been taken the same day as the one of mother and child. And of the little girl and her doll.

Beneath the photographs were letters. Six of them. And beneath the letters, three locks of hair. Light blond. Darker blond. And chestnut. The last was short. Each lock was held together with a ribbon.

Emma stared at the letters. "We have to read them," Cara said. "We have to know what this was all about."

Emma looked for postmarks. They'd been put away in order.

The first was a letter from the Confederate army, informing Mrs. Barnett of the death of her husband during battle, and informing her that his body had been buried, but that his personal effects would be sent to her. Telling her that he had died bravely, and sending regrets.

The second was another sort of letter entirely.

Cara read it aloud.

My dearest, darling Mattie, I am broken-hearted at the news of my brother's death. If he was a hard man, still, in the end he proved honorable, dying in a just cause. And with his death, we are freed of our secret and our shame. We need no longer hide our feelings for each other, and if some truths can never be told, still, now we need never fear that they will be uncovered.

I will live through this war, my dearest, and will find my way home to you, whole and strong. I swear it, though all the devils of all the battles that will yet rage upon this planet stand between us. And when we are together again, we'll marry, and we will have at last the future we should have had from the beginning.

With all my heart and soul, I declare myself yours,

Sam

"Oh, that's not good," Emma said. "That's not good at all."

"No. It isn't." Mike said, "So is the soldier in the pictures her husband, or is he her husband's brother?"

"He must be her husband," Emma said. "I mean, her husband died in the war. So imagine that the brother, with whom she had some sort of relationship before the war, went off to war with the husband. The husband dies. The brother writes to her and says, 'Ah, now we can be together forever.'" Emma frowned. "Only, what if she decides while he's gone that she'd rather be with someone else. She's a widow, after all. Free. If she can find a better man, all of a sudden she's free to marry him. So . . . say she does. And the brother comes home, and finds his wife-to-be already married to someone else."

"That could very well lead to murder."

"It might have."

"Murder?" Cara asked.

"The sense of tragedy that surrounds these people," Emma said. "We've all felt it. What else could it be?"

All the color blanched from Cara's face, and she scooted her chair back and put her head between her knees.

"Cara, are you okay?"

"No," she muttered. "I feel like I'm going to faint."

"You, too? Emma fainted when we pulled this out last night."

"The connection," Emma said. "You and I feel a connection to this place, and so does Cara."

Cara's brother squatted beside her and said, "You feel a connection to this place?"

"Emma didn't tell you about the doll?"

He glanced over at Emma. "You're a veritable font of not passing on the information," he said.

"We found a doll when Cara and I were up in the attic, talking about how I could redo it. Well, she found it, and it made her cry. The way just about everything in this place has made me cry at one time or another."

"That makes a little sense," he said.

"I think maybe it has something to do with reincarnation," Cara said.

"I don't believe in reincarnation," Emma told her.

"Neither do I," Mike said.

"If we're all three reincarnated here, then it doesn't really matter what you believe, does it?"

"That doesn't make any sense."

"Have you read about reincarnation? I have. People reincarnate in groups in order to work through things in their lives that didn't go right the first time. If for some reason Emma and I got killed, and if the two of you were supposed to be together, it would make perfect sense if we all ended up back here."

"No, it wouldn't," Mike said. "The whole idea is just nuts."

Emma, though, considered her life to date. She'd always felt like she was looking for something, and in finding the house, and then Mike, and then Cara, she believed she'd found it. She'd been born in this town. She'd been meant to be here, but the problem with her mother—either her mother's insanity, or perhaps her mother's choice of college boys with rich parents—had changed everything, and moved Emma away from her fate. And perhaps her destiny?

Either way, what if, however unlikely it seemed, she and Cara and Mike had reincarnated in the same place together, at the same time, so that they could work out their pasts. What of her mother, the teenaged girl whose pregnancy and death had stirred up such trouble twenty-five years later? Did she have a place in this past that seemed to have drawn in Emma, Cara, and Mike?

And what about Mike? What was his role in this mess? She could guess that she was Mattie and that Cara was the little girl. Perhaps it was the other way around, but if she was supposed to make things right with a man she had somehow misused in her previous life, it made more sense if she had been the mother than the daughter.

But *who* did that make Mike? The husband she'd cheated on? The brother she'd cheated with? The man she might have married instead of the brother (assuming that was what had happened)?

She vaguely remembered when she and Mike were making love the second time. The sex had been wonderful, she had been out of her mind, and then right at the end, something strange had happened. What was it? He'd called her . . . Mattie.

She shivered, and her skin started to crawl.

He'd called her Mattie, and she had called him . . . Sam.

How had she forgotten that? How had she not jumped screaming from the bed. Why had they not been sitting there afterward, glaring at each other, saying, "Exactly who is Sam?" and "Right—and who the hell is Mattie?"

Mike was Sam. The one the letters were from, the one Mattie had evidently cheated with.

If Emma was Mattie, and Mike was Sam, what was Emma supposed to get right this time around? Was she supposed to be faithful to the husband Mattie had cheated on? Who might he be? Or was she supposed to marry this lifetime's Sam, or was she supposed to turn down Sam in order to find a third man who had taken his place?

And if Mike was the re-embodied spirit of the man who had sworn on his eternal soul to find his way to her again, did that also make Mike the reincarnation of her killer?

If people were dying in town, and Emma was somehow involved, and her mother's death was somehow involved, was the man who had killed her in a past life also somehow involved in these new murders?

Was Mike a killer?

This was craziness.

Being with Mike felt so right. So perfect. They felt like they'd been made for each other.

But her head was screaming *Danger!*, even as her heart was whispering *Love*.

She could listen to her heart, of course. And maybe everything would be fine. But maybe she would end up like uncounted women who had ignored their heads, who had told themselves, *He loves me. I'm special. He could never hurt me,* only to end up dead in ditches or bathtubs or vats of lime. She *could* listen to her heart.

But she thought she'd buck the voluntary victim trend and listen to her head. Until she knew Mike *wasn't* a danger to her, she would treat him as if he was.

Innocent until proven guilty, some voice squeaked in her mind, and for an instant, she hesitated, uncertain. But while the law owed everyone the presumption of innocence, a woman with her life in danger would get her proof of guilt by being murdered by someone she trusted. Emma didn't want to be that woman.

So. Paranoia it was, then.

She didn't believe in reincarnation, she reminded herself. But she did believe in two murders in one week. And nobody yet knew who had committed those. She was pretty sure whoever it was knew her, though.

"We need to read the other letters," she told Mike and Cara, and then she had the thought that it was entirely possible that she had gotten pregnant the night before. Mattie had gotten pregnant in a previous life, and odds were she had not been married to the father. Sam. Who had promised to find his way back to her, to stand by her.

Mike had promised to stand by *Emma.*

In that earlier time, Mattie, or her child, or maybe both of them, had almost certainly been murdered.

Would Emma replicate the horrors of the past even to the point of providing another daughter to die by a jealous man's hand? To the point of dying herself?

I don't believe in reincarnation.

Cara, Emma realized, looked upset and shaken. She said, "I'm not up to reading any more of these out loud. How about you, Mike?"

Mike took them, though he didn't look thrilled, either.

The two letters back from Mattie to Sam were as joyous and loving and passionate (and occasionally regretful and guilty) as were the three from him to her.

The final letter in the sequence told her he was coming home. It rejoiced that they were going to be together again. That he was so excited to see her, that he couldn't wait, that he had missed her so much.

Emma could feel Sam's excitement, his hope, his yearning. She wondered if a man so full of joy and hope could turn that passion into hatred and murder.

She wondered what Sam's brother, Ian—named in the letters—who had been the dead husband, had been like. She wondered at the fact that Sam and Mattie spent so few words on him.

"I can't imagine what went wrong for the two of them. They seem so perfect for each other," Cara said.

"They got together wrong," Mike said. "Maybe the two of them should have been together. Maybe they were perfect for each other, but the other guy—the wrong guy, the husband—was already there."

"But he died," Emma said.

Mike nodded. "The fact that the two of them had been sneaking around behind his back lived on. They never came clean with the guy. They never said, 'We were meant to be together, and we're going to be together.' "

"Nobody did divorces back then," Emma said.

"I know," Mike said. "But I still bet that's what went wrong."

The diary lay unopened in the box.

"Should we read that?" Cara asked.

Emma said, "Not tonight. I don't want to think about this anymore tonight."

Actually, Emma wanted to read the diary when she was alone. She wanted to find clues about personalities, so that she could see if she could piece together the old tale of life and love and betrayal and murder in which she seemed to have become entangled, whether for the first time, or again.

She wanted the house to herself for the night. Mike had already mentioned staying over as protection, but Emma realized she did not want him there. Not while it seemed that he might have murdered her in the past. The past was not the present, and perhaps this was his chance to make things right, but . . .

She closed her eyes and rubbed her temples, warding off pressure that felt like an impending headache.

She wanted to be alone. No Cara. No Mike. No one but her.

And then her phone rang.

It was Susan's husband. "Sue's in labor, and we're at the hospital. There are problems, and she's been asking for you. I know this is a terrible time, and you're a long way away, but . . . could you come up?"

Emma said, "I'll be there as soon as I can. I'm not that far from an airport. I'll get on the next flight. Tell her I'm out the door."

Even though Emma was terrified for Susan, it was with an immense feeling of relief that she turned to Cara and Mike. "I have to go. Now. My best friend has gone into labor, and there's some sort of emergency. She's asking for me."

"Where is she?" Mike asked.

"Back in Wisconsin. I'll drive myself to the airport in Greenville. It's only forty miles." She looked at the two of them. "Be careful while I'm gone, okay?"

Both nodded.

Mike said, "I'll drive."

But Emma shook her head. "No. It would just complicate the car situation. I want to have my car there when I get back, and I don't want to inconvenience anyone for a ride. I don't know how long I'll be gone, or what's going to happen."

"All right," Mike said. He seemed calm enough about her refusal to let him take her to the airport.

"I have to go pack. I'm going to put all this stuff someplace safe." She bit her lip.

Cara said, "Send your friend my best wishes, would you? That's a terrifying situation to be in."

Emma said, "I'll tell her." She hugged Mike, and when she melted into his arms, all her doubts about him faded away. He kissed her, and her knees went liquid, and all she could think of was how much she wanted to be back in bed with him again. Or on the couch. Or in the shower. Or someplace different, like . . . the kitchen table against which she was balancing herself.

Could she possibly feel that way about a man who had killed her before?

Maybe.

Things change, she reminded herself. And they don't always change for the better.

"Be safe," Mike whispered in her ear. "And hurry back to me. I'll miss you like crazy while you're gone."

"I'll be careful," she told him. "And I'll miss you, too." The thing that made her crazy was that what she said was absolutely true.

He and Cara left, and Emma carried the box full of mementos from the attic wall upstairs with her. She took the diary out of the box and put it in her carry-on, along with two changes of clothes, two of underwear, and one sleep shirt. She made sure she didn't have any nail clippers, fingernail files, or other items forbidden by airlines in her purse. And then she took a deep breath.

She wanted to hide the box and the things that she and Mike had found. She didn't know where, until she thought of the bedroom at the top of the stairs, the one that scared her. She could put it in the closet there, shoved into the corner where it would be hard to see.

She didn't like going in there, but then, neither did Cara. And she would bet Mike wouldn't want to slip in, either. Something about that bedroom was . . . terrible.

She forced herself to go in to hide the box, but the atmosphere in the room—the feeling of being watched, the feeling of terror that seemed to be coming from the room itself—was so frightening Emma almost fled with the box in her arms. The closet was empty. The room was empty. But still her heart skipped and skittered as if it would stop at any moment.

Her hands shook as she placed the box on the closet floor, jammed into the corner out of sight of the main door, and closed the closet door. Her hands were still shaking moments later when she locked the front door behind her and ran across the porch to her truck, her bag banging on her hip.

She should have been glad to be leaving the place. Between murders in the present and in the past, and the haunting echoes that seemed to arise from the ground she walked on and to seep out of the walls, she should have been thinking about ways to never go back.

But she wasn't. Leaving her house, leaving Cara and Mike behind, she felt like she was tearing herself into pieces, and that nothing but being back with them again would set her right.

The airport wait, the screening, the flight, and the worry would have all been an ordeal. But because Emma had the diary, she had something she could think about while she waited. And the diary was fascinating. Compelling.

Mattie, who had been born Martha Lancaster, had written it, and she'd started it on the day she became engaged to the man who would be her first husband, Ian Barnett. Mattie wanted the diary to be a record of her new life. As she put it, "My life, now that I have become a woman." Emma found that young, and naive, and rather cute. Mattie mentioned a previous diary; Emma found herself wondering what had become of that.

Mattie wrote cautiously about her fiancé. Ian Barnett was a doctor, a well-respected professional man with a rich, supportive family. He had been a doctor for five years already, and had a good practice. He was fifteen years older than Mattie, and he had a reputation for being firm. *Firm* being Mattie's word.

Emma found herself wondering if firm, in this case, meant that he liked things neat, and he appreciated having people listen to him the first time he said something, or if firm meant he was a jackass.

The image of David Halifax flickered through the back of Emma's mind, and she immediately wished it hadn't. She would have described *him* as firm, if she had to be polite. She would have described him as a misogynistic, egocentric asshole if she was talking to friends.

Mattie had resisted the marriage to Ian. She hinted that she had her eye on a wild boy, a rakehell with dark eyes and a fine smile. She didn't mention Sam by name, but Emma guessed that she meant Sam—knowing, as she did, how things eventually turned out. Mattie's parents and grandparents on both sides had told her Sam's older brother Ian would be a good match for her; he was established, he was building her a house, he had a fine future ahead of him, and as his wife, she would not want for anything. Mattie wrote about hard times ahead, about everyone's fear of a war with the North. Fear and pressure from her parents led her to marry a man she did not love, though she did respect him. She talked about caring for him. She hoped in time she might come to love him.

Emma already knew it was not going to be enough. Her good intentions toward Ian were going to fall by the wayside. The question Emma hoped the diary would answer was *why*.

Emma put the diary down and stared out the window of the plane. She hated flying. She hated the whole idea of flying, but flying away from Benina and the strangeness going on there seemed like a good idea. She was learning about Mattie, and she was becoming a little more sympathetic; in a world where women were second-class citizens, basically voiceless and powerless, being nineteen and being pressured into marrying a man fifteen years her senior could not have been any treat. Marriages for love were not yet seen as sensible or particularly practical, but neither were they unheard of. And Mattie had someone she loved.

Emma found it hard to imagine a young woman marrying one brother—the older, powerful, "firm" one—and then fooling around with the younger brother, hoping everything would be all right.

Everything had ended all right for Mattie and Sam, though—at least where possible conflict with Ian was concerned. He'd died in the war.

So the problem had to be with Sam, and what happened after.

Emma started back into the diary again.

And quickly found herself skimming. The diary made for uncomfortable reading, because Mattie was not happy, and her life was not good. Ian was away a great deal, and in Mattie's eyes, that was the good news. He was already an important man in the community, and as the nation headed toward war with itself, he became active in the cause. When he was at home, he was demanding and distant, and when he wasn't distant, he was cruel. He clearly felt himself within his rights to hit her; on several occasions she reported being ill following punishment by him, and having to spend the day abed. The household had servants, and Mattie, who had not come from a home with servants, had no idea how to manage them. Ian was constantly berating her for having let them get the better of her on one point or another.

And then the war started, and Mattie reported that Ian had done his husbandly duty, something Mattie reported erratically and with distaste, and went off to join the army as an officer and a physician. He anticipated making a place for himself in the new government, and perhaps leaving medicine for politics.

Emma silently cheered with Mattie when he left.

The tone of the diary changed immediately.

Mattie noted that Sam had come to stay on the property, living in the little apartment above the carriage house, in order to protect her and work the property. She wrote cautiously, but Emma caught her happiness spilling through the cracks in her caution like sunlight through spaces in a boarded-up window. She read between the lines.

Mattie and Sam were in love, were living together, were sleeping together. Four months after Ian left to go to war, Mattie discovered she was pregnant. Eleven months after he left, she gave birth.

At home. She padded out her belly the instant she discovered her pregnancy to make herself look farther along than she was. She stayed in seclusion as much as possible. And when the baby was born, she claimed to everyone that the little girl had been born two months earlier, and was very small. Her husband was in the thick of things, and would not be able to come home, so she would not have to have a doctor look at the child and realize she was far younger than claimed. Mattie also noted in the diary that she'd written him a letter, backdated it, and announced the birth of a healthy baby girl at around the time the child would have been due, had she been Ian's.

Emma held the diary in her hands, frowning. Sam, or someone, had hidden away the diary and the letters after he'd killed her. After he'd killed the child. Emma could see where the contents of the diary would offer definite motives for murder. The diary proved that Sam had cheated with his brother's wife, had fathered the child that should have been Ian's, and had been relieved about his brother's death, even if he hadn't precisely rejoiced.

Ian had been no prize. That was evident from two years of sad little entries by a girl who had hoped for much more. Sam, however, was looking like a nightmare. A handsome, charming, rakehell of a nightmare whose carefully suppressed mean streak, when it came out of hiding, was going to be terrifying.

Mike was in the kitchen with Cara, sitting at the table and snacking on a Red Devil cake she'd made, when Drew dragged in from a call to the ER.

"How did it go?" Mike asked.

Drew grinned wearily. "It was hell, but we came through it. Family of five T-boned by Stony Markham, who was drunk again. Fortunately, Stony's foot came off the pedal when he passed out at the wheel, and his car went pretty slowly into the car that was going through the intersection."

"Why isn't that bastard locked away for life?" Mike growled.

"Because the other bastard is his lawyer, and as long as Stony has the money to keep the wheels greased, David has the tricks up his sleeves to keep him free. And driving."

"Can't you do something about David?" Cara asked.

Drew said, "I talk to him. I do my best to convince him to hang criminals like Stony out to dry. But we're family, which means I have the right to nag, but he has the right to ignore me. Where work is concerned, he does."

All three of them shared a commiserating look, and then Drew plopped down at the table and said, "How 'bout some cake for me, too, darlin'?"

Cara kissed the top of his head. "Cake it is. You want a meal first?"

"No. I want to let my poor dogs rest, and I want to eat something sweet, and I want to hear any news that isn't some friend of mine dying badly."

Mike said, "I have a question for you, actually. What ever happened to Dr. Pendergast's patient files and records when he died?"

"Jim's stuff? His practice split up. His receptionist and his nurse kept the office open long enough for living patients to find new physicians, and then sent records to the appropriate offices."

"What happened to the records of patients who were already dead?"

Drew raised an eyebrow. "He'd requested that all of those come to me. Why?"

Mike glanced over at Cara to see if she thought bringing Drew into Emma's situation was a good idea. Behind Drew's back, Cara shrugged.

"Okay. Here's the thing. Emma discovered not too long ago that she was born here in Benina. Dr. Pendergast's nurse took her up north and, with the help of a lawyer who was evidently in on it, sold her to a couple there who were willing to overlook certain irregularities in the adoption process."

Drew paled. "Oh, God. There were rumors about Jim when he died, and about the nurse right after she left town. She left a cryptic message in her apartment—the police took the message as evidence in a case they were building on her that involved blackmail and embezzlement and things that were only rumored. I don't think black market babies were ever part of the rumors. But . . ." He frowned. "Who's Emma's birth mother? Does she know?"

"Maris Kessler."

Drew was quiet for a moment.

"What's wrong?"

"No, she isn't. Maris Kessler's baby died. Jim Pendergast attended, and there was a review of the case because both the mother and baby died. The other GP and I alternated rounds on Maris with Jim in the month or so she was on the locked ward, before she delivered her baby. But then the baby died, and the girl died, and then the girl's mother killed herself. It was an ugly mess."

"More than you'd think," Mike said. "Emma's parents had a detective backtrack the case. He named the nurse on duty as the one who brought them the baby. No other names, but it looks like she was a black-market baby."

Drew sat quietly at the table, playing with crumbs on his plate, dragging a fork through them. "I'm pretty sure Maris's records would be in the office, Cara. I don't think you'll be the only one looking for them—I ran into Dris at the morgue and he told me the police were reopening the investigation of that girl's death, so I imagine we'll be subpoenaed for the records pretty soon. If you can find them, you'll save us time later, and in the meantime, we can go through them and see what we can deduce from the care she received. Make sure, as far as we can, that she received good care, and that some of the rumors about Jim being responsible for her death weren't true. I'm sure Emma would want to know that. The whole thing was such a tragedy."

Cara said, "Emma seems to be dealing with it well. She's worried, though, because she talked to Gwen, who put her in touch with Aileen Wilkes. She never got to speak to Aileen, but . . ."

Drew looked thoughtful. "But Emma clearly sees a

connection in the deaths, because she was asking about her mother, and then the women she was asking died. I suppose I can see where Dris would reopen the case. There's probably no connection, but he'd have to check."

"I'll go through the files tomorrow," Cara said. "The unopened Pendergast files are the ones clear in the back, aren't they?"

"They're all in blue folders. Everything that came to me from his practice but that was closed was in a blue folder. If we get a break in patients tomorrow, I'll help you look," Drew said.

Cara hugged him. "You're the best."

He laughed. "Oh, I *know* that. I just want to make sure you know." He winked at Mike, who chuckled.

But Mike wasn't feeling too happy inside.

Something had changed with Emma. As she was hurrying Cara and him out the door, he would have sworn that she had withdrawn. He hadn't felt it when he kissed her good-bye. But he'd felt it even before she got the phone call that took her away from him.

She'd been thinking. About what Cara had said, he'd bet. About the whole reincarnation theory, and Emma being Mattie, and him being . . . Sam?

And Ian being someone who didn't matter, because he'd died before he ever found out that Mattie had cheated on him with his brother.

And that would mean . . . what?

Mike drove home lost in thought. Not so lost that he wasn't watching out for another drunken Stony on the road, but still as deep as he dared go.

He'd thought Cara's reincarnation theory was stupid. Initially, anyway. But he remembered Emma calling him Sam, and him calling her Mattie, and that had been at a moment when they were both lost to themselves, when they had been at their most vulnerable to the forces at work in the house. It had also been before either of them had discovered the names of the house's previous inhabitants.

So he was Sam. Had been Sam once, anyway. Maybe. He sighed. And from everything going on, it seemed horribly likely that someone had killed Mattie, or maybe the daughter. Or maybe the daughter and Mattie.

And the only suspect they had who might have committed two murders, at least at that moment, was . . . Sam.

"Holy hell," he muttered. That was why she'd gotten distant. She'd run through the whole thing, she'd followed the same logic he had, and clearly she'd come to the same conclusion. The odds were good that Sam had killed Mattie—violently, horribly.

He got out of his truck and walked up to his front door, but he wasn't seeing his house. He was seeing that image he'd seen when he ran, panic-stricken, into the carriage house. It was so sharp and horrible; the woman dead in the barn, her curly golden hair matted with blood, part of her head smashed in, her body in its prim, long-skirted, old-fashioned dress limp and crumpled and still.

Had Sam killed Mattie?

Had *he*?

That was why Mike was seeing the images he was seeing, he decided. That was why he was hearing things in the house, why if Emma wasn't there he felt horrible and alone and sick inside of the house. Because there was something inside of him that had once been crazed enough to murder a woman he loved. It wasn't *him*. It couldn't be him. He was sure of that. But it was someone connected to him. Someone whom he had been once.

If he had killed before, could he kill again?

He was cold inside. How could he let himself near Emma until he understood better what had happened between Mattie and Sam? How could he trust himself to touch her until he could be sure that the same poison that had led him to commit the unthinkable was no longer a part of him?

He had to go back to the house. He had to find the diary, read the letters again, and see if he could figure out what had happened, and why it had happened.

He wanted to put his feet up and rest, and a good night's sleep wouldn't have gone amiss. But he needed to know what had happened right after the end of the War Between the States. Something had gone wrong between Sam and the woman he was supposed to be with for the rest of his life. That something now stood between Mike and the woman *he* loved.

With a sigh, he turned around, got back in his truck, and drove over to Emma's place.

She wasn't there, of course. He didn't have a key, either; he wasn't the sort of man who would keep a key to a house he'd done work on.

But that didn't mean he didn't know a way into the house.

He had his flashlight with him. He walked around to the back of the house, and dropped to his hands and knees, and went underneath. It was a little crazy, he knew. The undersides of old houses were fine places to find hunting snakes and black widow spiders and brown recluses. And possums, and maybe rabid raccoons, and God only knew what else. Nighttime was the right time, where unfriendly vermin were concerned.

He used his flashlight, and he didn't see any eyes looking back at him as he crawled toward the center of the house. Doing work on the flooring and joists, he'd discovered an access door there—a trapdoor that someone, at some time, had used for modernizing the plumbing, heating, and electrical wiring, and had never built over. The trapdoor and crawl spaces looked like they might have been used for something illegal in the past. Moonshining, maybe. They had been useful for getting at the plumbing in the modern age, though. They eliminated, of all things, crawling around under the house in the dark. If you knew the top trapdoor was there, you went at the crawl spaces from the inside.

He fiddled with the latch, and worked the bottom trapdoor open. And crawled up and inside.

He was still in the dark, of course. He'd come up into the tight crawl space beneath the water heater and the furnace that came out into the little utility room set dead center in the house.

Mike pulled the bottom door shut behind himself, feeling incredibly guilty that he was doing what he was doing.

But he was scared. Scared for himself, scared for Emma, scared because he had never had so much to lose before, and scared because there was a part of him that was telling him he had to do the right thing and walk out of her life before someone got hurt.

Before he did the right thing, though, Mike was determined to discover the truth. To make sure leaving was the right thing to do.

He crawled left, straight, right, and pushed himself up through the top trapdoor, into the utility room, and opened the door into the rest of the house.

Her studio was to his right, the kitchen was to his left, the dining room was in front of him to the left, the living room was in front of him to the right, and the staircase and foyer lay dead ahead.

In the center of the foyer sat the cat.

"Son of a bitch," he said softly. "There you are again."

The cat flicked its ears at the sound of his voice, and its tail began to swish back and forth.

"You don't like me?"

The cat watched him, unblinking.

Emma had been right. The cat did look like he belonged to somebody. He also bore an air of ownership that Mike found disconcerting. Mike had the distinct feeling that the cat knew he wasn't supposed to be where he was, and that the animal was unhappy with him.

He watched it, and began walking toward it.

The cat didn't move. It didn't make a sound, either. It just sat, watching, as he moved closer and closer, one cautious step at a time.

But when he'd split the difference between the utility room and the cat, the animal stood up.

"Stay," he said. "Come on, give me a break, will you?" Mike wasn't sure why he wanted to get a good, close look at it. He just knew that he did.

But the cat wasn't playing that game. It glanced at him over its shoulder, and then walked at a sedate pace under the staircase.

Mike watched it carefully. The staircase was closed off—a neat little alcove with no way out except the way the cat had gone in. Emma had a few boxes shoved under there that she hadn't gotten around to unpacking yet, but though the cat would be able to crouch on them, Mike was pretty sure he would be able to see it wherever it might try to hide.

He moved closer slowly, not wanting to disturb the animal.

Except that, when he got there, it wasn't there.

He'd seen it go into that alcove. He knew he had. He'd watched the alcove, and the cat had not come out. He'd been in the alcove when he was checking the house for damage, and if he hadn't exactly gone over every board with a fine-tooth comb, it was only because the woodwork had been solid, and the stairs had been solid, and a cursory inspection had been good enough.

So he checked behind and around the boxes, but the cat was not there.

He checked again.

He knew the cat hadn't run out in front of him.

He climbed under the stairs, certain that when he did, the cat would shoot out from some unseen nook and race across the hallway, or tear off toward the back of the house.

But no cat.

Mike swore softly. And then, crouched down and with one hand braced against the back wall of the alcove, he started having the feeling that he was being watched. He could feel something staring at the back of his neck. He felt his pulse start to pick up. He shivered, and felt his mouth go dry.

He consciously took a deep breath, trying to force himself to calm, but that didn't help at all. The feeling that he was being watched, that something was behind him, grew stronger, and stronger, until it was so over-powering that he almost couldn't breathe.

He gripped the flashlight tighter. It was heavy, rugged metal with a long handle and the weight of a handful of D-cell batteries inside to make it a formidable weapon.

The only thing behind him was a wall. He knew that. The side wall of the alcove. That was it. In front of him were the stepped decreases in height that mirrored the stairs above.

Nothing could be behind him. He turned so that he was facing the foyer, and nothing and no one was in there. He turned further, his flashlight shining on the blank face of the woodwork.

And the flashlight cast the shadow of a seam along one edge.

He froze.

The flashlight picked up a tiny unevenness in the way two pieces of wood came together. He would never have noticed it in daylight, because he would never have seen the tiny shadow that the flashlight cast.

He swallowed hard, his mouth feeling like the Sahara in a dry spell, and he placed the palm of one hand flat against the panel closest to him. He pushed. Lightly.

It wiggled.

His heart did a couple of theatrical double-shimmies. He pushed a little harder. The panel wiggled a little harder. He knocked on it, and was rewarded with a hollow sound. Just to be sure, he tapped to the left and right. He definitely had a door in front of him.

What he needed was a doorknob.

He shined his light around the overhead portion of the alcove, running his fingers along every promising protrusion and irregularity in the woodwork, but without results. He then pressed everything on the wall that held the door, and then on the wall to his right.

And then he looked down. One board in the beautiful old floor was made of a dark wood different in grain and texture from the cherry-stained oak of the rest of the floor. He knelt and tried to find a way to pull it up. That did nothing. He pushed down on it, though, and with a soft click, the door slipped open about an inch.

He stood up, and tried working the secret latch with the toe of his boot. It worked beautifully.

He was impressed. And infinitely curious.

He opened the door, and shined the light inside, and found himself face-to-face with a chamber of psychotic horrors.

Six hours after she walked onto her plane at the Greenville-Spartanburg airport—and after one wait, one transfer, and the usual interminable lines—Emma disembarked at Dale County Regional. She was tired and worried, and she had only made it through the first half of the diary. She found Jennifer, a mutual friend of hers and Susan's, waiting for her.

They hugged, and Emma asked, "Have you heard any news?"

"Still no baby when I left to pick you up. They were just putting her on pitocin to make the contractions harder. The doctor said she wasn't progressing, and they were concerned that the placenta would do something it wasn't supposed to." Jennifer looked both frazzled and bewildered. Like Emma, she'd never been pregnant, and the whole process was alien territory.

"Poor Susan," Emma said. "How's she holding up?"

"Not great." Jennifer took a curve too fast, and Emma

felt like she was going to meld with the car door. Or explode right out of it. "She's in horrible pain. The pitocin seems to make the whole thing worse." Jennifer shuddered. "I don't think I ever want to go through that."

I might be pregnant, Emma thought. *I could be, anyway.* "I guess you just get through it," she said to Jennifer. "I mean, people are born every day, so *somebody* is going through it and surviving."

Jennifer, clearly not impressed by this logic, just looked at Emma as if she'd lost her mind. "Tad's been going crazy. He's in a complete panic, absolutely certain that she's going to die and he'll have been the one who killed her."

Emma tried to ignore the echoes of those words—*she's going to die and he will have been the one who killed her.* Susan wasn't going to die. Tad was a great guy—even with a wimpy name—and none of this related to Mattie and Sam. Or to Emma and Mike.

"Anyway," Jennifer continued, "her parents are there, his parents are there, Susan is screaming and climbing the walls. She's waiting for you. Tad told her you were coming, and that is the first moment of calm she's had since things started going badly."

Emma closed her eyes. She'd left Susan so that she could go chasing after a house, and she had ended up in the middle of something she couldn't explain and that scared her, and all the while, Susan had needed her best friend close by.

"I should never have left."

Jennifer said, "Because you have X-ray vision and prescience, and can tell that a pregnant woman is going to have problems during delivery, even if the pregnancy was perfect and the doctor thought the delivery would be, too." Jennifer made a face. "You're good."

"Just guilty," Emma said.

They got to the hospital, and a nurse helped Emma scrub and put on a cap and scrubs and shoe covers and gloves, and then she led her in to see Susan.

Susan didn't look like herself. Her face was gaunt and strained, lined with pain. She was pale, and soaked with sweat.

She saw Emma, though, and said, "You made it," and managed the frailest of smiles before another round of pain hit her, and she screamed.

Emma nodded to Tad and took a place on the side of Susan opposite him. And then Susan's blood pressure dropped, and the room filled with medical people. She and Tad were chased out into the waiting room, and grim-faced hurrying nurses raced the abruptly still Susan to OR.

Emma held vigil. She prayed, knowing that Susan's parents and her in-laws were doing the same. She talked to Tad and tried to offer encouragement. Of all the people there, she was the fresh one, even after the flight. She had more energy than anyone else because she hadn't been living with the fear and the worry and the hope for the last nine hours.

The first good news, when it came, was that the baby was all right. Tad disappeared into the nursery to be with his son. Everyone else waited.

The second good news was a long time coming. Susan had nearly died from internal hemorrhage, and there were complications. But she had pulled through. An hour after the news that she was out of surgery came the news that she was out of recovery. And a couple hours after that, after Susan had the chance to visit briefly with family and rest and hold her baby, Emma finally had the chance to see her again.

"I knew you were going to make it," Emma told her. "You promised you were going to come down to my place with Tad and the baby."

Susan said, "I was pretty sure I was going to die, actually. I drifted off the operating table, and for a moment I could see them working on me. And then I floated toward a bright light, and met my grandma."

Emma shivered.

"She told me I had a baby to take care of, and said she'd see me when it was time. And she had a message for you."

"Your grandma? She had a message for me?"

"She always liked you." Susan held the sleeping baby close, her face radiant, and for a moment she looked like she might drift off to sleep, too. Then she opened her eyes and said, "Your father killed you once. Don't let him do it again."

"What?" Emma stared at Susan.

Susan said, "That was her message. It was what convinced me that I was dreaming the whole thing, actually, and wasn't about to die." She laughed a little. "It didn't make sense. Your dad was great, and he sure never killed you."

"Not my real dad. But maybe she was sort of referring to my birth father. Maybe it was a . . . metaphor, or something."

"You think?"

"I don't know." She took Susan's hand. "I'm just so glad you made it back," she said. "This would be a crummy world without you."

"You don't think I was dreaming?"

"The message makes sense, in a weird way," Emma told her. "I'll thank your grandma, but thank her for me, too, okay?"

The nurse came in then and told Emma she had to go. On her way out the door, Emma pictured Susan's grandmother the way she'd been the last time Emma had seen her alive—out in her tomato garden. *Thanks for getting Susan back safely,* she said. *And thanks for the warning.*

She breathed easier. Susan and her baby were going to be okay.

But in the back of her mind, a clock had started ticking—the clock that was counting down the days and hours until she would be back home again.

Chapter 9

Mike stood in a surprisingly long, narrow secret room that ran between the foyer and the formal dining room and kitchen. The main rooms of the first floor had been cleverly designed around the hideaway to fool the eye into thinking the space they took up made sense. On the outside wall at the far end, he knew, there was a built-in kitchen cupboard. And the stairs, of course, created the excuse for the living room to be set in.

The dead space wasn't wasted space though.

It was full of paintings: grim, angry, frightening paintings of people dying. A man in a rocking chair watched through a high window as bodies burned in a bonfire below him; a man strangled a child in a bedroom; the same man beat a woman to death with a candlestick back in the carriage house.

Two men fought, mirrored images of each other. Dark shadows chasing each other across a Möbius strip, so that he could not tell who was pursuing, or who was fleeing, and the painting left the impression that each might have been doing both.

The colors of all the paintings were stark, the textures were coarse, but they were all so skillfully done that he could not tear his gaze away.

Four of the pictures were portraits. Three he guessed as haunting, or perhaps haunted, looks at Sam, the wife, and the child. The fourth he had to guess as either the woman's first husband or an unidentified third man in the scenario.

Emma had painted them, Mike realized. She had painted them and had hidden them in the stairs. And then she had acted surprised and horrified when she saw the photographs of the house's first inhabitants—but she had clearly already seen pictures before. She had already known who they had been.

He stared at images of violent slaughter, of hatred and rage and shock, and he shivered.

Why had Emma done the paintings? Why had she hidden them? Why had she lied about her knowledge of the previous inhabitants? What was going on with her?

He looked at those ugly, evil paintings, and he imagined himself in bed with the woman who had done them. In bed. Asleep. Naked and vulnerable.

What was going on in her head? When he saw her, she was the light in his world. Apart from her, though, staring at the paintings she'd hidden away, reason had better luck getting past his gonads to his brain, and he started feeling sick.

She'd mentioned going to the police about someone messing with her art supplies. She'd made some off-hand comment about possibly having done that herself while she was sleepwalking. He'd been able to overlook the strangeness of that. But . . . sleep painting? He didn't think so.

If he'd killed Emma in a previous life, was he facing some sort of karmic plan that she go crazy and murder him in this one? Was that how he was supposed to pay his debt for what he'd done?

Was he the killer in those paintings? The man who'd strangled the child and bludgeoned his love, and sat in a high room, rocking and watching their bodies burn?

Emma was gone for a while, and Mike discovered he was grateful. He needed to talk to Cara, and maybe pull in Drew, who could take a look at the paintings and perhaps tell Mike if they might demonstrate an underlying psychosis. They didn't fit Emma's other work, they didn't fit the woman he knew—but how well did he know her? The paintings were graphic, sick, obscene in ways that shocked and disturbed him.

Between Cara's suggestions of reincarnation and the discovery of Emma's chamber-of-horrors paintings, Mike felt roped into a story he wanted nothing to do with, tangled into long-ended lives that scared him and confused him and made him feel guilty and evil. He was—he had always been—a decent guy. He made it a point to treat customers fairly, to treat friends well, and to end relationships with women without being an asshole about it. He'd been a Boy Scout, he was an irregular Methodist, he liked himself. Or at least he had.

And then his life had gotten tangled up in Emma Beck's, and all of a sudden he was feeling like a criminal and like prey, all at the same time. A shadow on a Möbius strip, both pursuing and being pursued.

Chapter 10

All day Sunday, Emma had immersed herself in the moment, and spent as much time as she could with Sue and the baby, watching as her friend went from ragged and weepy to momlike and scared.

On Monday, though, Emma realized she couldn't pretend Benina didn't exist anymore. She missed her home, she missed Cara, she missed Mike more than she could say.

She had no idea what would happen when she got back, or how she fit into her own future. She couldn't begin to guess how she should approach Mike with the information she was discovering in the diary. She had no idea what to do about her father—finding him, dealing with him, or maybe just hiding from him.

All she knew was that Benina was home, and it was time to go back.

On the flight, she dug back into the diary. And things immediately took a turn she had not expected.

Mattie began writing about how bitter Ian's letters were when he wrote home. About how angry he was that his political star was not on the rise, that he had not managed to become a private physician to a general, that instead he was doing disgusting, depressing work on horrible injuries in a war that he described as a meat grinder. There was no glory, he said. There was no triumph. It was relentless slaughter and endless after-battle butchery as he and other physicians and nurses attempted to save lives, and worked with tools and procedures that offered little in the relief of pain, the prevention of infection, or the restoration of health. He said the whole of the Confederate Army was starving by slow degrees. He had lost faith in their cause, in their battle, in the future of the South. He supported the defense of southern land, but told Mattie that when the war was over, they were going to move out west, where men could still be free.

Mattie reported his complaints with varying responses. She was concerned about Yankee invasion, and frightened of what might happen if the soldiers went through their region. She'd heard the tales of Yankee violence to women and children, just as everyone else had, of burning and rape and slaughter. She thought Ian should have been willing to serve, and should have borne his lot with the same stoicism that she faced having little food, and having to work in the field herself to grow most of what she and Mary Caroline had. Mattie milked the farm's two cows, made cheese, fed pigs, sold piglets to neighbors, helped with the slaughtering and the smoking and curing of the pig she'd fattened, did laundry and put up fruits and vegetables against the coming winter.

The family didn't own slaves, Emma realized. Most of the people that Mattie knew didn't own slaves. They hired such help as they could afford, and when times got hard, they did without. Benina was not a town built around plantations of cotton or tobacco. It had been a little crossroads trading center nestled between small outlying farms where subsistence farmers worked the poor soil, raised pigs and horses, and spent their little free time between church and neighboring farms.

Sam had enlisted and been gone for some time, and Mattie was getting by as best she could. She was out from the town, with her nearest neighbor a mile away, alone with her little girl. The old men and boys from her church came out and helped in the field when they could. But mostly she and her little girl, who grew from age one to age three while Sam was away, were all alone.

In the midst of the hardship and isolation, Ian's dream of becoming a powerful political figure didn't sit well with Mattie, nor did his ambitions to move away from Benina to some primitive camp out west. Mattie loved Benina. She liked her hills, her high ground, and her neighbors. She liked being close to friends she'd had all her life.

Mattie worried about having heard nothing from Sam, and wrote angrily about a letter in which Ian said he had taken as much as he could. Benina was cut off from trade, fighting was close, and people were terrified. They lived in dread of what might happen to them and their children, to their farms and their livestock. Yankees had stolen both cows and one pig from Mattie's barn during a night raid, and she found that she could only be grateful that they hadn't broken into the house and raided that.

And then she got the letter from the army telling her that Ian had died. She expressed only relief.

Shortly after that, she got the first letter from Sam, and rejoiced.

The Yankees moved on, and she rejoiced at that, too, even though the news on the war was dark, and she and Mary were constantly hungry. Friends who had been burned out of their house moved into hers while they waited for the war to end and the men to return.

She recorded more dead from the town, and how their mothers or wives or sweethearts had taken the news.

She wrote about her next letter from Sam joyously.

And then the war was over, and even in defeat, the men of Benina who still lived would be heading home.

Sam returned.

Emma clenched up, expecting the rest of the pages to be blank.

But they weren't. They went on for almost another year. Bewildered, she read about Mattie's and Sam's joyous reunion, their marriage, getting the farm back on its feet again, how happy she was and how happy Sam was and how wonderful their life was. She drew a sketch of her planned rose garden on the south side of the house. She talked about how beautiful Mary Caroline was becoming, and how much she looked and acted like Sam.

She reported a second pregnancy.

And then there were no more entries. Emma realized Mattie must have died at that point, but she was no closer to understanding how or why than she had been before.

She flipped through the last pages of the diary, hoping for some answer. When she found it, her hands started to shake.

Carefully inserted, a page at a time, into the last five

pages of the diary, was a letter from Ian. It was dated well after the letter reporting his death in battle.

In it, Ian told Mattie that after he had switched uniforms with a badly mangled corpse and deserted the war, he'd gone out west to make his fortune. He'd gotten into gold panning in Montana, done well because he was neither a drinker nor a gambler, parlayed his gold fortune and money he made by doctoring into connections in the growing region, worked his way into a position of some importance. He saw himself as a future governor of Montana, or perhaps a man of importance even farther west. He saw Mattie as first lady of the territory that he assured her would one day be a state, but he wrote that, even if that never came to pass, the place would make a damned fine country.

He told her that he had a little surprise for her, and by the time she received the letter, post by ship being what it was, she would probably already have the surprise.

"Oh, God," Emma whispered. Her fingers traced the edges of the last page of the letter. She knew—she just knew, in her heart and in her gut—what Ian's surprise was. He was coming home to get her, to take her west.

"I bet she never got the letter," Emma whispered.

She could see the scene. Sam and newly pregnant Mattie, and their beautiful little girl Mary Caroline, all at home. Ian arrived. Perhaps he had already been to Benina and knew what he would find in his home. Perhaps he saw his wife with his brother, and discovered firsthand how they had betrayed him.

He was never a gentle man, Emma recalled. He considered himself within his rights to beat Mattie for failing to keep the servants in line, for breaking a china knickknack that he'd obtained from some far-off place, or for what he considered being fresh.

He would not be interested in explanations. Or maybe he would have listened. But at some point, he'd found the diary. Sam's and Mattie's letters to each other, betraying the truth that they had been with each other while he was still known to be alive and acknowledged by all as her husband. He would have been able to figure out that Mattie had given birth to a child that was not his.

Were they still alive when he had found all these things, or were the details of his cuckolding something that he discovered only as he was cleaning up from murder?

Three murders, Emma thought. He would not have saved the child, who would have almost certainly known he'd killed her mother. And her father.

Emma's understanding of the whole scene changed, abruptly, painfully, and with horrible clarity. Sam was not and had never been the enemy. Sam had died at his brother's hand, hadn't he? Mary Caroline had. Mattie had.

She closed her eyes, fidgeting with the last page of the letter. It came out in her hand, and she opened her eyes to put it back. Under the page, written in what looked like dried blood, was the word HARLOT!

Emma shivered, and put the page back into the diary, hoping her seatmate had not noticed. He was sleeping, though, as he had for most of the flight.

She cautiously lifted each of the preceding four pages, and found four more words.

YOU
DESERVED
TO
DIE

*   *   *

"How's the hunt going?" Mike asked his sister.

She'd been writing in an appointment. "Hang on," she told him. "You need to get your prescriptions filled, and make sure you take them every day, Mrs. McCammon. We'll expect to see you for a checkup in one week. I have you scheduled for next Tuesday at three p.m."

The old woman nodded. "My son said he'll drive me in whenever I need to be here."

When Mrs. McCammon left, Cara turned her attention to Mike. "Terrible is how it's going. Drew and I have been through every file he got from Dr. Pendergast, and I have to tell you, I think the bastard destroyed the files on Maris and her mother. I don't think they ever landed in Drew's office—and since there has never been a call for them, how would we have known?"

"So there's no real information about Maris, or her mental state? No records of why she was admitted, or what was going on with her?"

"I don't think so," Cara told him, and arched an eyebrow at him. "Why? You've been acting funny since Emma went back to Wisconsin, but now you look really odd."

"Can you knock off work for a few minutes?"

"We'll be closing for lunch in half an hour. Can you hang around that long?"

"Yeah. I can. Can you see if you can get Drew to come, too?"

His sister frowned at him. "Come where?"

"Out to Emma's house. There's something strange going on there, and maybe if both of you see it, you can give me an opinion that will help me figure it out."

"Is she back?" Cara said.

"No."

Mike watched Cara's head tilt slowly to one side. "She left you a key?"

"No," Mike said. He felt uncomfortable admitting the truth. "There's another way into the house. There are a lot of strange things about the house, and you need to see this. Before she gets home, though. Because . . . just because."

He waited around, and then Drew and Cara followed him out to Emma's place. This time he was working in daylight, and he knew exactly were he needed to go. He popped in through the center of the house, trotted to the front door, and let Cara and Drew in.

"We shouldn't be doing this," Cara said.

"It's breaking and entering, even if she is your girl-friend," Drew said.

Mike was grim. "Just look at what I found. This is . . . it may relate to the murders of Gwen and Aileen. Some-how. I'm not sure how."

Cara and Drew exchanged glances, and Mike led them to the hidden room under the stairs. He opened the door, and both Drew and Cara gasped. And then Drew edged past him, and the sound that came out of his throat was almost animal in nature. He backed out, pale and tense, and Cara squeezed past him. "Oh, my God!" she said, and she too backed away.

"I can see what they are," Drew said. "But . . . ex-plain. What . . . what the *hell*?"

"I think Emma might be psychotic. Maybe a multiple personality—though that's where I'd need your opin-ion, Drew—or maybe something else. But from these paintings, and . . . other things . . . I think there's some-thing wrong with her. I have a small suspicion that she might plan to kill me. Revenge for what she sees as a past life. She'd done all of these before we looked at the photographs. So she already knew about this place and its past, or she suspected, at least. She had some other source for the history of the Barnett house."

"There were people murdered here?" Drew asked.

"We're almost certain of it."

"And somehow, she has tied the house's past to her own present?"

Mike said, "I'm a little shaky about how the past and the present relate. There's a . . . well, if you want to play around with reincarnation theory a little, at least . . ."

He faltered. Drew was not the sort of man who appreciated wild fandangos into the realm of the paranormal. He was a great believer in common sense, and if Mike floated the *I think I might have murdered her in a previous life* theory past him, Drew would not be amused.

Drew was watching him, waiting expectantly. Mike shook his head. "We got into a discussion of parallels between our lives and the lives of the first inhabitants of the house. About . . . ah . . . working out karma and things of that nature."

"A serious discussion, in which you were considering these speculations as possible in any way?"

"There's a lot about this house that you don't know, Drew," Cara said. "It has an effect on me. On Mike. On Emma. Each of us has had memories of times before we were born—memories from another life."

"There have been some supernatural events happening here," Mike offered. "Or at least inexplicable ones. Voices whispering on a tape recorder. The feeling of being watched. The . . . the memories Cara mentioned.

Some things between Emma and me that I'd rather not get into. Sounds I can't explain."

He was watching Drew's eyebrows make a valiant attempt at crawling right into his hairline.

Mike said, "It sounds ridiculous on the face of it."

"I'm willing to look at those paintings," Drew said in a gentle, quiet voice, "and believe that Emma is a disturbed young woman. But I am not about to stand here and listen to the two of you, whom I know to be sane and sensible individuals, attempt to tell me that you think you're . . . what . . . acting out past lives in this century? That you were both inhabitants of this house in a previous life? Do either of you realize how totally ludicrous you sound?"

He drew back from Mike and Cara, a frown deepening on his forehead, the corners of his mouth twisting downward.

His voice remained even, but a slight flushing of his face told Mike that Drew was genuinely upset. "I am appalled. I am . . . I am simply not going to allow you to get dragged into this. Suggestions of reincarnation and the paranoid fantasies of a sad, disturbed young woman, and you two are both acting like this is something that deserves serious consideration. You're both Methodists, for God's sake!"

Mike told Drew, "I've had things happen to me while I was in this house that have convinced me the Methodists might not be sole owners of the truth of the universe."

His sister was nodding vehemently. "This is outside of all of that," Cara said. "This has nothing to do with religion, or belief. This is something real. A phenomenon that I can't explain, because I don't have the words.

But it's real, Drew. It's completely real. And I was the one who suggested reincarnation, not Emma."

That's right, Mike thought. *She was.*

He told Cara, "He can't believe it because he hasn't experienced it," Mike said. And then he saw the cat, sitting on a box behind the paintings arrayed around the room.

"That cat is back in the house again," he said, and pointed, and Drew looked past him, into the room. Mike saw him shudder.

"No cat in there," Drew said.

"Sitting on the box. Right where I'm pointing."

Drew looked again. "No cat."

Cara said, "I see a cat."

And then overhead, footsteps walked down the hall. Slow, ponderous, heavy. Mike felt his heart do a stutter-step and he looked sidelong at Cara. She'd shivered, and he could see the goose bumps on her arms.

Drew looked up and frowned. "Who's up there?"

Mike hated to do it, but he said, "Let's go see."

"We're not supposed to be in this house," Drew reminded him in an angry, anxious whisper.

"But here we are. And you can bet your life whoever is up there is not Emma."

Mike heard the door at the top of the stairs open, then close. He didn't want to go see what was going on. He knew in his gut that he wanted nothing to do with whatever it was up there.

And yet . . .

He dragged Drew out and to the foot of the stairs in time to hear the footsteps, now heavier, now sounding exactly like they were dragging something, head out the door at the top of the stairs and straight toward them. They stood there, he and Drew, and stared upward. It was the middle of the day, the light was clear, vision was perfect. And there was nothing. There was absolutely nothing on the stairs.

Drew looked quickly at Mike. He set his jaw and wrapped his arms across his chest and said, "I don't know how much trouble you went to in order to pull off this little stunt, but I'm not amused. The sort of personality it takes—"

The footsteps had reached him. Mike stepped back—a good five steps, all the way to the front door—but Drew held his ground. Mike heard the footsteps walking right where Drew was standing. They stopped briefly, and Mike saw Drew shudder, and saw his hand whip up and around to grab the back of his neck. He turned to where he'd thought Mike was to snarl at him, but Mike wasn't there anymore, and when he turned the rest of the way, and saw where Mike actually was standing, his mouth dropped open. He shivered again.

He looked around the house. He backed away from the footsteps, which had turned and headed down the hall toward Emma's studio and the kitchen.

"What the fuck was that?" he asked.

It was the first time in all the years that Mike had known Drew, first as his physician when he was a kid, and later as his brother-in-law, that Mike had ever heard him use that particular bit of profanity.

"This is what we were telling you," Mike said. "There's . . . stuff going on in this house."

Drew wasn't interested in hearing any more, though. He went around the steps, grabbed Cara's arm, and started dragging her toward the door. "We're leaving," he said, "and you're never coming back here again. There is something terrible here. Terrible."

He walked past Mike, glaring at him as if he would have punched him into a wall if he could have, and stopped at the front door.

Emma had just opened it.

She looked shocked. With Drew looking enraged, and Cara looking scared of Drew, and Mike in the background wearing an expression of guilty, freaked-out idiocy, she came to an abrupt stop in the doorway and said, "What in the *world* is going on in here?"

"We're leaving," Drew said. "We won't be back. I won't be purchasing any more of your paintings. We will not—any of us"—and there he looked at Mike as if to include him in the blanket order—"be having anything further to do with you or your house. You need to visit a good psychiatrist." His voice was venomous. Mike had never heard anything like it. "And I think you need to be put on some strong antipsychotic medications. You're a danger to yourself and others."

And then he dragged Cara out the door, shoving past Emma and actually pushing her back onto her porch, and stalked down to his car. Cara looked like a rag doll in his grip. Drew opened her car door, shoved her inside, got in his own side, and drove off before either he or Cara had a chance to put on seat belts.

Emma came back through her door again. "Mike?" she said. "What just happened?"

"I don't know," Mike said. "He was scared. One of your resident ghosts just walked through him, I think."

"Why are you here?"

"I found something, and I wanted Cara's and Drew's opinion on it. I'm . . . I'm scared for you to see it, Emma."

*   *   *

Emma hadn't been sure whether she should call the police, or offer iced tea to everyone when she saw Cara and Mike and Drew inside her house. She'd parked beside Drew's truck. She was afraid at first that one of them had discovered something wrong at the house, or that there had been a break-in while she was away.

And then she had realized that they were in her house, though none of them had a key, and she started to be upset.

Following that, of course, Drew had blasted past her dragging Cara and snarling dire remarks, and she had simply been dumbfounded.

Mike was looking at her like he'd discovered she'd been murdering kittens in her spare time, and all she could do was follow along while he led her under the stairs and asked why, if she'd known the history of the house, she hadn't just told the truth about it.

And then she'd been confronted by her painting boards. Her painting. The ugly color palettes that she would never have used in a million years, put into ugly, obscenely violent, gruesome paintings in a dark, scary impasto style that had nothing in common with her work.

And still she recognized her own sense of composition. Her own approach to techniques. Her own voice, if painting could be said to have a voice.

It was as if she'd gone from singing opera to singing Goth rock. She still knew that she had done the work she was looking at.

She just didn't know when. Or how.

How?

"The sleepwalking?" she whispered. "The paintings I was working on never secured first thing in the morning, my palettes tossed in the trash, my palette knives and painting knives left out of place, my materials not properly cleaned up or put away . . . because I was doing these?"

She traced her fingers over the secret door that led into the hidden room. "How did I ever get in here? How did I not notice a door here?"

Mike was watching her. "You're telling me that you knew nothing about this? About the paintings, or about the room?"

"I knew someone was messing around in my workroom," she said. She felt scared in ways she couldn't even describe. "I told you that. I knew something was wrong, and I was worried enough about it that I went to the police. Remember?"

She stepped into the room and walked from painting to painting. "So sick. So angry. So horrible."

She stopped in front of the portrait of the man who wasn't Sam. She said, "This is Ian, I think."

"Ian? This is the same guy who is fighting for his life with Sam."

"That isn't quite how it went," she said. Emma turned to Mike and said, "I'm so sorry. I was thinking horrible things about you when I left. I thought you might have been the person who killed me. Or . . . you know. That you might have been Sam, and that Sam had killed Mattie."

He was watching her. "I thought the same thing was likely."

She shook her head. "Ian killed Mattie. And Mattie's and Sam's daughter, Mary Caroline. And, I'm pretty sure, Sam."

"He couldn't have. He was dead."

She fished around in the carry-on bag that was still slung over her shoulder, and said, "Not as dead as everyone thought." She pulled out a book, and watched his face for signs of recognition. After an instant, he said, "The diary."

"Right. There's a lot in it, and I've read almost all of it. So here's the story, short and quick. Ian was reported dead in battle. Sam made it home from the war, he and Mattie married, Mattie got pregnant again, they were both deliriously happy. And then Ian sent this."

She'd thumbed through the diary while she was talking, and found the pages at the end where Ian had tucked away the letter he'd sent. The one that Emma suspected neither Sam nor Mattie had ever seen.

She handed the diary over to Mike, and then she stood there and watched while he read.

His expression went from bewildered to stunned to horrified. When he was done reading, he started to hand the diary back to her, but she shook her head.

"Lift each of the letter pages and look underneath."

Mike did as she'd suggested. He found the message. "Oh, God, Emma."

She said, "It had to have been terrible. I can't even imagine. Mattie and Sam were so happy, and so in love, and then the husband who had been cruel to Mattie before he went off to the war sort of came back from the dead. He came home and found out the truth. Or maybe he didn't. Maybe he just found the two of them together and killed them first, and *then* he discovered everything that had happened. I think he killed them before they even knew he was still alive. It makes sense—from the feelings I've had in this house, and from the little I was able to piece together about his character. And everything else."

"He was a deserter from the war."

"Right. Not a hero who died saving the lives of the men who counted on him. But a creep who changed identities with someone else, then fled and left the men he was charged to care for without someone qualified to help them."

Mike started pacing. "So. You aren't here to work out your karma by getting retribution for what I did to you, because I didn't do anything horrible to you. And I'm not here to keep myself from killing you for a second time, because I didn't kill you the first time. We're both here to be together." He stopped and smiled over at her. "We were here to find each other, and fall in love, and spend the rest of our lives together. Raise a little family, maybe."

She smiled back at him. "Yes."

His smile fled, though. "But we have to figure out what's the story with those paintings, Emma, because they're . . . horrible."

"And we have to talk to Cara and Drew and convince them that I'm not crazy."

"But you don't remember doing the paintings?"

"No."

"So when I saw you sleepwalking, you'd also been sleep painting?"

Emma didn't want to think about that. "It might have been sleep painting, I suppose. I don't know of anyone, anywhere, who's ever painted while sleeping. And certainly not something coherent."

"I have to agree. I think there's more to it than that. Something a lot scarier than painting while you're asleep."

"Like what?"

"I can think of one explanation. Maybe you suffer from multiple personalities."

Emma said, "I've read about those cases, and they were always kids who were horribly abused or molested—they formed alternate personalities to deal with the terrible things happening to them."

"Okay." He looked at her, curious. "And that couldn't be you because . . ."

"Because I've never been abused."

"If you had multiple personalities, the personality that is you wouldn't remember being abused, right?"

Emma considered that for a moment. "I don't think that's it. Alternate personalities don't walk around like . . . like zombies, or whatever it was you said I looked like. They look just like everyone else."

Mike said, "Then I'm out of ideas."

She bit her lip. She didn't even want to suggest the idea that had come to mind, but now that she'd thought it, she couldn't escape the thought that she'd hit on the truth. "How about possession?" she asked.

He raised an eyebrow. "Like in *The Exorcist*? Voices coming from your body, and your head spinning around, and you vomiting pea soup?"

"Sort of." She felt her way through the land mines of the concept she was exploring. "What if my previous self was possessing me? Or . . . the house, which remembers what happened here before. What if when I fall asleep, the house, or the ghosts in the house, can enter my body and use it?"

Mike looked a little sick. "I hate that idea."

"I wasn't too crazy about the multiple personalities one," she said, and heard the defensiveness in her own

voice. "This one would at least mean that I'm not dealing with serious psychological problems."

"It would also mean that there are things in your
house that are able to use you for their purposes. That
you're vulnerable. Maybe that I'm vulnerable, or that
Cara is vulnerable. If the house ghosts—or even the
house itself—can connect with you because your . . .
what . . . your soul lived here before, then it might be
able to do the same thing to me. Or to Cara."

"Only if you slept here, I think."

"I *did* sleep here." He looked a little panicked.

"The house likes us. It isn't dangerous to us."

"We aren't the only people who lived here," he said.
"Ian Barnett lived here, too. And what if his spirit is still
hanging around? What if his murderous spirit is watching you right now? Have you thought of that? What if
the bastard is just waiting for someone he can move
into, so that he can kill you again?"

"No," she said. "No. Not possible."

But she was thinking of the warning from Susan's
grandmother. *Your father killed you once. Don't let him
do it again.*

For the warning to make sense, she had to accept past
lives. But she had no memories or clues that would suggest a past life in which her father had killed her. However, the message felt real. Emma had the sick feeling that
her present-day biological father was involved in the
killings of the two Benina women, and that her questions
had set him on that path. That he had left some sort of
awful secret in the past that she was awakening.

But what did that have to do with *your father killed
you once*?

Ian had killed Mattie. Emma was cautiously willing

to concede that she shared a bond with Mattie, and that the bond might have been one of reincarnation. Did this suggest that her father in this life had been Ian in the Civil War life? Did her danger from him come from more than the activities of this life?

"It's not possible," she repeated, but with much less assurance.

"You sure? You have something that is dragging you around when you're asleep, having you paint things that happened a couple of lifetimes ago. You have something that *can use you* to do what it wants. If a spirit can use you, Emma, it can use someone else. If we're right, then you were Mattie in a previous life. So Mattie—or something that echoes Mattie—is working through you. And I was Sam in a previous life, so something that echoes Sam might be able to work through me. Maybe. We haven't seen any evidence of that."

"No. We haven't."

Emma positioned herself so that she didn't have to look at the paintings. "We have no evidence that Ian has reincarnated. No reason to think he has anything to do with any of this."

"We don't have evidence," Mike agreed. "We don't have evidence of reincarnation, either. But, Emma, if Sam and Mattie and Mary Caroline are back in order to work out something that went wrong before, it only makes sense that the thing that went wrong would come back. So that they could fix it."

"The thing that went wrong?"

Mike grimaced. "Ian. And," he continued doggedly, "we've seen plenty of evidence that something can work through you. If Ian were going to carry out his evil a second time, he could do it through his reincarnated self."

"Assuming he is back, we don't know who Ian's reincarnated self is," Emma said.

Mike nodded. "I'll bet anything he knows who you are, though."

Emma hadn't given any thought to Ian when the subject first came up, because he had died in battle, and therefore couldn't have been involved in later events. Then, when she'd learned the truth, she'd simply written him off as a past problem only, because Mike didn't have a brother. So clearly, there could be no brother-to-brother drama or violence or misery. But if Cara was Mary Caroline, then daughters could reincarnate as sisters. And brothers could reincarnate as anyone. Even fathers.

"So our challenge in this life, if we're going to believe in such things," she said, carefully choosing her words, "might be more than just being together. It might be—making things right with Ian's spirit."

"Or surviving a second round of Ian's vengeance," Mike said.

"You have a deep streak of pessimism in you, don't you?"

"Deep," Mike agreed. "It comes from seeing the woman I love being marched through the house like a puppet, and discovering paintings that she insists she didn't paint, and suspecting from those paintings that she and I and a daughter we both loved died horribly in a previous life, at the hands of some vicious psychopath." He said, "Forgive me if I notice drought, and hawks overhead, and hurricanes on the horizon."

She closed the door to the hidden room under the stairs.

Mike said, "I think about things like, what if the father who was responsible for your mother dying, and for you being shipped off to buyers of a black-market baby, and maybe for the death of your grandmother, and possibly for the murders of Gwen and Aileen, is the same person who was Ian in a previous life?"

Emma had been thinking the same thing, but she wasn't sure she wanted to admit it out loud. "It . . . doesn't seem likely."

"Likely? Is anything that has happened to us likely?"

Mike led her toward the kitchen. "No one has any idea what sort of person Ian was when people weren't watching him. Maybe as a doctor back in the eighteen hundreds, he was an unethical scumbag even before he changed identities with some poor soldier, leaving that guy's family to never know what happened to him. Maybe Ian was a creep before he deserted the war, and before that, before he was cruel to his young wife, and maybe even before that. Maybe there were other people besides Mary Caroline, and you, and me, who died at his hands back then."

Emma nodded. "That makes sense. Decent people generally don't turn into the sort of monster he turned out to be."

"Right. So. Say that he's been here for a while in this lifetime. Longer than you and me. Maybe long enough to be the sort of creep who would get your mother pregnant, then have his parents see to it that she was locked away as crazy when she wouldn't abort you." He paused. "See, if it's him, then he's already tried to kill you once. Before you were born. And even if he didn't cause it directly, he was responsible for your mother's death."

"We don't know that. That's just speculation." Emma closed her eyes tight and wrapped her arms around herself, shutting herself away from Mike's words. She could believe that her father was that cold, callous lawyer, that he was someone nearly everyone in town hated, and that he'd done everything in his power to have her mother abort her, and when that had failed, that he'd enlisted his parents to get rid of her anyway.

But she didn't want to think that this was something that was haunting her. That it might have haunted her all the way from a previous life. That it might haunt her into future lives, where he'd keep on finding ways to kill her until she found a way to stop him. Maybe that her mother had died twice already, repeating the same nightmare loop that had encircled Emma. Who might her mother have been back then? A sister? A friend? A parent? One of Ian's patients?

Emma realized she may never know. There were pieces of the puzzle she may never find. She didn't want to think she may be living with the echoes of having cheated on her husband in a previous life—no matter how much he'd deserved it—and that his payback had cost her not just her life, her second husband's life, and her daughter's life long ago, but a mother, a grandmother, and spending her life in a place where she truly belonged in her current life. She didn't want to think that her choices back then were affecting the lives of people she cared about in the present—Gwen and Mike and Cara, and even the florist she'd never had the chance to meet.

She didn't want to think it.

But something about what Mike had said resonated inside her. It *felt* like truth, even if it sounded deeply and ludicrously far-fetched.

Emma stared at the wood tabletop, looking at the grain in the boards that held it together, wondering how long ago that tree had been a sapling, and what events had happened in its lifetime. Wondering whether it had been around long enough for her past life and her present life to be connected through the rings in its wood.

People were so transitory. They were born, they lived their lives in a flash, and then they were gone. But something about them remained. Something about them held on, from time to time and life to life, bringing baggage from past mistakes, stepping into new lives determined to make better choices only to forget the mistakes they'd made the first time.

Only to make them again, and again.

The first thing they had to do, as far as Mike was concerned, was straighten out the mix-up with Drew, and fix things up with Cara. Both Drew and Cara needed to realize that Emma was neither crazy nor dangerous, because someone bad was out there with Emma in his sights, and Mike wanted all the help he could get in keeping her safe. And Mike didn't want to see them at odds with each other, either.

So he talked Emma into getting into his truck and riding over to the doctor's office with him. They got there before closing, but not by much.

Cara raised her eyebrows when she saw them. "He's still really upset, Mike," she said. "He's been seeing patients, but he hasn't been talking to me."

"I've come over to fix things up," Mike said. "Stick both of us in a room and squeeze us in between appointments, would you?"

"We're down to the last three patients for the day,"

she said. "They're in the back and Drew is seeing them, so it won't be much longer. Just sit tight out here, will you?"

Mike looked at Emma. She nodded. "I don't want to be the cause of any hardship between you and your family," she said. "I'm fine with waiting. I'll wait outside if you want, and let you get everything fixed without me in the way."

Cara was looking at Emma with curiosity. "Why did you do those paintings?"

"I have no memory of doing them, Cara. None. You saw them before I did," Emma said. "As far as Mike and I can figure, the house is haunted. I know it sounds crazy, but the only explanation that I have is that it—or someone left behind in it—has been using me."

"That's bizarre."

Emma nodded.

Mike said, "Creepy. But we think the house is trying to tell us something important, that may affect you and Emma and me. That the past is tied to the present somehow, and that the same spirit that moved in Ian to kill Mattie and Mary Caroline and Sam is moving now in someone to kill the three of us."

Cara told Mike, "This theory is going to calm Drew down? Are you crazy? He's already half-convinced the two of you are going to become paranoid, gun-toting lunatics who will kill everyone around you, whether accidentally or on purpose. He's still going to think she's dangerous." She turned to Emma. "He's afraid you've inherited a mental disorder from your mother."

Emma said, "I'm pretty sure there was never anything wrong with my mother. I think her doctor and his nurse and David Halifax's parents were in on the whole thing."

"That's quite a conspiracy."

"It is. But parents will do a lot to smooth out problems for their kids. And I'll bet David Halifax's father was the same sort of shark as he is."

"His folks are still around. It kills them that he has never married, and never given them grandchildren. They're nice people. Kind of sad, and nowhere near the vultures they were when he was the spoiled only child that he was."

"You see them?"

"Drew and I go out to the country club from time to time," Cara said. "David is there frequently. So are his parents, though they're getting on in years. They're older than Drew." She rested her chin in her hands and looked glum. "Though not by much."

"It would help so much if you could find that chart on my mother," Emma said. "If we could just get the names of the people who were involved in my birth— nurses, technicians—someone must have seen something. Someone must have some idea of what happened to her. It just wasn't all that long ago."

Cara said, "Drew and I tore the place apart. Are you wanting to pursue criminal charges or something like that?"

Emma shook her head. "That seems so hopeless. And pointless. I just want to know the truth. It keeps changing on me, and I'm to the point where I can't be sure who I am, because I don't know who my mother was, I don't know who my father was, and I don't know what happened to either of them." She leaned on the counter. "Everyone I met who knew my mother swears that she was never crazy. Never psychotic, never dangerous, and that she wanted me more than anything. If I'm the daughter of that woman, it's a lot different than if I'm the daughter of someone who was in a straitjacket or a padded cell because she was trying to kill her baby, or herself, or random strangers."

Mike said, "You aren't crazy. I don't believe your mother was, either."

Emma gave him a warm smile, then looked at Cara with hope that she would see empathy there. "You know what I mean?"

"Yes," Cara said. "But I don't know that we'll ever find out the truth. That chart is nowhere in this office. Dr. Pendergast must have destroyed it right after Maris's death. But I won't give up. And you shouldn't, either."

Drew stepped into the office, and saw Emma and Mike talking to Cara, and his face turned dark. "I meant it, Mike. I don't want her anywhere around Cara. If you're going to be with her, I don't want you anywhere around Cara, either."

Cara turned to him and said, "Drew, calm down. There are strange things going on in Emma's house. But she's fine. Not crazy, not dangerous."

"You're qualified to make this diagnosis?" he asked.

Mike said, "Drew, I'm not going to put my sister in danger. Or you, or me, or anyone else I care about. You know this about me, right?"

Drew turned and studied him. Some of the anger seemed to drain out of him. "You're about as good as brothers get," he admitted.

"Right. I am. I know this about me."

Drew stood there for a long moment, and Mike saw him change. He stopped being the angry, bitter man he was after Hannah died, and became the warm, happy man he'd evolved into when Cara came into his life. After a moment, he shook his head and laughed. "And just as modest as you've always been." He turned his attention to Emma. "I'm sorry about my outburst, dear. Your house had just finished frightening the everlasting life out of me, some cold thing blew into the back of my neck and walked right through me, and those paintings were disturbing, to say the least. For a while, there, I wasn't myself."

"It's okay. I understand. Inexplicable things happened to me in that house, too. But I want to see if we can find out how I'm doing the paintings," Emma told him. "I'm not doing them while I'm awake, so we're looking into sleepwalking, and . . . other less pleasant possibilities."

"Have you considered moving out of the house? Getting away from whatever it is that's going on there. Maybe going back to Wisconsin, where you were doing wonderful paintings, and where the sort of strangeness that has surrounded your presence in this town would not be an issue? You were safe there."

"As long as she's with me," Mike said, "she's safe here."

"If she could live in your pocket, I'd agree with you," Drew said.

"I'm not leaving," Emma said. "There are too many stories in this place that have me in them. I need to know why."

Drew shook his head. "If people hadn't already died, I'd be more supportive. I understand the rashness of youth, and as a collector, I have to acknowledge that if something happened to you, my investment in your work would show a quick rather than a slow payoff."

He gave her a sad smile. "But I think your best work is ahead of you, and if you won't listen to me as a friend, try understanding where I'm coming from as a connoisseur of fine art who sees something special in you. Move away from the danger and live, Emma."

Mike frowned at him. "I'm happy with a woman for the first time in my life. And you're trying to run her off."

"You could be happy anywhere, Mike. I know you."

Mike stared at him. "Drop it, Drew. Seriously. I don't want to be at odds with you. You're a wonderful man, and you make my sister happy, so let's move on to things we can agree on. Emma is staying, I'm staying with her, and she's going to be fine because I'll see to it that she is." He took a deep breath. "And we're going to find out who her father was, and who killed two women who might have known, and how all of what is happening now ties into the murders of people who lived in Emma's house a long time ago."

"You're bothered by Drew," Mike said.

They'd pulled into her driveway after picking up drive-through to have for a quick supper.

"I'm bothered," Emma agreed. "I don't want to think that someone to whom I could someday be sort of related doesn't want me around."

"Drew has always been a little difficult," Mike told her. They got out of his truck and went inside, walking hand in hand. Emma liked that. Her hand fit into his in wonderful ways, and his touch made her feel happy and needed and at home.

"Difficult how?"

"You have to understand that he suffered a horrible

loss back when he was a lot younger. Twenty years ago.
He had a wife who was beautiful, and charming, and
sweet, and devoted, and he and she and their two kids
were . . . well, according to my folks and other people
who knew them pretty well, they were the perfect
family."

"And then she left him? Or something like that?"

"He would have been able to deal with that. She had
been complaining about the car sounding funny, and she
asked him to look into it. He kept putting it off, and one
day, something went wrong while she was driving to pick
up their kids from school. She swerved into oncoming
traffic just in time to go head-on into an eighteen-
wheeler. That was it for her."

"God." Emma was horrified.

"It was all anyone could talk about for ages. According to my folks, Drew buried himself in a bottle for a
year or three, and then, when he finally sobered up, he
buried himself in his work. His kids grew up on their
own, and blamed him for their mother's death—as
much as he blamed himself, I guess. He was angry, bitter, obsessed with his work and nothing else. They had
a lot of problems, and when they were old enough, they
took off. One of them lives in California, at least the last
anyone heard, and the other one is in a Buddhist
monastery in India, or someplace like that. Neither of
them will have anything to do with him. They don't acknowledge that he's alive, and on his part, he returns the
favor."

Emma frowned. "That's so sad. They could have
helped each other and meant so much to each other."

"Could have. Didn't," Mike said. "After Hannah's
death, Drew didn't even look at other women. His job

was his whole life, and he was sort of an enraged saint about it. He donated his time, he did the free clinics, he was the doctor the hospital would call if they couldn't get anyone else, because he would always come in. He'd cover for anyone."

"A saint."

"Yeah. A miserable man who devoted his life to the good of others."

They sat at the table, and Emma spread out their fast food fare—fried chicken, potatoes and gravy, coleslaw and corn on the cob. "No. That wouldn't be the way to live." She dished food out onto two plates, and passed one to Mike. "So then Cara came into his life."

"She was like a stealth fighter working its way below the radar. She got him to hire her; my parents were still friends with him, even if they almost never saw him." Mike took a bite.

"Cara," Emma reminded him.

"Right. Cara. She organized his files, she improved his payments received from patients and got him on a pretty solvent footing. And then she started making sure that the people who had been using him as their automatic fallback for almost fifteen years didn't do that anymore. He started having a little personal time. She claimed all of it."

"And the fact that she's young enough to be his daughter—"

"Granddaughter, almost."

"Granddaughter, then."

"She didn't care. She loved him. He'd saved her life when she was a kid, and she was determined to give him a life in return. But he still has his prickly moments, and he still has some reclusive habits that drive her nuts."

"Like . . . ?"

"He still lives in the same house he and his first wife lived in. He won't let her change any of the furniture, or redecorate. No new curtains, no new colors on the wall. Cara says it's like living in a museum. He has a study that he keeps locked. He will not let anyone in it. Ever. He says it was his private place when he and his first wife and their kids lived there, and it is still his private place. He built on a hobby room for her, and he doesn't go in that, but Cara never actually wanted a hobby room."

"She wanted Drew to be her hobby."

Mike raised an eyebrow. "That's one way of putting it. I'd never thought of it that way, but . . . yes. She wanted to make her life around him, and he still has big parts of it that he won't share."

"That can't be much fun."

"I doubt that it is. I know she wanted to have kids, too, and he's not willing to consider that at all. I can't really blame him. He's old. But . . . she isn't."

Emma sighed. "Ow."

"It isn't a perfect relationship. They love each other, though, and she truly is happy being with him. So I'm happy for her."

They changed the subject and chatted about other things while they were finishing their food. And they washed and dried the plates together, which Emma found hilarious.

And then they were done, with the empty house all around them, and the mysteries in it hanging over them.

Emma said, "We should look through the box again. Maybe we can find something in it that will help us figure out what we should do next."

Mike shrugged. "There are other options. The Benina newspaper closed years ago, but they donated their morgue to the library. The old newspapers might have something about the Barnett house. Seems they would if Ian Barnett's brother and wife went missing. I think all those papers are on microfiche now. I think Gwen wanted to scan the whole archive digitally, but she never got around to it."

"But the library is a crime scene until the police figure out if anything in the library is connected to her death."

"If we haven't found something else before then, we'll go when it isn't."

Emma dragged him with her to the top of the stairs. "You think the little girl died in here?" she asked as they stood outside the bedroom door.

"I don't know," Mike said. "I really would rather not have had to think about that as I was walking in the door. Really."

Emma smiled. Walking in, though, she felt the smile freeze. The room sucked the air out of her lungs, and left her cold and shivering, and made her heart race and her skin crawl. She went to the closet by sheer force of will and dragged the box out of it, and turned to find Mike standing in the center of the room, his body rigid, tears rolling down his cheeks, and an expression of anguish on his face.

"Mike?"

He didn't respond to her. She hurried past him, put the box in the hallway, and then went back and grabbed him and half led, half dragged him out.

"Don't ever make me go back in there," he told her when the two of them were downstairs again.

"What happened?"

"I could hear her screaming. And begging someone not to hurt her. And then—" He shook his head. "If the things we hear in this house have anything to do with what actually happened here, then yes. Mary Caroline was murdered in that room."

Emma closed her eyes. "That could make me not want to live here. Knowing that. It's the only place in the house that feels terrifying."

"Have you been in the carriage house yet?"

"No," Emma told him. "I haven't had any reason to go in there."

"How about to park your truck?"

"I'd rather have it close to the house."

"Instead of out of the weather."

Emma raised an eyebrow at him. "Have you seen my truck?"

"Point taken. Weather is not really an issue. But, you own the carriage house. Aren't you curious about what's in there?"

She studied him. "I'd have to say . . . not really. I look at it, and I don't want to go in there."

"I think it's because that's where Ian Barnett killed Mattie."

"And I'm Mattie reincarnated."

"You're at least sensitive to her spirit and what she's doing in the house."

"Right. I think I'd rather think that."

"So would I," Mike agreed.

Emma started pulling out the items from the box. She set the lockbox on the table, and beside it the paper money and the gold. And the uniform. And the shoes.

"What are you doing," Mike asked.

"I thought, if we could get impressions from being in a room, maybe we could get impressions from holding these objects. Maybe we could figure out why Ian boarded them up in the wall along with the diary."

"Where is that, by the way?"

"My dresser drawer."

"Could you go get it?"

"Sure." She got up to go after it, and while she was heading up the steps, Mike went back to the room beneath the stairs and started dragging her paintings out.

He set them up around the counters, surprised again by how gripping they were, and how completely they disturbed and frightened him.

When Emma came back into the kitchen, she jumped. "You should have warned me," she told him. "I wasn't prepared to see those things again."

He said, "I'm sorry. I just thought we could compare them to the pictures in the box."

They pulled out the photographs, and looked at each one. "Definitely Sam," Emma said, pointing to the man in uniform fighting with the other man in one of the paintings.

"And probably Ian," Mike said, pointing to the other one, and then pulling the portrait of Ian beside it.

"Do you think he looks like David Halifax?" Emma asked out of the blue.

"You mean the painting of Ian? Not much. But then, I don't think that Cara looks much like Mary Caroline. Or that you look like Mattie."

"But you look a lot like Sam."

"Maybe that's coincidence."

"Would I look like Mattie if I were blond?"

Mike studied her for a moment. He picked up the

picture, and frowned, and said, "Pull your hair back from your face."

Emma caught it in her hands and pulled it back.

"The bangs, too. She had the little curly things around her face, but nothing on her forehead."

Emma smoothed her bangs back with her other hand.

Mike moved closer to her, holding the photograph, frowning. "Look right at me. And don't smile even a little bit."

Emma tried to duplicate the stiff, unsmiling expression that people in those daguerreotypes always ended up with. She tried, at the same time, to read Mike's expression.

"Not much," he said at last. "You both have faces, you know? Eyes, ears, mouths, noses in pretty much the usual places. But—" He shook his head. "That's about the only resemblance."

He looked at the picture of Mary Caroline again. "You mind if I take this one over to my parents' house tomorrow, to see if I can compare it to pictures of Cara when she was a kid?"

"I don't mind," Emma told him.

"Thanks. Could I take the portrait of the man who's probably Ian, too? I want to have my folks look at it. I don't know if they'll think it looks like David Halifax, but it's a younger version of whoever it is. They'd be a lot more likely to see similarities, if any exist."

Emma shrugged. "That's fine. I don't know what the point is, though. If I don't look like Mattie, and Cara doesn't look like Mary Caroline, what point is there in seeing if Ian looks like David Halifax?"

Mike was looking at the Ian portrait. "I don't know. Maybe it's just men who resemble themselves from life to life."

"Maybe," Emma said, "we aren't who we think we all are. Maybe I look like a female version of Ian. Maybe Cara looks like Mattie. Maybe David Halifax is really Mary Caroline." She made a face. "We're all just guessing, and the whole thing doesn't make sense. The house should help us out."

Mike turned from studying her paintings to stare at her. "The . . . what?"

"The house should help us out." She looked around at the walls, and up at the ceiling. "You've been calling to me since I was a kid," she said. "You have been with me since I can remember. You wanted me here. So. You should show me who is who. You should give me a sign—who is Ian? Who is the danger to the rest of us?"

Mike, she realized, was looking nervous. "Don't do that," he said.

She turned back to him. Suddenly, though she couldn't begin to explain why, she was angry. "Why not? This house has been haunting me since I was five years old. Five. You cannot imagine what it's like to feel pulled in two directions all the time. To dream people who know you, though you've never met them. To see the eyes of the dead watching your every move, and not understand what you're seeing. Or why." She felt her body tightening, her hands clenching into fists, her face flushing. "You aren't the one who's had someone or something moving you around like a toy, using your body to create messages so vague no one can under- stand them." Her voice was getting louder. "Something horrible happened here? Right. I get it. We all get it. But what does it mean to me, what does it mean to any of us? What are we supposed to do about it?" She was, she realized, shouting. She didn't stop herself. She felt like

she was a runaway train, all holds gone, nothing but relentless gravity and a steep hill and some awful crash at
the end of it ahead of her.

"I want to know what all of this means!" She
screamed. "The house can tell me things. So let the
damned house tell me. Let it tell me who is the danger.
Let it tell me what I'm supposed to do about it. I'm here.
I came," she screamed at the ceiling, no longer making
a pretense of talking to Mike. The tears were pouring
down her cheeks. "I'm here, and you have something
that I need to do for you. Or something that I need to fix.
What is it? What IS it? Show me, damn you. *SHOW
ME!*"

Mike wrapped his arms around her and pulled her to
his chest. She fought against him, but he held her
tightly, whispering, "Breathe. Calm down. It will be
okay," into her hair, until at last she stopped shaking,
and her body relaxed. "Don't talk to the house, sweetheart," he told her. "You don't know which of them
might be listening."

She pressed her face to his chest and inhaled the scent
of him. Lightly musky, soapy, masculine, clean. He was
warm. Real. With her.

He would keep her safe.

Upstairs, footsteps moved along the hallway, into the
spare bedroom. Then out of the spare bedroom, and
down the stairs. She shuddered.

"Don't talk to the house," he whispered again.

"No," she told him. "I won't. Not anymore."

When she closed her own eyes, she could feel other
eyes open inside her. The eyes of the dead, for so long
nameless, but bound to her across miles and time. She'd

felt them watching her. She'd heard their whispers in her sleep. She let them into her, and they had touched her.

"My other paintings," she said, and pushed away from Mike.

"What?"

"Come on. I want to see something, and I want you to come with me."

He followed her down across the hall, into her workroom. It was, she noticed, a much less friendly place in the dark. She worked there only in the daytime—evenings had always been her downtime, and she'd made no exception when she moved to Benina. It had never occurred to her, therefore, that her studio felt different after dark. It felt . . . occupied.

She thought, *Maybe Drew Jackson was right. Maybe I do need to get out of this house.*

Or maybe she needed to have a ghostbuster go through the place and do a spiritual cleansing. Or . . . maybe she just needed to not talk to it.

She got into her storage closet, and pulled out her printed portfolio.

"Here are my prints of work that I've sold. The originals are all either in private collections or in little art museums—places that would let me donate work—or with the art dealer who sells them for me." She dragged it back out to the kitchen—a huge, heavy leatherette case filled with full-scale reproductions of paintings she'd done since she turned pro.

She spread out the portfolio in the middle of the kitchen floor. And then she started flipping through pictures, looking at each painting as she did. She pointed out to Mike the places where she'd hidden the bits and pieces of the house she would one day buy.

She also started pointing out faces to him.

"Mike, look at this," she said, and pointed to a picture of a woman who was Cara's blond double.

She showed him the other pictures she'd done of Sam, and some of them looked more like Mike than like Sam.

She froze. "Oh, God," she said.

He followed her gaze, and then got down on his hands and knees. "Holy hell, Emma, when did you paint that?"

She pointed out the little glyph at the bottom that included her signature, her logo, and the date. "Two thousand," she said.

"That's Gwen."

"The librarian. I know."

"You have her surrounded by books, even though she's next to a barbarian."

"It was the commission. The publisher told me what to paint. I just—painted."

"But it's Gwen. In some sort of library."

"I know."

"How is she tied in to this?"

"I don't know," Emma said. "I don't understand how any of this is connected to any of the rest of it, but it seems like most of my paintings have been visited by the dead."

"She wasn't dead when you painted it."

"No. But whoever she had been in an earlier life was."

Mike sat back. "Start over from the beginning. I want to see every single painting you have in there. And I want to take a few pictures. Just of details. Of the faces, of the house, of things that I might recognize later, or that Cara might, or that my folks might."

"Take pictures?"

"My cell phone has a pretty good camera," he said. "And my flash card is almost empty." He shrugged. "All the fancy ring tones just sound stupid to me, so I only use the flash card to store photos."

"Okay," Emma told him. "Take whatever you need."

She slowly flipped from page to page, watching what he ignored and what caught his attention. She didn't have any idea why he took some of the pictures he did, but she was intrigued. He seemed worried. Scared. But he wasn't giving much away, and he certainly wasn't saying anything.

"Are you all right?" she asked him.

"This is the scariest thing I've ever been witness to in my entire life," he told her. "And if I could, I'd take you away from this and make it go away." He kept snapping pictures as she turned pages. "But this has been with you longer than . . . well. And it's with me, too. And Cara. We have to see it through, because it isn't going to be done with us until we do."

He paused, and lifted his face to look at her. "I hope it's done with us after that."

She thought about that for a moment. "Yes," she said. "I don't want to do this again."

Mike had no intention of telling her what he thought he was seeing in her paintings. He didn't see anyone who looked like the David Halifax he knew, or had known. He might have been mistaken, so he took a few pictures of random men from Emma's paintings, just so

that he could show them to his folks and get their opin-
ions.

He'd had a bad minute, though, when he'd realized
that with her hair pulled back, and with blond hair and
light eyes and a paler complexion, Emma and Mattie
could have been the same woman.

It was when he made that discovery that he also realized that the pictures of Mary Caroline resembled Cara
when she was little. Only Cara had never sat still, and
she'd never been solemn. That made it hard for him to
be sure.

He didn't know why he didn't want to confirm that
Emma looked like Mattie, at least until he caught the portrait of Ian out of the corner of his eye, and realized that it
bore more than a passing resemblance to Drew Jackson.

Which was ludicrous, of course. Emma had told him
her sources had been very clear that Maris Kessler had
fallen in love with a college boy. Drew Jackson had
been a practicing doctor when Maris got pregnant. He
had a wife and Mike was pretty sure he had already had
two kids.

Drew's son wouldn't have been old enough to be
Maris's college boy. He might have been in her grade,
or a few years behind her.

Mike tried to remember if he'd ever seen a picture of
Jack Jackson. He'd been over at Drew's and Cara's
place a zillion times, and Drew still had a few pictures
of his dead wife around. The pictures of the kids,
though, had gone away after they'd marched out of his
life, shouting epithets. Mike hadn't exactly been around
for that, either. But he'd heard the stories from his parents, who sometimes worried about Cara being married
to such an old man, and one who had lost so much.

He couldn't make sense of it. But . . . maybe he didn't need to. Emma had painted a woman who looked like Gwen, and Gwen's role in her life had been to give her some useful information. And then to get killed.

Maybe the pictures were some channeled image of Drew. Drew's role could be something similar to Gwen's. He had the connections that might let him find out the truth about Emma's mother, if only he could figure out where to look or whom to ask for the information. In which case, he might be in as much danger as Emma. Or Cara. Or Mike himself.

Or he could have been Ian in a past life, and be just as much of a killer in this one.

"You've gone away," Emma told him.

"I'm tired," he lied. "I'm worried about you, and this has been one really stressful day. If I could talk you into going to bed, I'd be the happiest man ever."

She looked over at him and smiled. "I could be convinced."

"Oh," he groaned. "You want . . . more than sleep? I don't know about that."

But he scooped her into his arms and held her close. He wanted her, and the more he thought about her naked in the bed, the more he wanted her. He didn't intend to fall asleep afterward, but . . . he was in the mood for a little fun. A little passion and craziness and lust and . . . love.

Afterward, he watched her sleeping. She was beautiful, lying there with her face bathed in innocence. Her hair spread around her like a fan, dark and glossy against the white sheets. He admired the curve of her hip and the sweet fullness of her breast. He stroked

her, wondering at how right the two of them felt together. How magical she was, how complete and how
forever the two of them were when he was inside her,
when she was moving against him.

He had never thought love at first sight had any
meaning. He'd written it off as the excuses people in
shallow relationships made for going to bed on the first
date. He thought even claiming such a thing was cheap.

And there he was, sitting on the side of the bed with
a woman he had fallen in love with the first time he laid
eyes on her.

He didn't even feel apologetic. "I knew you for at
least a hundred and fifty years," he told her. "That's
long enough to wait." She made a little sound in the
back of her throat and slid back, against him. She was
asleep, but not yet deeply asleep.

He ran his hand along her rib cage, down the curve of
her waist, over her hip and the round, firm flesh of her
buttock. He would love her forever, he thought. He
would know her anywhere, any-when. His heart would
always bring him to her, and her to him. They would
find each other.

If they got their lives right this time.

Maybe that was the stakes of this thing they were
caught up in. Maybe if they didn't solve this puzzle of
their lives, and if they didn't resolve the trouble between them and Ian, they would not get to be together
again. They'd die here, maybe soon, and then they
would just not see each other again.

Or maybe they would be destined to be murdered by
Ian time and again until they stopped him.

He wondered if they had been through a second life
together since the Civil War. He didn't think there had

been other chances for them. He didn't have any memories of other times in between. He caught images of
the house, of her in it, of her dead in the carriage house.
He could hear the voices and the music in the place, the
echoes that reverberated after all that time. He'd always
had a bad feeling about the Barnett house, and at the
same time, he'd always felt tied to it, though he hadn't
identified that connected feeling until Emma came into
his life in the flesh.

He couldn't deny that he had known her the moment
he first saw her, even if he hadn't immediately understood what she meant to him and his life.

He wanted to get this right.

He covered her and tucked a pillow behind her back
to take his place until he finished doing what he needed
to do. He got up and put on clothes and went down to
the kitchen, where he sat staring at all those paintings
she'd done. He looked at the ones that looked a lot like
a young Drew.

Emma had always painted him as the villain.

Why hadn't he come back in this lifetime as her husband? That part puzzled Mike. If Drew was Ian, then
why were things so messed up? Why was he Cara's husband? What relationship, aside from being connected to
Mike through Cara, did Drew have with Emma?

He'd met her in Wisconsin, at an art show.

Mike considered that for a while. It had seemed one
of those amazing small-world coincidences when he'd
first found out about it, and then briefly it had seemed
like a cover for an affair between Drew and Emma. But
the relationship between them was clearly platonic. He
could see nothing at all between them that was more
than artist/client.

He thought about it some more.

Drew had met Emma in Wisconsin. Drew did from time to time go to medical conferences. He did from time to time buy art. Mike tried to remember a time when he'd gone to a medical conference, though, and come back with art, other than the time he'd taken off for Wisconsin. He couldn't think of any.

Cara would know, of course. Cara did all the bills and finances for them. She'd be able to track any expenditures to dates. She was a careful, organized bookkeeper, and she made sure the business part of Drew's medical practice and the bill portion of their lives stayed spotless. Drew, according to Cara, was horrible about keeping track of money.

He looked at the time. Pretty late to call—just a little before midnight. But Cara sometimes stayed up late.

He went to Emma's phone and dialed.

Cara didn't answer, though. Drew did, on the first ring.

"What the hell, calling at this hour, who is this and what the fuck do you think you want, you stupid bastard? You think just because you're awake at this hour that other people are, too? Or are you so drunk you can't see the numbers?"

Mike quietly hung up the phone.

Drew had been drunk. Very drunk. Mike had heard him like that only once or twice before, and the circumstances had never been good.

He considered sending a text message to Cara, but something about Drew's mood made him think that it would be a bad idea if the message, however benign, was intercepted. Something was wrong over there. He couldn't be certain that it involved Cara. Sometimes, after all, she went to bed early. He certainly didn't see Drew getting drunk in front of her.

He frowned.

He was going to have to go see her the next day. He had to show her what he'd discovered, and he needed to have her opinion on his questions about Drew and his association with their, well, *problem* for lack of a better word. And he wanted her to have a good look at the pictures he'd taken of Emma's paintings. He didn't want to spook Cara, but he needed to know if she saw the similarities he did, or if she thought he was making something out of nothing.

He couldn't do anything about it at the moment, though.

So he put everything back the way Emma had left it, and went upstairs and crawled into bed with her. He was grateful for her warmth, and her solidness, for her presence in his life. He was grateful that they had managed to find each other. He wanted to do anything he could to make sure they never lost each other again. It would be hell to have her slip out of his reach.

He wondered, as he fell asleep, if the people who spent their lives fruitlessly looking for the person they were just right for, the person who fulfilled them, were people who had once had something wonderful—in an earlier life—and had screwed it up so badly that their soul mate vanished to another part of the world, or another time, forever out of their reach.

He had to make sure he didn't screw this up, he thought. It was a second chance. He didn't doubt that for an instant. And damned near nobody got second chances.

*   *   *

The house had been listening. Only moments after Mike fell into a deep sleep—far deeper than was natural—Emma arose. Her eyes were still nearly closed, and she was essentially asleep. Nevertheless, she made her way down the hall, past the bedroom at the top of the stairs from which plaintive, weakening cries emanated, and down the tricky curving staircase, and down the long hall to her studio.

With jerky movements, she put another canvas on her easel, and squeezed paints onto a palette, and began applying them with painting knives, quickly, furiously.

The house was answering the question she'd thrown at it, giving her a picture unlike anything she could have anticipated. It was, unlike the previous pictures she had done under the influence of the dead, a picture from the relatively recent past.

It would be waiting on the easel for her in the morning.

She would not find it until it was too late.

Chapter 11

"Hey, gorgeous. Wake up and smell the coffee."

Emma opened her eyes. Mike was standing beside the bed, fully dressed, holding a plate of remarkably good-smelling food and a big cup of coffee. He hadn't found her bed tray—but she couldn't blame him. She had it hidden in the back of a kitchen cupboard because when she unpacked, she hadn't actually planned on using it.

"You're awake," she groaned.

"Is that any way to greet breakfast beside the bed?" He pulled her nightstand forward, cleared off everything she had on it, and put down pancakes, bacon, hash browns, a big glass of orange juice, and an enormous cup of coffee.

She said, "I don't have any pancake mix."

Mike laughed. "That's okay. I don't know how to make pancakes." He shrugged. "I went out. Got myself a couple of ham biscuits and a cup of coffee, and got you a few other things. I have more ham biscuits if you want them."

"This is more than I'll eat in a week." She grinned. "You did a great job of making it look like not fast food."

"It's one of my skills." He sat on the edge of the bed. "I can make Chinese takeout and just about anything else look homemade, too." He sighed. "It was something I did to impress dates. It was cheap of me. Very cheap."

Emma laughed. "I can't imagine you doing that."

"Women love men who cook. I don't cook. But I wanted to be loved—at least a little."

Emma did not pursue that line of thought.

She yawned, and tried to stretch. Every muscle in her body protested. "Why am I so tired?"

"I wore you out," he said, grinning at her.

"You sure I wasn't sleep painting again?"

"Certain. I'm a light sleeper. If you'd gotten up, you'd have woken me. You just haven't caught up with all the sleep you've missed yet."

"That makes perfect sense." She grinned at him and ate breakfast, which was about as mediocre as fast food got, and drank the coffee, which was excellent, and she was still exhausted when she was done.

He said, "I have a couple things I need to do today. I've already got my guys going on one job, but I have to check out another one. I have my cell phone with me. Call me or message me if you need me, and I'll get here as quickly as I can."

She leaned back in the bed. "Don't worry about me," she told him. "I'm going to sleep for a while. I'm too tired to do anything useful, or functional. I'll call you when I wake up, just to let you know everything is okay."

He kissed her. "Sounds perfect. Get some rest, and I'll wear you out again when I get back. And maybe afterward, we can run into Greenville and I can take you to a great restaurant I know there."

"I love you," she told him.

He paused, looking a little surprised. "I love you, too."

She got up long enough to wrap a robe around herself and walk him to the door. They hugged and kissed good-bye, and she went back up the stairs. She left the robe on; she always felt strange sleeping with nothing on, but she didn't want to take the time to put on pajamas. She went back to bed, and within minutes was soundly asleep.

Mike had gone out to the site and made sure his men were working. But after that, he called Cara. "I need to talk to you. Something's . . . wrong."

"I know," Cara said. "I told Drew I was sick, and I stayed home today. You need to get over here."

In his stomach, something twisted horribly. "How was Drew this morning?" he asked.

"In a foul mood. He had a headache, but he was determined to go in and work. He acts like this around the anniversary of Hannah's death, but this isn't anywhere near the time she died. I don't know what his problem is."

"He was shit-faced drunk last night," Mike told her. "I called to talk to you, and he answered the phone, and chewed my ass out for calling, but his words were slurred and he was thoroughly messed up."

"Drunk. That's not good."

"I didn't think so either. I'll be there in five," Mike told her.

"Park in back. If the neighbors are watching the place, or if Drew drives by for some reason, I don't want your truck to be easy to spot."

"Will do."

Cara met him at the back door. The first thing Mike noticed about her was that her eyes were swollen and her nose was red. She'd been crying, something she rarely did. And not that he knew of since she and Drew got married.

"What's the matter?" he asked her.

"You know about Drew's room."

"Of course."

"I went into it after he left for the hospital this morning."

Mike was stunned. Cara had been religious about not prying into the parts of Drew's life that he wanted to keep to himself. She'd found out that he was terribly sensitive about his dead wife and his absent children, so she kept away from those subjects. She discovered that he needed time to himself most nights, so she found other things to do during those times. She didn't try to invite herself along on his medical convention trips, though Mike knew she had once hired a detective. She'd found something odd in his luggage, but she never would tell Mike what. Drew's explanation had matched the detective's report, which Mike had seen. The detective had found Drew to be the dedicated, if difficult, medical saint she'd always believed him to be. The report had reassured Mike, too.

So for her to go into his study without his invitation or permission or knowledge suggested that something terrible had gone wrong.

"Why?"

"Because I stopped believing him. He told me he was worried about Emma doing something to hurt me, and that was why he didn't want me to have anything more to do with her. But his eyes were lying to me, Mike. I saw his face, and as good as he's been ever since we got together at convincing me that he was telling me the truth, this time I just didn't believe him."

"I can understand that. But we came in yesterday and patched things up."

"No," Cara said. "You thought you did. And I thought you did. But when we got home last night, Drew told me that I wasn't to have anything more to do with Emma—that I was to make polite excuses, or be busy, or whatever it took, but that he never wanted me to be alone with her again."

Mike couldn't believe what he was hearing.

"And me?"

"He said you'd get over her. Or she'd go back where she came from. Or she'd get herself into the same sort of trouble she got Gwen and Aileen into—but that if she did, at least I wouldn't be involved. At least I wouldn't get hurt."

"And you told him . . ."

"I lied right back to him," Cara said. "I said whatever he wanted was fine with me, and that I knew he was looking out for my best interests, and . . . I don't remember everything I said, but I convinced him that I wouldn't have anything else to do with her."

"And then you went into his study this morning after he went to work, and you . . . found something?"

"I found a lot of somethings."

Cara grabbed his arm and led him through the house to Drew's office.

"The first thing I found was this," she said, and opened a photograph album that started with pictures of a little girl, and followed her through youth into her teen years, and then into young adulthood. Mike was staring at Emma. The album contained outdoor pictures that were clearly taken with a telephoto lens, and that had been taken with the subject unaware. It held newspaper clippings of Emma's placement in various class award programs, and her high school art awards, and a handful of classroom pictures, which gave way to more personal pictures of her attending college, sitting with a young man (who had a large X scratched through him), painting on an easel, walking across a well-manicured green while talking with evident animation to another young woman.

"What is this?"

Cara pulled a folded sheet of paper out of a space between the binding and the endpaper of the album. She handed it to him.

It was a birth certificate. Baby Girl, 7 lbs, 1 oz, to Maris Kessler, age 16, mother, and Andrew Jackson, age 40, father. Signed by Dr. Pendergast. Witnessed by the nurse who had handed Emma to her adoptive parents.

"Oh, my God," Mike said. "Drew's her father?"

"Apparently he has been, at least from a distance, a fairly interested father. He hired a detective to check out the young man to whom she was engaged, and paid the same young man a lot of money to go away. He paid a gallery to show her first paintings, and bought some of them himself. He didn't have to do this for any of her later work . . . I'm guessing it got better."

"It was all good," Mike said. "There's some of it,

though, that could use a bit of explaining." He pulled out his cell phone and keyed through to the picture files. He showed her the close-ups he'd taken of various faces. "You have to realize that she painted all of these years before she came here for the first time."

"That's Gwen," Emma said.

"Looks like her. How about this one?" He showed her the face of a little girl.

"That looks a lot like I did when I was that age, doesn't it?"

"From the pictures I've seen of you at that age, yes." He showed her a few more of the relatively innocuous ones. She was as unnerved as he had been.

Then he showed her the pictures that he thought looked like Drew.

Cara's response was sharp and shocked. "Oh, my God," she said. "That's Drew. Oh, Mike, that's a picture of Drew."

"There were a lot more of them. They were all pictures of villains. You were never pictured as a villain, and neither was I. But every picture she ever painted that had his face in it had him as some menacing nightmare figure. Wielding a knife, or a sword, or strangling someone, or standing like the vanquishing barbarian with his foot on the throat of some innocent young woman."

"He never noticed that in her work?"

"She said these were commissioned book covers, and generally she sold the original to the author of the book following making posters and other things with it."

"So he never saw the ones that had him on them."

Mike said, "As closely as it looks like he's followed her career, he probably did. But when the pictures are small, it's hard to make out the details of the faces. They're much clearer at full size." Mike paused. "Or maybe he did recognize them, but maybe seeing you paint people he knew you'd never met scared him enough that he watched you more closely."

Cara said, "Maybe. I wish I could tell you that his strange little baby book on Emma was the only thing I found."

Mike sat down on the arm of the couch Drew had in his study. "Tell me," he said.

"Maris Kessler's chart was in here. So was her mother's. I haven't had a chance to go through either of them, but I did find a copy of the two new birth certificates that were done for Emma. On one, she was born dead. On the other, the father is listed as unknown. The signature on the "born dead" one says Dr. Pendergast, but it doesn't match his real signature. The other signature, the one with "father unknown," is Drew's.

"How in the world did he get Dr. Pendergast to go along with not telling anyone that Maris's baby had lived?"

"I'm guessing blackmail," Maris said. "But we're going to need to go through his office for more information before we can be sure."

"Couldn't we just call the police?"

"Not yet," Cara said. "We're definitely calling them, but I have a strong suspicion that Drew killed Maris. And maybe her mother."

"Why?"

Cara looked at him like he'd lost his mind. "Even in the late seventies, being a married, professional father of two who fathered a baby with an underage girl would not have been good for his career. And above everything else, Drew has always put his career first. He has spent his whole life being a doctor. It wouldn't have worked out too well for him to have lost his wife and his children by divorce, and ended up in prison for statutory rape. It's hard to be a member of the AMA if you're a convicted felon in prison. They still don't think too highly of that."

"No," Mike agreed. "I guess they don't."

Cara looked sick, and scared, and betrayed. And angry. Deeply, deeply angry. "So help me look. I'm not sure what we're looking for, but whatever it is, we need to find it soon."

"You expecting him back?"

"Not for hours," Cara said. "Half the patients in the hospital are his today. Rounds are going to take him forever, and then he has to go into the office. And since I'm not there to keep everything organized, Nancine is going to be stuck doing everything herself, and you know Nancine; everything will take twice as long as it usually does, and half of that will have to be done twice."

"Then why are we hurrying?"

"Because I have to get away from here. Him. I thought I knew him. I thought I mattered to him. And everything I based my life on has turned out to be a lie. As soon as I find out everything I need to know, I'm calling the police and then I'm packing a bag and getting the hell out of here."

Mike looked at her, and then looked at the house. It was the same as it had been the day Drew's wife died. The same as it had been when his kids had marched out the front door and never looked back.

"Good plan," he said softly.

"I'm going to stay at your place until I can find one of my own."

"Really?" Mike said, and raised his eyebrows. "Do I have any say in this?"

"You're moving in with Emma, right?" Cara said, and he could hear the strain in her voice. "I'll use your place until I figure out where else I can go." She managed a weak smile. That smile about broke Mike's heart.

He started with the bookshelves, taking down each book, looking into it to make sure it held no surprises, and then moving on to the next. Cara opened his filing cabinet, and starting at the bottom and the back, began working her way forward and up.

The process seemed to take forever. Drew had a lot of books, and they were mostly medical texts, some from earlier centuries, some current. They were, along with an eclectic mix of other books, filed alphabetically by author, not grouped by subject matter, so there was no real coherence to the system. Occasionally Mike would run through a cluster of novels, invariably a collection by the same author. Most of these were well thumbed. Drew had a penchant for crime thrillers, something that Mike, in all the years he'd known Drew, had never suspected.

He kept going.

Cara got lucky first.

"Oh, Mike. Oh, God, Mike, he killed Hannah."

Mike turned to stare at her. "He *what*?"

"He killed Hannah. He gave her a combination of drugs that were designed to lower her blood pressure dangerously, and then he sent her out in the car."

"How do you know this?"

"He filed his diaries. I found the date that his wife

died. And right in here, he says that she had started asking too many questions about Maris Kessler. Someone apparently talked to her about his involvement in the girl's death, or . . . something. I'm not sure what set him off. But he writes in here that he's tried to make the dose so heavy that when she goes out to pick up the kids from school, she'll have an accident on the way. He doesn't want her to have the kids in the car when things go wrong." Cara looked up from her reading and said, "He calls them 'acceptable losses, if it comes to that,' though."

Mike felt his blood chilling in his veins.

"This is your husband? And the man who has been taking care of half of this town for the last thirty-five years?"

Cara said, "Mike, I'm so scared. What else has he done?"

"I don't know. But you have enough now that we can call the police."

She nodded. She picked up the phone and dialed. Mike went back to the bookshelves, but this time he didn't just go through every book. His gut was telling him there was something in those stacks he needed to see.

He checked in the Ks. For Kessler. Then he went to the Ms.

One big book, leather bound but with no writing on the spine, caught his attention. He pulled it out, noticing that the pages did not lie evenly against each other. He riffled through carefully, and ran across photos he wished he'd never seen. The girl in them looked a lot like Emma. He would have recognized them as mother and daughter, he thought. She was pretty, dark haired, dark eyed. She had the feathered, blow-dried Princess

Di hair of the era, and in the first picture, she was wearing a T-shirt, shorts, and sneakers. She looked terribly young. Thin, fragile, a child out of her depth. Her smile in the photo was tenuous and heartbreaking.

The next pictures, though, were far worse. They were taken through some sort of peephole, and they showed Drew, nearly forty, seducing a child for the camera. The camera showed the child's initial resistance. Fear. She had, after all, been a good girl, raised right, and it was evident that as much as she admired Jackson, she didn't want to take her clothes off, and she was uncomfortable with the way he was touching her. The next shots showed him giving her alcohol, getting her drunk, and finally undressing her, and raping her.

The cameraman moved out from behind his peephole for the last bit. The girl was by that point unconscious, so he took the sort of shots that wouldn't have been acceptable in any but the hardest-core porn. And then he posed for a few himself, and Mike discovered the second member of the duo who had buried this secret for a quarter of a century. The other grinning child rapist.

David Halifax. Drew's cousin. Not more than twenty at the time.

Mike had to look away for a moment. He felt sick. He wondered if, along with the series of still photos, Drew Jackson had a couple of VCR cassettes hidden away so that he could watch the whole thing happening again, and listen. He wondered what other horrors the bastard had hidden away.

When he got his stomach under control and managed to look back at the book, he got sicker. Because somehow Jackson and Halifax had continued their photo sessions with the girl through much of her pregnancy.

Emma said she'd heard her mother was deeply in love with her father, and the pictures seemed to bear that out. Even in late pregnancy, even when he was doing things to her that made Mike so queasy he had to sit down, her expressions toward him remained almost worshipful.

Then, however, something must have changed, because the final series of pictures were of her in a straitjacket in a padded room. And there was hatred in her eyes.

The last picture was of her dead body, laid out on an autopsy table.

Mike closed the book and stood there with tears running down his cheeks, with his hands clenched into fists. He wanted to kill Jackson. He wanted to grab him by the neck and strangle him, or rip him apart piece by piece. For Cara. For Emma. For Maris.

Cara said, "The police are here." And then apparently she caught a glimpse of him, because she said, "Mike? What's wrong."

"Go pack," he told her. His voice sounded like death. "Do it as fast as you can. You're never coming back here. Trust me. You don't want to."

Cara stared at him a moment longer, then went to answer the bell.

Dris Cavanaugh walked in, followed by Amos Hill in his uniform, and their presence triggered something in Mike. He leaned over in a corner and puked out his guts into the philodendron.

He pushed the book at Dris and said, "Start here. Maris Kessler."

And then he staggered out to the living room to sit down.

The phone rang. In the distance, almost a world away,

he heard Cara answer it. He didn't intentionally follow the conversation, but when he heard her say, "What do you mean he never came in?" his blood froze.

He stood up, and turned toward her.

"Drew never went in to the hospital," she said. "He never showed up at the office."

Mike would have fainted, but he knew where Drew was. If he wasn't there already, he would be headed there soon. He would be going out to the Barnett place, and he was going to kill Emma.

She was asleep. She was helpless. She wouldn't know she couldn't trust him; she would think everything was all right.

He forced himself to go back into the study. "Drew Jackson is on his way out to the Barnett place to kill Emma," he said. "She's his illegitimate daughter, born to Maris Kessler. The girl in those photos."

Dris was leaning against a wall wiping the tears from his cheeks. Amos wasn't. He was beet red and furious. Amos spoke into the radio on his shoulder and told the dispatcher he was heading out to the Barnett place, and to get the sheriff and anyone else who was available to meet him out there for an attempted murder in progress. County-wide, he said. Fastest response.

Mike didn't pray too often. He prayed then.

Emma woke up abruptly, to find the cat staring at her from inches away. He was standing on the bed, and his fur was bristled out so that he looked like someone had plugged him into live current. He was hissing.

She jumped out of the bed and stared at him. He started stalking toward her, and she backed up.

It was then that she realized that she could feel him hissing inside her head. But she couldn't hear him hissing.

She lunged at him and tried to grab him.

He vanished, and only a cold spot remained in the air to mark his passing.

She screamed. Downstairs, someone was pounding on the door, roaring profanities. She tried to make out the words. Aside from "bitch" and "slut," and a handful of swear words, she could make out "you harlot" and "I'm going to kill you."

There was no place in the house where she could see onto the front porch except for the foyer, where she could look out through one of the sidelights. To see from there, she'd have to expose herself.

She knew she didn't want to do that. She pulled a pair of jeans on under her robe, but didn't have time to find a shirt. Downstairs, she heard glass shatter, and then the front door banged open.

The cat was in front of her again, hissing and snarling silently. Backing her into a corner. Her hand came to rest on the closet door, and she opened it, and slid inside, and pulled it shut in front of her.

And then she stood there, listening while someone rampaged through her house, looking for her, screaming that he was going to kill her, the tramp, the harlot, the whore that she was.

The pull chain brushed Emma's cheek. She knew the intruder was still downstairs. She would hear him when he started upstairs. She turned on the light for an instant, looking desperately for a place to hide in the little closet.

And the cat was there. This time not hissing. This time looking at her over his shoulder, expectantly, as if he was certain she would follow him. She watched, and he disappeared into a wall.

She studied the wall. At the bottom of it was a little crawl space.

"Yes," she whispered. She made a pile of stuff in front of the crawl space, and then climbed in, and pulled the clothes and boxes as close to her as she could. Then, carefully, she put the door back into its place and pulled it tightly shut.

When she was sure she had done her best to hide her means of disappearing, she turned around. She was in pitch darkness, except for a narrow rectangle of light around it. She was looking at the inside of the window she'd asked Mike about, she realized. It hadn't been a dummy window at all, but something else. She fumbled through the darkness toward the feeble light, and ran her hands over boards nailed together to fit inside the windowsill, and in the center of the boards, a metal handle like a barn door pull, making her wonder if the barrier was intended to be . . . pulled out?

She gave it a tug, and it wiggled. A harder tug, and the weight of it dropped onto her. She staggered, praying that she wouldn't drop the heavy window barrier on the floor and alert Drew to her whereabouts with the ensuing bang.

She managed to lean the barrier against the wall. The room still let in very little light. The curtains were covered with dust. Emma pushed them out of the way, then turned to survey her hiding place.

The room she found herself in had a door that would have led into her bedroom, but when she opened it, plaster and lathe covered the exit. That door had been hidden a very long time ago. The room itself was narrow—it must have been a sitting room, or a changing room. Maybe a quiet room for nursing a baby. It still had a rocking chair in one corner.

Her heart thudded and skipped.

There was something—someone—in the chair.

Her skin started to crawl. She looked out the window, down to the carriage house and the ground below. It was the angle she'd seen in one of those horrible possession paintings—the one with the man in the rocking chair and the bodies in the bonfire.

Emma knew suddenly what it was she'd found. She didn't want to believe it. She didn't want to think it.

She crept to the side of the chair.

The man—the skeleton—in the chair wasn't Ian, gloating over the burning bodies below. This man was tied to the chair, sitting in ragged clothes and his stocking feet. His wrists were manacled together, as were his ankles, and the chains that bound him had been run through the rocking chair and anchored to the floor.

He had been forced to watch out the window. Emma looked from as close to his position as she dared get, and saw that he'd had a clear view of the carriage house. If the doors had been open, he would have had a clear view of the inside of that, too, and the scene where Mattie was murdered.

"Oh, Sam. Poor, poor Sam," she whispered.

She felt certain that he had been alive to see his beloved Mattie dragged out to the carriage house and beaten to death. That he had watched the bonfire in which his wife's and child's bodies were burned—in the painting she had done, that had been in front of the carriage house and behind the main house, too. Ian had made sure Sam had seen it all.

And then . . . what?

Had Ian boarded over the door with lathe and plastered it to make it look like it had never existed before or after he had murdered Sam's whole world? Had he crawled through the little hatchway from time to time so that he could watch Sam die? Or had he stayed away, content in the knowledge that his brother was never going to see another face or hear another voice? When had he slipped his shield into the window, leaving only the faintest crack of light to bleed through. Had Sam still been alive for all of that?

Emma could not imagine which way of dying would be worse.

She wondered what had become of the remains of Mattie and Mary Caroline. Wherever they were, they had not been next to Sam. No wonder the ghosts in her house had not rested easy.

She ached for them.

And him. Pinned to the wall next to him was a newspaper story about his disappearance, and that of Mattie and Mary Caroline. The article's headline said, "BIGAMY," and the first paragraph said that the bigamists and their daughter had fled when Dr. Barnett had returned home, after beating him senseless and robbing him.

Emma stared at that article. Had Sam been alive to read it? Or had it been pinned there by Ian to mock the corpse?

She raged at the monster who had destroyed them.

She listened to him downstairs. Whoever he was, he had returned.

Emma made no noise. She was sure if she could just be quiet, he would not be able to find her. She hadn't left the light on in the closet, she hadn't left the doorway open, she hadn't given any clues to her whereabouts. And the hunter outside her hideaway would not even be certain that she had been in the bedroom. He would see that she wasn't there when he went into the room. He'd check the closet. Maybe kick the pile of clothes and things she'd left near the crawl space, but if he did that, he'd only do a better job of hiding it.

She didn't dare hope too hard, but she thought she had a good chance of living through this.

From downstairs, she heard a piercing, almost girlish scream—he sounded like he was almost beneath her when he made it, which would suggest that he was in her studio. She wondered what he'd found in there.

"You knew it was me? You knew all along? I'll burn you and this painting, you whore!"

And something cold and fleshless and dead whispered in her ear, *I'm coming for you now.*

She buried her scream in her robe and squeezed her eyes closed tight. The temperature around her fell so quickly it seemed to suck the air out of the stuffy room. Within an instant, she could see her breath curling in front of her, and she could feel the hateful, malignant presence of Ian Barnett, Mattie's killer. Sam's killer. Mary Caroline's killer.

I'll kill him. I'll kill her. And I'll kill you, Ian's ghost whispered again.

But he wouldn't. He couldn't touch any of them, though he could scare her nearly to death. She told herself if he could have killed her, he would have done it already.

Emma dug her fingers into the soft blue terry cloth of her robe, and willed him away from her. She knew no tricks for getting rid of ghosts, though she did pray; maybe, she thought, that was what finally sent the horror on his way.

She knew he was gone when the air got warmer.

She stood up, and looked around the room. Nothing had changed. Outside her hiding place, though, the real threat to her life was thundering up the stairs, still roaring, "I'll kill you, whore! I'll kill you!"

She frowned. The voice was familiar. But, "whore"? She thought she was hearing Drew, and yet, she wasn't. She heard drunkenness, and rage. And an accent that suggested another time, perhaps another century.

Her heart hammered with the realization that she was not necessarily facing a would-be killer in his natural state. If sleep had made her vulnerable to the house spirits, would drunkenness make Drew vulnerable to Ian's wrathful ghost? Would Ian tell Drew where to find her? Would he bring Drew to her?

And why Drew? He was too old to have been Maris's secret love. He'd already been married, a father, and a physician for a long time when Maris conceived Emma.

But he sounded like Drew, and Emma realized that Drew, a respected doctor, could have altered records, made charts disappear, and gotten a baby into the hands of would-be parents eagerly awaiting an orphaned newborn.

Emma started looking around the room for another way out. She might be able to kick through the lathe and plaster, but Drew—and Ian—would be able to hear her do that.

She did not dare go out through the crawl space. Ian had been in the secret room with her, and he knew where she was. If he was in control of Drew, then Drew would know, too, and he'd kill her for both of them.

She looked at the remains of Sam Barnett, still staring at the window that had been the last thing he ever saw. She looked at the window, too.

It hadn't been opened in more than a century. It might have been painted shut, it might have been nailed shut. Opening it would probably make a lot of noise.

But it might work.

She undid the latches and tried to push it open. It wasn't moving.

She looked around the room for something that might wedge it open. At Sam's bare, bony feet lay a sword that had been placed out of his reach by Ian. No doubt to taunt him, to offer him a means of saving Mattie and Mary Caroline, or perhaps a means of ending his own life before it became unbearable.

Mercy withheld.

Emma picked up the weapon. In a pinch, she might be able to use it to defend herself, but it was dusty, and dull, and she had never touched a sword before in her life. She didn't know if she would be able to do any damage with it.

On the other hand, it might make a decent pry bar. If she could get out the window, she would land on the roof of the back porch. She could crawl from there to one of the posts, hook her feet in some gingerbread, shimmy down, or if she had to, jump and aim for azaleas.

She heard Drew in the bedroom. She was running out of time.

She worked the blade between the sill and the sash, and started carefully rocking it back and forth. She heard a soft crack, and saw the window move upward fractionally. She braced her hands under the inside sash, right at the top, and shoved. Hard. She pushed harder, and it still resisted her, and she heard the closet door opening. It resisted her, and she heard Drew, sounding nothing like Drew, say, "I know where you're hiding, you strumpet. You harlot. You cuckolding daughter of Eve. I know."

And then the old paint gave way, and the dirty window slid up, the noise it made covered by Drew screaming at her. She kept the sword, shoving it through the belt of her robe, and scooted out onto the roof.

Tin roof, kind of slick, very cold. She was in her bare feet, which gripped the surface well, though. She shoved the window shut and prayed that Drew got hung up in the crawl space, and then, belly down, she scooted toward the edge of the roof and a place where she was pretty sure she would be able to find support for her trip down.

The gingerbread she'd hoped for was there, but it was too far under the eaves for her to use it.

Emma felt panic grip her, but she kept low and crawled around the corner of the house. She could use the downspout, maybe, she decided, and made it to the corner where the porch joined the outside wall. The drainpipe was there, and it looked sturdy enough. If it wasn't, she'd have a fast trip down.

She grabbed it with both hands, carefully swung her feet off the edge of the roof, and dangled for a moment. The saber rapped against the wall, and she felt her hands beginning to slip.

Her feet were close to the porch rail. She needed to slide just a little.

Above her, she heard the window slam open and her hunter screaming invective.

She swung her left leg out to reach for the porch rail, and missed. Her hands slipped a little, and it felt like the palms of them snagged on old metal. The pain was awful, but she didn't let herself think about it. She kept hanging on. The slip had moved her closer to the porch rail, and she tried again. She heard footsteps on the tin roof, slow and careful.

Her hands slipped again, and she could see bloody streaks on the drainpipe above her.

She clenched her jaws against the pain in her hands and made one more attempt for the porch rail. Her toes hooked over it, and she put enough of her weight on her left leg to relieve her hands of some of their burden. She managed to shift around so that her toes pointed toward the drainpipe, and she backed her other leg onto the porch rail. She couldn't hear Drew moving. So maybe he got to the edge and discovered he was afraid of heights. She managed a tight little grin, and got her balance on the rail, and then walked her hands backward along the wall, ignoring the bloody handprints she was leaving on the pale new paint.

Safe, she told herself. She was almost safe.

And then she was all the way onto the porch rail.

Drew grabbed her from behind and dragged her down into his arms.

Emma screamed.

Drew clamped his hand over her mouth, and Emma sank her teeth into the palm of his hand and bit as hard as she could, going for bone. He squealed like a pig, and lost his grip with that hand, but not with the arm he had clamped around her neck.

Emma kicked backward as hard as she could, aiming for a direct hit on his kneecap. She missed, and he didn't give her another chance to hurt him. He picked her up, so that she lost all of her leverage.

He shouldn't have been so strong, she thought. He was sixty-five years old. But when she looked into his eyes, she didn't see Drew there. She saw eyes the other part of her remembered.

"Ian," she said.

He threw her over his shoulder, and walked toward the carriage house. She could feel the saber still banging against her leg. She wasn't in any position to draw it, but she did manage to hook the back of her leg around it so that it wouldn't hit Drew. Ian.

Either of them.

She wanted it to still be there for her to use, if she got the chance.

"He's still up there watching," Ian's voice said.

"You can't hurt him anymore," Emma said.

And from Drew's mouth, Ian laughed. "Of course I can, my little tea cake. I can bash you into porridge in front of him, while he is helpless to do anything but watch. And then I'll burn your body in front of him, and your daughter's, and I'll let him rot up there forever."

"You're dead," Emma said.

"Not me. I'm right here."

It was hard to argue with him. But she said, "I'm not Mattie. I'm Emma. I'm Drew's daughter."

"I don't know any Drew."

"You're carrying me with his body."

Perhaps the spirit would have argued, but the body faltered. Drew was not far from the carriage house, but suddenly it seemed he would not be able to carry her anymore.

He put her down, and said, "Emma."

"Oh, thank God, Drew, it's you."

"You . . ." He looked bewildered. "How did we get out here?"

"You chased me. You were threatening to kill me. You thought I was someone else."

"I . . . yes. I've . . ." He smiled at her, and it wasn't a good smile. "I've had a lot to drink, and things in my head are a little . . . funny."

He pulled a gun out of his pocket and aimed it at her and said, "Not so funny, really. Very dark, in fact. I'm looking at my whole world falling apart, and I have worked so very hard to keep it together. I'm worth the keeping."

"What?"

"Back into the carriage house, darlin'. I don't want us to be out where everyone can see us."

"No," she told him.

"I could shoot you right here and leave you in the dirt. But the carriage house is . . . better. Somehow."

"That's where Ian Barnett killed Mattie."

"Means nothing to me. I have other issues. I tried to make things good for you. Your mother was a tramp, and she absolutely refused to have an abortion. Which, I suppose, you appreciate. But I couldn't have her telling people I was your father. I would have lost my career. And there aren't any other doctors better than I am, or more dedicated. As good as I am, certainly. There are a few. But not better."

"How modest of you," Emma said.

"Talent runs in my family, and I was pleased to see that you took after me as you grew older. But then, for whatever reason, you came back here, and you started asking questions, and a lot of problems that had fallen away into forgetfulness came back in a rush. And, with them, people asking the wrong questions."

He frowned at her. "I tried to save your life. I got you away from this place, and I made sure no one would ever send you back to me. And you still turned up."

Emma suddenly felt warmth and comfort surround her—and assurance that she would be all right. She wasn't sure why or how, but she grabbed the saber and yanked it up and out, certain that, with Drew's weaving and the way the gun in his hand was shaking, she would be able to get him before he got her.

She was wrong.

She felt the bullet hit her in the chest, and she felt it knock her back. The saber flew out of her hand. She felt horrible pain, and a sense of failure. Of terrible loss. And then Sam's ghost standing over her, looking down at her. Smiling. "Almost finished," he said.

And then she felt nothing.

Drew's car was already there when Mike pulled into the yard. Driscoll Cavanaugh was right behind him, and Amos was behind *him*, and the sheriff was on his way, and Mike kept telling himself that everything would be all right. They would get to Emma in time, and she'd be fine, and the police could lock Drew away forever for the horrible things he'd done.

But as he was jumping out of his truck, with Cara hopping out the other side, he heard a gunshot.

He yelled, "No!" and ran back along the drive. Toward the carriage house, which was where Drew would be, where Emma would be.

Maybe it was a warning shot, he thought.

Cara was panting behind him. He shouted, "Stay back, Cara. Stay out of this!"

But she didn't slow down, or hesitate. She just kept running.

Blood. He could see it in his mind's eye. The woman he loved crumpled along the back wall, her head bashed in, and blood everywhere, spattered and flung and horrible to contemplate.

That was then. This was now. He launched himself through the archway of the carriage house, and heard another shot, and didn't feel it. But behind him, Cara screamed. He got Drew's hand, the one that held the gun, and lifted it, and the old bastard fought with him. He was stronger than he had any business being. He was shouting about a harlot, a scarlet woman, a strumpet and a doxie, and he didn't sound like Drew. Mike tried to pull the gun away from him, and as he did, Drew's eyes focused on him, and he said, "I killed you, you cheating whoreson. I made you watch her die, and your daughter die, and then I killed you. You're up there, dead. You're dead."

"I'm right here, shitbag," Mike said.

Mike was pretty sure he'd been talking to Ian, but then Ian went away. And Drew was there. And he said, "I'm a good man, Mike. I made a mistake with Maris. I made a mistake, but I've spent the rest of my life repenting it."

His gun steadied a little. It seemed to Mike that Drew was a bit less drunk than Ian had been.

He tried to figure out what the right thing to say would be, and he realized that he could hear Dris and Amos behind him. He could hear the sheriff, back a ways calling on his radio for ambulances, and backup, and all cars, hostage situation. He realized that he was the hostage, not Emma, and not Cara, because they were both down and not moving.

He was going to get them both to safety. Somehow.

He said, "Drew, you and I have been brothers-in-law and friends for a long time. Long time. You are a good guy. And I know—" He almost choked on the words he was going to say next, but Emma was bleeding in the corner, and the gun was on him. So he went on. "I know you didn't mean to get Emma's mother pregnant. Mistakes happen, and I know this was just a mistake."

"A mistake," Drew agreed, his eyes wide with innocence. "I loved my wife, and that girl pursued me. And I was weak. Once. Just once, but that was all it took. And then she had an allergic reaction to a standard labor medication, and I managed to save the baby, but I couldn't save her. It was a tragedy, and it broke my heart."

"I know," Mike said. "You're a good guy, Drew, and this isn't the way you want to do things. You're the doctor everyone looks up to. You're the hero of most of the folks in Benina. A good man."

The gun wavered. Drew looked so tired. So beat. Mike kept his voice calm. "You and I will get past this, and we'll go out and play another round of golf. We'll go fishing for largemouths, and we'll sit back in the seats with good cold beer and hot dogs."

Drew nodded.

"But first we have to save Emma, you and me. Because nothing good can come of you leaving her there to die."

And the gun came up with a sharpness that scared the hell out of Mike. He heard Driscoll behind him roar,

"Get down!" and he dropped to the dirt, and above him, guns fired.

He started crawling toward Emma. All the other men—the sheriff, the deputies, Dris and Amos, were out there with Cara, but no one was taking care of Emma.

He found her in a pool of blood. Her face was covered in blood, her blue terry cloth robe looked for a minute like a long dress from another era, and . . .

. . . and she had a saber in her hand.

A saber?

It had a huge dent halfway down the blade. A round dent, like someone had just clobbered the hell out of it with a ball-peen hammer.

He touched her head. It wasn't caved in. She had a vertical slice on her forehead—a knife cut, or more likely a saber cut—and a goose egg that was already turning black and blue. The cut had bled like Niagara Falls. The goose egg was a little scary. But she was breathing. She was warm. Her color was good. Her pulse was okay.

He lifted her eyelids and looked at her pupils, ignoring the sounds of men shouting behind him. He didn't hear Drew. That was okay, then. He heard Dris, and he heard the sheriff.

He stayed focused on what he was doing. He tried to find out why Emma wasn't awake.

"Emma?" he said. He shook her lightly, afraid that anything he did might hurt her, but knowing that he needed to know how hurt she was.

She didn't move.

He tried to remember his CPR and Basic Life Support classes. Somewhere along the way, someone had said something about rubbing knuckles across the ster-

num to check for levels of unconsciousness—or had
that been Drew, talking about a patient in the ER?

Mike didn't remember, but he opened her robe to get
to her sternum, and got a shock. She had an enormous
bruise just left of her sternum. Mike stared for a second,
figuring it out. The distance from the saber tip to the
dent in its center was about the same as the distance between the cut and the bump on Emma's head and the
huge bruise on her chest.

As if she'd swung the saber up just in time to stop the
bullet.

Behind him, shuffling and grunting. Sirens coming,
dopplering louder and louder as they approached.

He felt his belly tense. He didn't know how Cara was,
and he needed to know that, too. But . . . Emma.

"Emma," he shouted, and rubbed her sternum, digging with his knuckles.

Her eyes popped open and she said, "Owwww!" and
pushed at his hands.

"Hey," he said. "How are you?"

She focused on him. And frowned. "My head hurts.
My chest hurts even more. But . . . I'm alive." She
seemed very surprised by that.

Mike was surprised by it, too. He'd figured that they
were doomed.

She tried to sit up, and immediately laid back down.
"God, I don't think I've ever been this queasy."

"You have a hell of a bump on your head," he said.
"And a cut. And a bruise on your chest that I think
would have been a bullet hole, except you evidently
have freakish reflexes with a sword."

"I think I had help. I think someone was watching
over me."

She looked toward the back of the house, over the porch, and in one of the upstairs windows, for just an instant, Mike thought he saw a man standing there, looking out.

He shivered, and the shadows in the window went away.

"I'm alive," Emma said, wondering. She raised her hands to him, palms forward. "How messed up are they?" she asked. "I'm afraid to look."

They were pretty torn up. "Just flesh wounds," he said, and slid an arm under her shoulders. "I'm going to help you up now, and get you out of here. There's an ambulance here, and you're not going to give me any nonsense about not going to the hospital."

"As long as Drew Jackson isn't my doctor," she said.

"I think the police shot him."

"I hope he's dead," Emma said. "He killed my mother."

"He did a lot of things—" Mike stopped himself before he could add *to your mother.* Instead he said, "And he killed a lot of people. Not just her. His own wife. People back then, people now. It's going to take the police a while to figure out just how much damage he did. And probably other doctors, and other people reviewing the hospital records. I'm guessing from . . . things I saw . . ." Mike swallowed hard. "I'm guessing there were other victims . . . other girls . . ."

And he stopped. He couldn't talk about Drew anymore.

He bent down and kissed Emma. And got her to her feet, and to the ambulance. And then he went back for the saber, to show the EMTs.

They stared at it, and agreed that it looked like it had made the cut. The ding in the metal, both EMTs and cops agreed, looked like it might have stopped the bullet.

Emma said, "Sam never quit waiting for the chance to make things right. He never gave up."

The EMTs wrote off her comment to the head trauma and shock. The cops ignored it. Mike, though, was pretty sure she was right.

Chapter 12

FIVE MONTHS LATER

It took Emma and Mike three months to find Mattie and Mary Caroline. Ian had buried their ashes and what was left of their bones in the rose garden. In a box. Under the fountain that Emma hated. Emma guessed that Ian did it so that he could sit on Mattie's bench seat and look at them, and know that he had punished them.

He hadn't, though. Mattie and Mary Caroline and Sam had come back, and they had brought the truth about their deaths to light. And they had, in doing so, revealed Ian as a monster for a second time. And perhaps saved a few more lives.

The town gave a funeral to all three; Sam, Mattie, and Mary Caroline Barnett were interred together as husband, wife, and child, and a surprising number of people came. No one but Mike, Emma, and Cara knew how deeply that funeral mattered to the living. The house was silent, the echoes banished, the horrors gone.

The truth about Drew Jackson, when investigators began unearthing it and putting pieces together, just kept getting worse. He could be traced to a number of deaths in the town, from patients who were old and inconvenient to young children with birth defects, to middle-aged women whose menopause symptoms apparently got on his nerves.

He'd killed Dr. Pendergast when he dared to rebel against being blackmailed over a medication error that had taken the life of a young farmer. He'd killed Maris with an IV bolus injection of potassium chloride right after she gave birth, and Maris's mother with carefully mislabeled drugs supposed to help her nerves following the deaths of her daughter and granddaughter. He'd killed Aileen and Gwen, and the nurse who had gone with him to deliver the baby to the Beck's, and a list of others that just kept getting longer. He was careful, he had access to drugs that made their deaths look like accidents, or heart attacks, and he was such an obsessively dedicated physician, no one ever suspected what he was on the other side, when no one was watching.

The biggest repercussions landed on David Halifax, though, who as the sole survivor of the duo had been exposed as a pedophile and compatriot of Drew's, and a frequent participant in his crimes. Halifax realized his legal talent couldn't save him; as the police were breaking down his door to arrest him, he put a bullet in his brain.

"I've been through everything I could find about the history of the house," Emma said.

She and Mike were sitting on the front porch swing, just relaxing. "I still can't figure out who my mother might have been in relation to Mattie and Sam and Mary Caroline, or how she fit in to all of this."

Mike's arm tightened around her shoulder. "Maybe

she wasn't even part of this. Maybe she was a new victim in this life. We might never know. We'll keep looking." He kissed the top of her head.

They watched Cara pull into the driveway and get out of her car. She was still walking with crutches—the bullet had gone through her lower leg, shattering both bones, and she was pinned together and getting physical therapy. And glad, like Emma, to be alive.

"There were more little girls," she said.

Emma braced herself. "How many more?"

"The police haven't finished tearing the house apart yet. They know about some. There were probably a lot."

They were quiet for a while. Then Emma said, "I have some good news. We've set a date."

"Really?"

"We figure before the baby is born would be good. So we're going to just do a little thing here. Next month."

Cara looked so happy. "I'm still your matron of honor?"

"Crutches or not," Emma said. "And Susan will be here. You'll get to meet her then."

They rocked on the porch swing, and Cara settled into the wicker chair. "Do you miss them sometimes?" she asked.

Emma and Mike glanced at each other. "Sam and Mattie and Mary Caroline? Not really," Mike said. "They got Emma out of bed at night."

"On the downside, I'm getting a lot fewer paintings done."

"On the bright side," Mike said, "your paintings are a hell of a lot more fun to look at."

Emma nodded.

She leaned her head on Mike's shoulder, and thought

about that last painting, the one she hadn't seen until after Drew was dead and she was back from the emergency room.

It had been a reproduction of what Mike said was Jackson with her fifteen-year-old mother. Mike said he'd seen the original. Emma had burned the painting.

It had been that painting that had elicited the scream from him.

It had been, as far as anyone could figure, a true painting.

It was ashes in the garden, though. The nightmare was over. Everything had been made right. Maris's reputation had been restored, and her mother's as well.

Jackson was dead.

Cara was finding her way through the ashes of her own life. She'd found a job in a doctor's office in Anderson, and a little apartment there. She was dating a nice younger man. She still made it home for Monday nights.

Emma thought she looked younger. Happier. God knows she deserved it.

They'd silenced the ghosts, they'd set right evils that were nearly a century and a half old, and some that were brand new, and Emma and Mike had found each other.

Emma leaned against Mike and rocked on the porch swing.

And then she turned her head just a little as a shadow caught her eye.

The cat jumped on the railing and sat watching her. He seemed content, so she didn't say a thing.

HOLLY LISLE

I SEE YOU

For paramedic Dia Courvant, each day brings
the possibility of facing blood and death. But
nothing can match the horror of the day she
was dispatched to the scene of a terrible car
accident and rescued the sole survivor—only to
find her own husband dead in the wreckage.
Four years later, a series of deadly car crashes
brings handsome detective Brig Hafferty into
Dia's life. She's drawn to Brig, but can she
trust him enough to tell him of the terror that
stalks her? For Dia has received a message
warning her of danger and death—a message
that seems to have been sent to her from
beyond the grave....

0-451-41221-4

Available wherever books are sold or at
penguin.com

HOLLY LISLE

LAST GIRL DANCING

Obsessed with discovering what happened to her missing sister, Atlanta detective Jess Brubraker is willing to disappear into a sordid nightworld to find the answer. But that means leading both herself and her lover into the most intimate and terrifying trap of all.

"ADD LISLE'S NAME TO THE LIST OF EXCEPTIONAL ROMANTIC SUSPENSE AUTHORS."
—*ROMANTIC TIMES BOOKCLUB* (TOP PICK)

"AN ENGROSSING READ."
—*NEW YORK TIMES* BESTSELLING AUTHOR
LINDA HOWARD

0-451-41197-8

Available wherever books are sold or at
penguin.com